*W*hat the critics are saying...

ॐ

"I highly recommend THE COWBOY AND THE CAPTIVE especially to those that have yet to sample Lora Leigh's very distinct style of writing of highly emotional, seductive, and passionate erotic stories that will engage you from the first sentence to the last." ~ *Romance Junkies*

"An interesting plot and story that will have one wondering if Luc will catch on. Extremely sensual but with a good love story that is not overpowered by sensuality. I especially enjoyed how Luc's character developed into a compassionate one. I won't give away the ending but I will say it's a good read and very entertaining." ~ *The Romance Studio*

"Lora Leigh has done it again. Cowboy and the Captive is a cheeky adaptation of one of Aesop's The Wolf and the Nurse. This book is guaranteed to satisfy time and again. The characters are lively, the dialogue is snappy, and the storyline will tug at your heartstrings. And the sex is hot, hot, hot. What more can you ask for?" ~ *A Romance Review*

"I have to admit that I am a fan of Ms. Leigh's and this book doesn't disappoint. The story moves along quickly and I finished in one reading. The characters were easy to care about and their actions rang true. This was a thoroughly enjoyable and very sensual romance novel." ~ *Sensual Romance Reviews*

LORA LEIGH
SHILOH WALKER

Cops
AND
Cowboys

ELLORA'S CAVE
ROMANTICA PUBLISHING

An Ellora's Cave Romantica Publication

www.ellorascave.com

Cops & Cowboys

ISBN 1419952021
ALL RIGHTS RESERVED.
Her Wildest Dreams Copyright © 2003 Shiloh Walker
Cowboy & the Captive Copyright © 2004 Lora Leigh

Edited by Pamela Campbell
Cover art by Syneca

Electronic book Publication March 2004
Trade paperback Publication June 2005

Excerpt from *Coming in Last* Copyright © Shiloh Walker, 2004

Content Advisory:

S – ENSUOUS
E – ROTIC
X - TREME

Ellora's Cave Publishing offers three levels of Romantica™ reading entertainment: S (S-ensuous), E (E-rotic), and X (X-treme).

The following material contains graphic sexual content meant for mature readers. This story has been rated E rotic.

S-*ensuous* love scenes are explicit and leave nothing to the imagination.

E-*rotic* love scenes are explicit, leave nothing to the imagination, and are high in volume per the overall word count. E-rated titles might contain material that some readers find objectionable—in other words, almost anything goes, sexually. E-rated titles are the most graphic titles we carry in terms of both sexual language and descriptiveness in these works of literature.

X-*treme* titles differ from E-rated titles only in plot premise and storyline execution. Stories designated with the letter X tend to contain difficult or controversial subject matter not for the faint of heart.

Contents

HER WILDEST DREAMS

മ

Dedication:

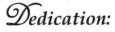

To my editor Pam, the Wondrous One
To my kids Cam and Jess — my world revolves around you
two. I love you both.
And to my husband Jerry.
My real life fantasy… I love you…

Chapter One
February 2001

∞

It's weird, the way a woman can go her whole life without ever really seeing herself. And the things that can flash through her mind when she's come face to face with a knife-welding punk out to snatch her purse, and end her life.

He was high; Alison had spent two years giving out Methadone at a clinic and she could spot high easily enough. Basically that meant her life wasn't worth the twenty dollars she had in her wallet—not to this guy.

Yet, in that moment—when seconds stretched out to a crawl—it wasn't any odd sentimental moment from childhood that rose to her memory, no poignant moment spent in a lover's arms.

Instead, she could see her reflection—as she had looked just twenty minutes before she had left the house to run to the bookstore—her nondescript brown hair pulled back in a loose ponytail, her glasses sliding down her nose, her long narrow face pale and listless.

The clothes she had on were baggy and simple—jeans and a flannel shirt—covered by a serviceable jacket of black wool. They hung on a frame so skinny, it could have belonged to a teenaged boy, not a twenty-six-year-old woman.

And that was what she saw.

Herself. Miserable, pathetic, lifeless.

Dimly, she heard footsteps and a shout.

With a jolt, reality snapped back into focus and her eyes, hidden behind huge plastic frames and lenses, narrowed, her mouth tightened into a grim line. She looped one wrist through the purse strap and drew the other one down, cocked back, the ball of her hand driving up—a trick she had learned long ago, back when she had still lived with her folks and one very protective older brother.

To her surprise, the boy—*God, was he even seventeen?*—went crashing down, shouting with shock. She was certain she had felt cartilage crunch under her hand, but the pain of that wouldn't faze somebody so obviously strung out. She drew her foot back, praying for forgiveness, and landed a kick square in his unprotected crotch.

That drew a howl from him…and a vicious curse. She dropped into a crouch she didn't even know she remembered, drawing her hands up, eyes darting around for a weapon.

But it wasn't necessary.

A body hurtled out from nowhere, tackling the boy who had rushed to his feet, taking him down. A large hand clipped the boy across the face, stunning him. Alison heard the clank of metal, followed by the quiet snick of handcuffs latching.

Her body had started to quiver and it took a long time to realize the voice addressing her was calling her by name. It took even longer to realize that voice was familiar.

Large hands closed over her shoulders and an irate voice demanded, "Girl, have you lost your mind?"

Slowly her lids lowered, then lifted once more and her gaze moved up, training on that face, her ears homing in on the rough, angry voice. It clicked and she smiled a dazed, rather dreamy smile.

"Why, Alexander O'Malley, how nice to see you," she murmured as her body went from subtle shivering to outright quaking in a matter of heartbeats. Her own heart started to kick, pounding heavily against the wall of her chest, causing her breath to catch in her throat.

His dark brown hair spilled onto his forehead, falling into his chocolate-brown eyes as he glared down at her in unsuppressed rage. His mouth—that sexy, sexy mouth she had always wanted one taste of — was grim and tight, his lean, tanned face stark with anger.

Her mind felt oddly disconnected as she stared at him, head cocked. Vicious, furious curses drew her attention away from Alex, but the angry narcotics detective barely even glanced at the struggling boy at his feet.

"Little idiot," he snapped out, giving her one final shake before drawing a cell phone from his pocket. She barely heard him barking into the phone. Instead, Alison focused on the battered boy who lay at their feet, moaning pitifully, crying and struggling to get up and away. Alex's feet were braced on either side of him and his glittering dark-brown gaze locked on the boy's face.

Alison's eyes were locked on the boy's face too, widening as she realized some of the marks on him had come from her — the meekest, mildest woman ever to stroll through southern Indiana.

A warm hand closed on her face and she felt her chin being lifted. Staring into Alex's eyes, the fog that had started to envelope her brain thickened. "I think I might have broken his nose," she said calmly.

"You little idiot, he was about to slit your damn throat," Alex growled. "Why didn't you just give him your fucking purse?"

Her eyes dropped to the object in question and her lips pursed. "I really don't know." A frown marred her face as she looked back up at him and said quietly, "It wouldn't have mattered though. He would have killed me no matter what I did. And we both know it, Alex."

* * * * *

Alex paced the small office, watching the silent little figure huddled in the chair. Every now and then, Alison Ryan would sip from the cup of coffee she held, but for the most part, her eyes remained locked on the wall in front of her. He seriously doubted she was seeing anything, but he had to admit, she was much calmer than he ever would have thought.

It wouldn't have mattered though. He would have killed me no matter what I did. And we both know it, Alex.

Damn it. Fuck.

The bitch of it all? She was right. The boy was so fucking strung out, he would have killed her and it wouldn't have fazed him. Oh, he would have been sorry — once it was too late.

Too late — Alex would have had to go see quiet little Allie one last time, right before her coffin was closed. She had saved her own neck. A sick, hot little ball of nausea slid through his gut and Alex clenched his jaw. *Fuck.* He had known her since she was a kid. There was no way to describe the rage he had felt when he had raced upon the scene and seen the teenager flashing that knife, so close to her white neck.

But she had handled it. Who would have thought it? Alison Ryan. She was such a, well, *mouse.* It wasn't the nicest thing to say about his best friend's baby sister, but what else could he say? It was the truth.

Her pale little face was a bit paler than normal, but nothing that was worrying him.

The signs of shock had faded and she was calm. Geez, how long had he known her? Going on twenty-five years now. And he didn't think he had ever seen her upset. Alex seriously doubted she had the passion it took to get upset. So why was it surprising that she wasn't upset now? Hysterical, even?

Why, Alexander O'Malley, how nice to see you, she had said, pushing her glasses up and staring at him owlishly, like she hadn't almost been killed.

Little fool, he thought. For the fifteenth time.

Her ponytail had been tidied at some point, pulled back tightly from her face. Every now and then, her eyes would glance at the plain watch on her wrist, but she still hadn't said much. "Why don't I call your brother to come get you?"

In her soft, hesitant voice, she said, "Mike's out of town until next Saturday."

Alex pressed his fingers against his eyes and muttered, "Tahiti. I forgot."

Forgotten that he had stood up for Mike in his wedding only four days earlier? Alison smiled slightly. She didn't doubt it; Alex looked strained. And she doubted it had anything to do with what might have happened earlier. She set aside the half empty coffee cup and stood, folding her arms across her chest. "I can call a cab," she said. "I just need to get back to my car, anyway."

A cab. He stared at her, his pen falling from his hand. *A cab? After damn near getting her throat slit, she was going to call a fucking cab? Mike would kill me. Shit, I'd kill me.* "No," he said slowly, shaking his head and lowering his gaze back to the report. "No cab."

"I don't mind," she said softly. "It's late and —"

"No cab, Allie," he said in a steely voice. "I'll take you. I've got a few things to finish up and then I can take you home." He scowled. *Home? Alone?* "Is there a friend you could call? Go stay with?"

She frowned at him quizzically. "Why would I do that?"

"Because you almost got your throat slit?" he snapped and then mentally kicked his ass as her eyes fell away and her mouth twitched.

His date had called and cancelled at the last minute, which explained why he had been in the area. He had stopped to pick up a book and on the way out had seen Allie's car. He had almost turned around to go find her, to see if he could talk her into grabbing a bite with him, thinking it was better than going home alone.

Actually, even though it would end up without any sex, it was better than a date. Once you got her talking, Allie was adorable, funny, sharp-witted. And unmistakable.

He would have seen her in the store.

She hadn't been there. The worry hadn't even had a chance to settle in his gut when he heard the scuffle and the muttered curse from the small alley between the old bookstore and the run-down grocery and had known—just *known*—that the little twit was getting in trouble.

So instead of settling down with his book, dragging the shy kid sister of his best friend out for some food, or looking up another date, he was writing up a police report because the idiot was too stupid to realize it wasn't safe to walk from one store to the other—not in this neighborhood. Allie was a cop's sister, for crying out loud. *She* should know better.

"I'm sorry. Look, just give me a few minutes to wrap a few things up and then I can take you home, okay? Hang around a little while. You don't need to be alone just yet, okay?"

She nodded, slowly, hesitantly, and lowered herself back into the chair. Alex went to his desk and finished typing up the report. As he whipped the paper from the old typewriter he preferred, his eye caught sight of a file.

Hot damn. About time, he thought as satisfaction slid through his gut.

Eyes gleaming, he flipped it open. This was it, all right. What he had been waiting for.

Within five minutes of poring over the files, he had completely forgotten Alison was there.

After another thirty-five minutes had passed, Alison realized he had forgotten her. Biting back a sigh, she rose and made her way to the door on silent feet. Glancing back over her shoulder, she released the sigh. She was so forgettable. She knew damn well if she had been a criminal under arrest, or any other woman, she would never had made it out of that tiny office without Alex's sharp eyes catching her.

But her? Quiet, mousy little Alison Ryan? He didn't so much as glance up as she slid through the door. He still had his nose buried in the file as she made her way to the woman occupying the huge desk up front.

It hurt, but Alex had always had the ability to hurt her. Since she had spent the majority of her life dreaming about him, it was no surprise. At first, they had been the sweet romantic dreams of a girl, him sweeping her away, vowing to love her forever.

He was so damn sexy, so adorable. so hot...but it was more than that. Not that being six-feet-four with thick, curly brown hair, melted-chocolate eyes, and a flashing white smile didn't help. And his shoulders, that wide chest...tapering down to a flat, muscled belly and a tight ass that filled out a pair of jeans like nothing she had ever seen.

And of course there was always the front view — long, powerful legs, muscled thighs, a sizeable bulge that Allie eyed when she knew he wasn't looking. Which was often — he never really looked at her.

Oh, yeah, there was a lot about Alex's looks to fuel her dreams.

In her wildest dreams, they were both naked and sweaty and wrapped around each other, his dark body covering hers while he rode her hard. She had dreams where he bound her hands behind her and mounted her. Dreams where she knelt in front of him and licked and sucked on his penis like it was candy.

Now any time she dreamed about him, she woke up and cried, because the likelihood of him ever touching her was nonexistent. Alex was handsome, arrogant, living sex appeal, with broad shoulders, and arms and thighs heavy with muscle. His mouth was full and sensual and usually puckered with a scowl when he looked at her.

She'd had entire dreams spun around that mouth. Entire fantasies about the things he would do to her, that she would do to him. Things that made her blush almost as hotly as they made her burn. Things she was too damn clumsy to do, even if he was interested.

It wasn't just his looks, though—there was something about him that seemed to call to something inside of her.

She paused long enough to make a call for a cab, her voice flat and even, showing no sign of the distress inside. But inside she was shaking. Trembling. Frightened and angry and bordering on desperation—feelings she wasn't very familiar with all.

She was on her way out the door when she heard Alex holler her name, followed by a quieter, "Fuck," as he grabbed his jacket, stuffed the file under his arm and caught up with her.

"Sorry, kid," he muttered, his dark cheeks flushed. "I've been waiting on that information for a while and...shit. I'm sorry."

She smiled politely, unaware of how bright and desperate her eyes were. "Go on back to work, Alex. I've called a cab."

"A cab?" he repeated. His mouth opened, closed, opened, and snapped shut. Then his eyes rolled heavenward, closing them as he sighed out a prayer of patience. "A cab. She's called a cab. Does she want Mike to kill me?" Then he opened his eyes and caught her arm, guiding her outside. "No. No cab. I told you, no cab. You could have been hurt, or killed. You shouldn't be alone; shit, Mike would kill me. Damn it, I think I'd do it before he could get to me, Allie. You're my friend, kid."

She followed in mute silence as he led her outside to his black truck—shaking inside, violently cold, teeth chattering, her green eyes glassy. Alex eyed her worriedly and wondered if he ought to take her to the emergency room for treatment for shock instead of taking her home.

They were only a few miles away from the station when a sob caught in her throat. Followed by another. And another.

Her seat belt was loosened and she felt a warm, strong arm go around her and heard Alex whisper in her ear, "It's all right. Go ahead and cry."

The tears wouldn't stop.

Finally, Alex curled her against him while he drove the scant mile to his house. He pulled her out and lifted her up. Damnation, she felt so fragile.

He left her crying softly on the couch while he hunted up tea bags and whiskey, a cool wash cloth, and aspirin. Then he carried the steaming tea with a generous serving of whiskey out to where she lay with her head buried in her arms.

Allie's body was rigid, resisting him when he lifted her up, sitting stiffly on his lap and dashing at her tears until he finally pinned her arms down and forced her body against the curve of his.

"Drink it," he told her, pushing the tea and whiskey into her hands when she refused to take it. "Drink it. You'll need it to sleep."

Exhausted, she took it and drank. One sip, another and another until the cold knot of fear and pain in her belly loosened and she relaxed against Alex, enjoying the sensation of being pressed so close to him. His scent, the feel of his hands stroking her back. The terror of the night started to fade and she felt her eyelids start to droop.

Alex could tell the second she fell asleep. The last of the tension faded from her body and her head fell back against his arm, her glasses going askew. He tugged them off and pulled the band that held her hair up so tightly. He idly stroked his hand through it, recalling another time or two when he had done this. The day Mike had to have emergency surgery right before she turned five — the day her dog passed away when she was eight.

With a sigh, he shifted her on his lap and rested his chin against her crown. Her dark brown hair was soft, silky against his cheek, and it smelled like peaches. His eyes felt heavy and he was too damn tired himself. The past few weeks had been rough. The small town he lived in didn't usually see too much outside the normal, but a crime spree had been taking place lately and he had been living on caffeine and adrenaline.

Within a matter of minutes, he followed her into sleep.

A click of metal, and she could feel the cold cuffs biting into her wrist as he looped them around the headboard before catching her other wrist. "Spread your legs," he whispered, rising to stand over her, fully clothed, while he stared down at her naked, bound body.

"You're wet," he told her.

She knew. She could feel it.

He reached out, slid one finger through her damp curls, and lower, until he could slide it inside her. Back and forth until she teetered on the edge of orgasm, until she was biting her lips and pleading.

"Tell me," he ordered. "Tell me what you want."

"You," she gasped. "Inside me."

"Tell me to fuck you," he said, freeing the buttons at his fly and then covering her body with his. He stared down into her eyes, his gaze hungry, hot and needy.

"Fuck me," she pleaded, staring up into his dark-chocolate eyes.

He drove the rigid length of his cock inside her. And held still. "Beg me," he whispered, nipping at her ear.

"Fuck me, please. Hard, fuck me hard. Harder, harder — "

Allie awoke with a moan when Alex trailed his lips down the curve of her neck. Somehow they had gone from sleeping sitting upright on the couch to sprawling on the floor, with his hands inside her pants, cupping her ass while he nuzzled and nipped along the line of her neck and shoulders. An irritated grunt fell from his lips and he withdrew his hands from her jeans to jerk her flannel shirt off her shoulders, to pull the turtleneck from her body with such force, her head flew back and rapped against the rug covered floor.

Then his teeth closed over one small, hard nipple and Allie cried out, her hands flying up to cup his head, threading through his dark brown curls and tangling there to hold him to her. He allowed it while he swiftly removed her jeans, but then he caught her hands and pinned them to the floor beside her head, wedging one heavy thigh between hers, dragging the rough material covering his thigh against her damp curls. He secured both of her wrists in one large hand and cupped her mound in his other, spreading the lips of her sex and plunging two long, thick fingers deep inside her.

Allie shrieked and rocked up against him.

His mouth crushed down on hers, his tongue driving past her lips, deep inside her mouth, swirling and tangling with hers. Pulling his fingers from her slick, wet pussy, he shoved back onto his knees and jerked his jeans open, ten thick inches of cock springing free to throb against his belly, hard, ruddy, and ready.

When he dropped his weight on her, she gasped, her head spinning, her body aching. When he used his legs to spread hers, she greedily wrapped her legs around him, bathing in his heat and warmth. When he drove his long, hard cock into her untried body, she screamed in mingled pain and ecstasy.

Alex grunted in pleasure as small, cool hands stroked over his shoulders and back before cupping the back of his skull and guiding his mouth to small, hard-tipped tits that tasted like peaches. He caught her hands and pinned her down, that hot writhing body pushing him near the breaking point.

He slid a finger through her wet curls, gathering the cream that had started to collect in her narrow, tight vagina. She whimpered and whispered his name, curling against him, her pinned wrists straining, her body lifting upwards to his. He shoved his jeans down, freed his trapped cock, and drove deep inside that hot little body.

It was the sound of her half-terrified scream that woke him up.

And the smell of peaches that had recognition stirring in his head.

"Allie?" he rasped, lifting his head and staring down at her sweaty, upturned face, at her dazed, almost drugged expression. "Fuck."

"Oh, please," she whispered, obviously unaware that he was, well, aware.

Her tight, wet little sheath was snug around his penis, convulsing and pulsating around him until he thought he'd go mad with it. Finding the kid sister of his best friend underneath his aroused body should have had his dick wilting. At least a little.

But her pleading voice and undulating body had him hard as iron and burning. He gripped one slender thigh and pulled it high over his hip, opening her wider, granting him access to a slim, smooth buttock and the crevice between the cheeks of that tight little ass as he pulled back out.

With a twist of his hips, he worked his way back inside her body, angling her slight weight with his free hand until he could feel the head of his penis rubbing that sensitized spot deep inside her body. When she was trembling and panting under him, he started to rock against her body with slow, deep thrusts, one hand gripping her ass, the other hand still holding her wrists down.

The wet silk of her pussy hugged him tightly as he surged back inside her, clung to him as he withdrew. His balls felt tight and heavy, burning and full, as he rode her, and she screamed, jumped a little when he smacked her upraised bottom with the flat of his hand. "You like that," he purred as he released her hands and cupped the back of her head, arching her neck and making her dazed eyes meet his. *Allie likes to be spanked…*

This ain't happening, a slightly saner part of him yelled.

Shut the fuck up, the rest of him bellowed as he sank his cock back into her creamy heat. The diamond hard points of her nipples stabbed into his chest and he pushed up to stare down at her, the image burning itself into his mind. Her breasts were small, but round, firm, topped with nipples that were red and hard. Her narrow ribcage and slim waist tapered down to the hips and ass he had always written off as too damned skinny, but right now, they felt awfully good as he squeezed one tight ass cheek and pressed his index finger against her anus.

"Christ, you're tight, Allie," he grunted as he worked his engorged cock back inside her waiting pussy. Burying his face in her neck, he drew in the sweet scent of peaches and smacked her butt lightly a second time. His eyes crossed when her inner muscles clamped down around him like a silken vise, and he groaned when he felt a wet flood pour from within her body. A wet slap filled the air each time he drove into her, harder and harder until they were scooting across the floor with each thrust.

After she came around him a third time, he let loose and pounded himself into her, pinning her down and fucking her with bruising force, until he lost it and spewed hot seed inside her quaking body.

He pulled out of her quivering pussy with a wet sucking sound a few minutes later and rolled onto his back.

What in the fuck happened? he thought, bewildered, his chest heaving as he lay on his back staring up at the ceiling. Allie? He had just fucked Allie. And unless he was even more sleep deprived than he thought, it had been the best damn fuck of his life.

With a savage, "Shit," he got to his feet, gritting his teeth against the lingering pleasure that had him wanting to sink back inside her body. This was *Allie*, for God's sake. Bookish, shy, dull little Alison Ryan. Under his breath, he muttered, "I don't believe this."

Clenching his jaw, he knelt and lifted her shuddering, skinny body and put her back on the couch. Faint bruises were appearing on her wrists already and a wave of disgust flooded him. This wasn't one of his women, who were used to rough sex and enjoyed it.

Allie, for pity's sake.

He walked away to get a wash cloth to clean her up—her cream and his come drying on his cock as he left the room.

He had to get her home.

If he didn't, he was pretty damn certain he was going to work his cock back inside her tight sheath and fuck her slowly, to see if it felt as good when he was fully awake as it did when he was half asleep.

But he lingered too long in the bathroom. Trying to get his brain in order, his cock under control, and his thoughts together.

When he came out ten minutes later, she had already gathered her things and slipped out the door. He jerked the door open, and stood there naked as he watched her climb into a cab.

Allie?

* * * * *

Later that night, she lay on her bed, sleeping with the courtesy of a couple of painkillers. In her dream, Alex was kissing his way down her body, pausing to kiss the faint bruises on her wrists, the faintly stinging flesh of her backside where he had smacked her while he rode her body.

Allie awoke on the verge of orgasm, a sob falling from her lips. Her body, needy and hot, clenched ruthlessly while her heart wept.

An impossible dream.

She could still see the shock in his eyes, the urge to pull away, when he woke up and realized he was buried inside her body. Could still see the scorn in his eyes as he looked over her scrawny, pale little body. Still hear the faint irritation in his voice as he muttered, *I don't believe this.*

Chapter Two

සං

It wasn't until nearly two weeks later that she lost it. She was wearing her plain blue scrubs as she worked her way down the long hall of the nursing home where she worked, handing out pills and emptying the bed pans her aides had conveniently forgot about.

When her supervisor approached her, Alison linked her hands behind her back, eyeing the other nurse who followed. Leslie.

Leslie was her replacement, supposed to come on shift in approximately twenty minutes. But from the look in Don's eyes, that wasn't going to happen.

"Leslie's got an emergency," Don started out.

Alison could guess well enough what the emergency was. Don had won tickets to a concert that night and he wanted to take his new girlfriend with him. Leslie smiled, showing off her recently whitened teeth, pressing her augmented breasts up against Don's arm as she said, "My mom fell earlier today. I need to get to the emergency room so I can take her home and sit with her."

Leslie's mom had taken off when Leslie was just a kid. Alison remembered overhearing that. She overheard a lot of things. When you blended in with the wallpaper that happened quite often. But she didn't call her on the lie, just apologetically said, "I'm afraid I can't."

"Oh, sure, you can," Don said. "You don't have a family at home, and it's not like you've got a date waiting."

The words were true, but it made them no less painful.

Carefully, not letting her feelings show, she said, "I'm sorry, but I can't. I have plans for tonight that can't be broken."

"I'm afraid I'm going to have to insist," Don said, getting more irritated. Alison never said no. And damn it, nobody else would stay an extra eight hours, not on a Friday night. "Unless you want to lose your job for refusing mandatory overtime."

Slowly, Alison's fingers loosened and came up to rest atop the medicine cart. "And I'm afraid I'm going to have to insist on calling the emergency department and verifying that Leslie's mom is actually there."

"Excuse me?"

Her body was shaking slightly and Alison had to force herself to continue. God, she hated confrontations. But taking a deep breath, she told him, "I can always go talk to Billie and ask her if she can look for ya'll tonight at the concert. You think she'll buy that emergency bit if she sees you two dancing down at Coyote's? She's been talking about that concert for weeks."

Billie Monroe, the Director of Nursing at Lindenwood Nursing Home, was a country music fanatic. And for some reason nobody could fathom, she liked Alison, not just casually, as a good employer likes a good employee, but nearly and dearly, the way a friend liked a friend.

"Are you threatening me?" Don asked, hardly able to believe his ears. This mouse didn't stand up to a little old lady trying to filch cookies. And she was standing up to him, her boss? The little bitch was threatening him. "We don't tolerate threats here."

Slowly, Alison nodded. "I realize that. As I said, I can't work for you tonight, Leslie." Silently, she pushed her cart away, finished her medicine pass up and made a few necessary chart entries, all the while feeling two pairs of eyes drilling into her back. Well, actually more. Several people had overheard and were giving her surprised glances.

She ignored them, finished her charting, turned her keys over to a very hostile Leslie, and clocked out. Then she made her way to Billie's office. Billie had just finished up the weekly administration meeting so she should be available now. *If Don hasn't beat me to it already*, Allie thought weakly, turning a pen over and over in her small hands.

The tiny redhead looked up from her desk, the phone propped on her shoulder. Holding up one slim finger, she mouthed, "Give me a minute."

Alison lowered herself into a chair, slowly taking deep breaths and releasing them, concentrating on the flow of air in and out of her lungs.

She had done it. She had stood up to her bully of a boss. She hadn't let Miss Prom Queen intimidate her. Well, Leslie and Don did intimidate her. But she hadn't shown it.

And now she was sitting here in her director's office.

She was going to do it.

She was really going to do it.

Billie lowered the phone, flashed Alison a bright smile and asked, "Change your mind, darlin'? Coming to the show tonight with me? We can get drunk, find us some rhinestone cowboys and you can loosen your strings and get laid, have some fun..."

Her breathing grew shallow now and she turned her head away.

Billie's eyes darkened with concern. "Honey, what's wrong?"

Footsteps from down the hall grew nearer and from the corner of her eye, she saw Don. Straightening up in her chair, she laid her fisted hands in her lap, took a deep breath and said it.

"I quit."

"Quit?"

"I'll work out my two weeks, but I quit," she said, the words coming through her raw, tight throat.

Billie nodded, slowly. "Okay. Okay, we'll get to that." Rising from her chair, she moved to the door and grasped the door knob. She saw Don approaching and said formally, "Don, if you need me, I'll talk to you in a few minutes. I'm busy now."

Don's eyes narrowed on the skinny nurse seated in the chair and he started to seethe. "Billie, this is —"

"Later, Don." Then she closed the door in the day shift supervisor's face and turned back to Alison. "Okay, sweetie. Now you're gonna tell me what's got you so upset."

Alison's face flushed and her hands were shaking but she repeated, "I quit."

"I heard you, and if you feel you need to do that, then you do it. But tell me what's got you so upset," Billie said, her voice level. Full of authority.

Full of concern.

It was just too much, Alison thought helplessly, listening to the retreating footsteps, the mumbling coming from outside the door. For some bizarre reason, she was also remembering the mugging, and Alex — that hot explosive sex, and that humiliating scene afterwards, when he had pulled away from her...oh, shit. A sharp, brutal pain slid through her gut, twisted and jerked and she gasped out loud from the intensity of it.

The dull haze she had existed in for the past few weeks was disappearing — like a painkiller wearing off — and Allie was starting to hurt more than she had ever hurt in her life.

Staring up at Billie, she whispered, "I just can't do this any more."

"Can't do what, baby?" Billie asked, starting to get worried. "Now talk to me, Allie. You're making me nervous."

Alison's eyes closed as two tears escaped to slide down her cheeks. "Billie, I hate my life. I hate it."

Smoothing a gentle hand down her back, Billie murmured, "We all get that way from time to time, baby."

"No. I mean it, Billie. I hate my life," she whispered, her voice shaking. Rising to her feet, she paced the small confines of the office. "I hate seeing my reflection in the morning, knowing how other people see me. A doormat who will let anybody walk all over me. A mouse. A pushover."

Her voice breaking, she whirled and stared at Billie with hot, angry, hurting eyes. "Damn it, I haven't had a date in nearly a year. Nobody wants to date somebody like me. I hide from my own shadow. Here, people treat me like a damned servant. Can't work your shift? Call Alison. Don't want to deal with that temperamental bear in 201A? Have Alison do it. Got a hot date and need to get out of work? Tell Alison there's an emergency. She'll never guess you're lying; she's too naive. And even if she does guess, she's too chicken to say anything."

When Allie turned around to stare out the window, a bright wicked grin slashed across Billie's face, but she subdued it and cleared her throat, forcing back the giggle of relief. "Honey, I don't think you're a doormat. You're dependable, honest, and kind. Those are good things." Heaving a sigh, she added, "Maybe a little too kind for your own good."

Lowering herself to her chair, she thought of how many times she had seen Alison's name appear on the work roster when it shouldn't have been there. "And maybe some people here do take advantage of you." Shoving her wild red curls back, she said, "But, baby, that's going to happen until you learn how to say no. No matter where you work."

Slowly, a smile crept across Alison's face and she turned around to face Billie. "I know. And I did." Pressing a hand to her still jumping stomach, she said, "It wasn't as hard as I thought it would be."

"Is that what all this is about?"

Alison barely hesitated to relay what had happened to Billie. Before, she never would have dared. But, now, it poured out of her. And other things. How Leslie had been badgering her for weeks to swap shifts permanently, brushing aside the college courses that Alison attended three nights a week. How her aides went off to lunch right before her noon med pass, leaving bedridden patients unchanged and unfed.

And then she told her about the attempted mugging.

"What the fuck are you talking about?" she shouted as Allison blurted out what had happened. Billie's brilliant green eyes narrowed and then widened and her mouth moved soundlessly. "Why didn't you call me, honey?" She shoved aside the hurt and concentrated on the wildness she saw in Alison's normally placid green eyes.

"I wanted to forget about it. I can't. The past two weeks, I keep thinking, if…if he had killed me, would my life have meant anything?" Billie started to speak, but Allie cut her off, her voice urgent. "Billie, I don't think I've done a damn thing in my life that I'm proud of. I could see myself in his eyes, and I looked so pathetic. Felt so pathetic."

Billie's sense of hurt faded under the misery she saw in Alison's face. "Oh, honey," she whispered, walking over to the taller woman and folding her arms around her.

But she didn't tell her about the worst of it. How she had gotten naked and sweating with the man of her dreams, only to have him pull away from her in disgust when it was over. How she had run away from his house at two in the morning, ashamed and hurt, still wet from him, her heart still pounding, her body still quivering.

And her ears still echoing from what he had said—*I don't believe this.*

As Alison cried her heart out, Billie stroked her hands down the narrow back—and had to hide a smile, had to hide that she wanted to jump up on the desk and dance a jig. Never mind she was going to have to tell administration they had lost one of their best nurses. She had started to think this day was never going to come.

After the tears passed, Billie briskly shook Alison's shoulder. "Tomorrow's not your shift to work, is it?"

Alison shook her head, mutely as she dashed tears from her face.

"Okay. I'm picking you up at nine. Get some rest, because we are going to be busy."

"Busy doing what?"

Billie smiled faintly. "You'll see. You will work out your two weeks, thank goodness," she said, lowering herself to her desk, flipping her calendar.

Alison nodded, hardly able to believe she had gone through with it. She had quit—she was walking away from this job that had broken her heart and left her aching.

"Good. That will leave a shift open on days. Hmm." Sliding Alison a sly glance, she said, "I'm sure Leslie would be happy with that. But Angie has been here longer. And she's made some noises about getting off night shift. We'll keep this thing quiet until I can talk to her. I'll swing by here in the morning after her shift."

Guilt started to settle in. "Billie, I know how short staffed we've been-"

Holding up her hand, Billie said, "Don't worry about it, Allie. That's my job, not yours." She finally released a sigh of regret. "You don't belong in a place like this, Allie. It's breaking your heart. You get too close to these little old people, and your heart's too soft. I love it here, and I love these people. But I'm cut out for this place. You are not. And I've always known you'd leave, sooner or later. This isn't what you need."

* * * * *

"Of course I have money," Alison said as she followed Billie out to the car the following morning. The breeze from the river blew her hair into her face and she absently brushed it back before reaching into her pocket for a scrunchy. As she pulled her brown hair into a ponytail, she eyed Billie warily. "Why?"

"Because you're going to need it," Billie said with relish, her eyes narrowed, an excited smile on her face. Shopping, in her opinion, took second place to two things—sex and chocolate.

A half an hour later, Alison stared at the storefront. "Contacts? No way."

"Yes," Billie said, herding her through the door and signing her in when Alison only stared dumbly at the clipboard.

Two hours later, her contacts in place, she reached up, brushing a hand across her face. "It feels weird," she said. The absence of the glasses she had worn since she was ten left her feeling naked somehow. She stared into the mirrored wall at her eyes, her face. The pale, skinny oval looked *too* pale and her green eyes looked lost in her face, in her hair. "I don't know about this, Billie."

"You look great," Billie said firmly. Then she steered her out of the shop and into the now bustling mall.

They bypassed the clothing stores and boutiques and once more, Billie herded her into another shop. A salon.

"Cut my hair?" Alison squeaked, one hand flying up to the heavy ponytail that fell half way down her back.

"Your face isn't right for all that hair," Billie said. "A friend of mine works here and put you in for an appointment."

"I didn't ask for an appointment."

"I did. Hey, Genni."

Genni was a massive black woman with braids wrapped around her head like a crown. She moved to greet Billie then turned her black eyes on Alison. "Layers. Short," was all she said before taking Alison's hand and gently but firmly guiding her across the salon to a chair.

Alison touched one fearful hand to her head and whispered, "I'm not too sure about this."

Genni smiled, a blinding flash of teeth in her wide face. "Don't worry, girl. You will be," she told her in a deep, oddly soothing voice.

Alison just closed her eyes and silently promised retribution as Billie moved to stand behind her shoulder. "What about highlights?"

"A rinse. I bet she's got natural ones in her hair. I got something in the back that'll bring 'em out," Genni said, pursing her lips as she smoothed her long fingers through Alison's hair – tugging the band from her hair and massaging her scalp as she went.

Beauticians had to go to college, right? Surely this woman who looked like an Amazon knew what she was doing. Didn't she? Alison, out of self-defense, tuned out the voices above and behind her, retreating into her mind.

It was kind of relaxing, she thought a little later as strong hands worked lather through her thick heavy hair. "Good weight, Billie. Hair's shiny and healthy. Just too much of it," Genni said, talking to Billie as though Alison wasn't even there.

She jumped slightly when she heard the first snip-snip. Genni laughed behind her and said, "I was waiting for that. Now you got it out of your system, girl, you hold still." And then a ten-inch long hank of hair fell into Alison's lap.

Alison's eyes closed and she whispered, "Oh, God." She was praying.

Praying Genni wasn't going to leave her bald.

Genni and Billie laughed. "Don't worry," Billie teased. "God's going to be mighty pleased when we're done with you."

Thirty minutes later, her hair chopped, clipped, rinsed, dried and combed, Alison stared at her reflection. "Oh," she said, her voice faint.

One hesitant hand reached up and touched her head. God, she felt so much lighter. And her hair was still long. In the back, it curved just past her shoulders, but around her face, it was cut in layers that curled and waved. She ran her hand over it, then through it, watched as it fell right back into place. And the color... "How did you get it to streak like that?" she asked, eyeing the random streaks of dark gold that mixed with the darker brown. "What did you do?"

"Not much," Genni said, pleased. "You got them highlights, all right. And to keep 'em, all you got to do is use this rinse I'm going to sell you about two or three times a week. You're gonna use the stuff I send home with you. All that department store crap is building up on your hair, keeping it looking so blah. And you need monthly appointments to keep your hair in shape."

Billie opened her mouth to insist, certain Alison would squawk. Instead, the younger woman touched her hair again, and said, "All right."

She looked so different. Her face—she looked, well, pretty. Without the glasses hiding them, her eyes looked huge. And her face—which had always seemed too narrow and skinny—looked cute, elfin.

Billie started to grin as she realized what Alison was thinking. "Not a mouse, honey. Definitely not a mouse."

* * * * *

"Start working out?" Alison repeated, glancing down at her rail thin body. "I'll fade away."

"You're working out to put muscle on. Weight lifting, I think. About three times a week. Can you afford a gym?"

Alison thought of the money her parents had left her, of her weekly paychecks that went mostly untouched. A small, sad little smile curved her mouth and she nodded. "I can afford it."

"Good. You'll join one, one that's close to your home; otherwise you won't ever use it. And maybe some aerobics, or something."

"Karate."

The word slipped out before Alison realized it and Billie's eyes turned her way, brows arched nearly to her hair line.

"I, uh, I took it for two years when I was younger."

"All right. Karate sounds good to me," Billie said, grinning as she watched Alison's hand once more go up to comb through her hair. Looping one arm through hers, Billie guided her away from the fountain and into a shop. "Now you need clothes. You ever think about getting your ears pierced?"

Her fingers crept up to touch her lobes and Allie shook her head.

Laughing, Billie seized a pale green spring sweater and held it up to Alison. "Think about it. You've gotta couple hours to get used to the idea."

Six exhausting hours—and nearly eight hundred dollars later—Alison walked through the door of her house, arms laden with bags. Dumping them on the floor next to the others, she walked across the room and flopped down on the wide sage green sofa, flinging an arm over her eyes. Small gold hoops sparkled at her ears and a delicate chain wrapped around the wrist she had lying on her belly.

Her head was spinning. Clothes, hair, make-up Billie had insisted she'd come over with a friend and teach her how to put it on. Make up…every day? It took Alison forever to get it to look right and she was expected to wear it everyday?

Rolling off the couch she made her way to her bedroom and opened the door to the walk-in closet. Flicking on the light, she studied her reflection in the full-length mirror, a tiny grin curving her mouth.

Still way too skinny. But maybe the weight lifting would help. She still looked uncertain, but not so much now. And that was something she could work on.

Reaching up, she ran her fingers through her chopped off hair, watched as it drifted down to settle into place.

An unbidden thought crept into her mind and she wondered, idly, what would Alex think?

Chapter Three
July 2001
Kells, Ireland

෨

The sun shone down warmly on her body but the air around her was cool. The hands moving over her were firm, hard and certain, strong and gentle.

She sobbed out Niall's name as he pulled his mouth from her sex and moved between her thighs, taking a condom and sliding it down his length before he covered her and started to enter her.

Staring up into his impossibly blue eyes, Allie wondered again if she was dreaming as Niall whispered against her ear in that low, sexy Irish accent about how good she felt. His voice alone was enough to make her wet and he wanted *her*.

His mouth closed hot and wet over one tight, swollen nipple and he suckled there as he rode her gently, shifting his weight so that he could circle his thumb over her clit. In the past ten days, since she had first taken Niall as a lover, or actually he had taken her, she had realized just how generous a man could be. He brought her to climax twice before he took his own.

He was handsome, he was attentive, he showed every sign of being infatuated. Even if he did live on the other side of the world.

So there was no reason for her to dream of Alex when she fell asleep later that night.

But, of course, she did.

Allie awoke early the next morning, sliding from the bed and stretching her arms high overhead. She hadn't slept as well—she had, foolishly most likely, spent four nights with Niall—and those had been the sweetest nights—but last night the doctor had been called in to work and she had slept alone at the inn.

And she had dreamed of Alex.

The cad.

Then she flushed and kicked herself.

It wasn't his fault—not exactly.

He couldn't help that she wasn't his type.

But he didn't have to be so fucking cruel that night.

She hadn't seen him since. Alex had been avoiding Mike and Lori's house. Nobody had outright said that, but he hadn't gone to the Fourth of July party or the cookout they had every year on Derby Day. Typically, they ran into each other four or five times a month, at least. They usually caught a movie together at least once a month, or went and got something to eat after Alex nagged her into it.

She would admit, under punishment of torture, that she missed him.

But she was still too angry, too hurt, to be anything other than grateful for his continued absence from her life.

At least up until recently.

The knock on her door was Niall.

When she opened it, and his eyes met hers, and he caught her face in his beautiful poet's hands and kissed her like she was some kind of treasure, she forgot about Alex.

At least for a while.

The lush greenery of the Irish countryside hid the truck from view. Allie lay in the truck bed, gasping and sobbing as Niall sucked ruthlessly at her clit, driving two fingers inside her pussy, almost roughly.

He had pulled over, a slightly feverish look in his eyes, after a glance at his watch. "I hate that ya have to go," he murmured as he pulled her from the cab. "Something to remember me by."

She shifted and squirmed until she could close her hand over his cock while he fucked her with his fingers. "Niall, please," Allie whispered, rocking against him.

He moaned and pulled away, jerking a condom out and putting it on before driving into her, rough and hard. Her breath caught and he froze. "Allie?"

"Again," she pleaded, pushing her hips up. "Please—"

Her words died in her throat as he started to drive into her, hard and rough and fast with the sun shining down on them. He caught her mouth in a deep kiss, hungry and desperate, as he threaded his hands through her gold-streaked hair, holding her thrashing head still.

She came, quick and hard and he followed, unable to hold off as he groaned "Alison," against her mouth.

Indiana

"Sorry," Alex lied into the phone, closing his eyes and pressing his fingers against them. "I can't, Mike. I've got too much going—"

"Alex, you have to," Mike insisted. "Lori's sick. I can't leave her alone. Her mom's out of town and I don't know who the fuck else to call. It's not like Allie has a whole list of friends to choose from."

Grudgingly, and silently, he admitted Mike had a point. "What time is her flight?"

He jotted the details down. "If Lori gets to feeling better—"

"She has to stay in bed for the next three days, Alex. Doctor's orders. And I've already called in for personal leave for tomorrow. Her mom will be home to stay with her after that, but she's not going to be better in the next five hours, bro. It's not like it's going to take that long."

"What's the problem, anyway? It's just Allie, for crying out loud. You pick up a couple of suitcases and take her home. And she won't even talk your ear off," Mike said, aggravated.

"The problem is I had things to do and I don't feel like picking up your baby sister," Alex snapped. *I feel like fucking her every time I even hear her name.* He grimaced and said, "Sorry. Look, it's not a problem. I didn't sleep well and I'm in a bitch of a mood. I'll take care of it."

Mike hung up on him.

Alex stood there, swearing silently and feeling his jeans grow tighter as he realized he didn't have any choice.

He was going to be picking little Alison Ryan up from the airport in a couple of hours. He hadn't seen her in six months, not in the flesh. But he had dreamed of her on a regular basis, and even the thought of seeing her, smelling her, was enough to have his cock standing at attention.

Okay.

Maybe this wasn't a bad thing.

He'd see her, realize that night was a fluke.

And he could get on with his life. Every woman he had been with since Allie had paled in comparison. And it was getting to the point where he just wasn't that interested in any of them.

Just her.

Sometimes he saw a dark-haired, skinny woman and his heart squeezed, his cock throbbed and he wondered, he hoped, but it wasn't her. For a fairly small town, they were doing a good job of never seeing each other.

Okay.

So now they would see each other.

He could apologize and get things back on level ground and get on with his life.

Yeah, that's it.

This could work.

Allie Ryan would never be right for him anyway.

Chapter Four

ঙ০

Allie Ryan floated off the airplane, smiling dreamily, her fingers caressing the gold Celtic knot at her throat.

Three weeks in Ireland, and the last ten days were spent with Niall—that tall, sexy blond doctor who had pursued her with a vengeance from the first glance. Her first real lover, a man so fabulous looking, he would have put Pierce Brosnan to shame. Slow, dreamy sex on a picnic blanket next to a lake with the sun shining down on them.

Niall had spent hours loving her by the lake, and even more hours in the nights that followed.

She had seen real, burning desire in his eyes, had felt it when he kissed his way down her body to drink from her like she tasted of the finest wine. Even now, the thought had her flushing—brought a rush of cream to dampen her skimpy silk panties.

She'd finally had a lover. Even if only for ten days.

A lover, not ten sweaty—if glorious—minutes on the floor. A gorgeous, generous man who had whispered sweet things in her ear while they ate dinner—and some not so sweet things while he undressed her.

She had made new friends, had invitations to return to the country and stay with them—as a friend—not a customer.

Allie had already decided she would return as soon as she could afford it. Her savings had been nearly wiped out by this trip, but the new job she had lined up was at nearly triple what she had been making as an LPN.

She snorted, knowing full well she wouldn't be doing a damn thing she hadn't already known how to do. But those two little letters, RN, made a world of difference when it came to payroll.

God, she was excited.

She was going to be working in the ER, something she had always dreamed of, but had never had the guts to go for. At least not until recently.

Her whole life had changed in the past few months. It hadn't been easy—forcing herself to come out of her shy little shell—but it had been worth it. The weight lifting hadn't been much fun, until a month after she had started, when she had noticed she had developed some curves where before, she had only been flat. And after a while, when her temper finally rose above her hurt, she fantasized about using those newly developed muscles to give Alex O'Malley a black eye.

And the three weekly classes of karate, once she had finished her courses at The Health Institute, had been nothing but fun. Hot, sweaty, muscle aching fun, but fun nonetheless.

Almost as much hot and sweaty fun as she had had with Niall in the cab of his truck on the way to the airport.

With a breathless little laugh, she blew her bangs out of her eyes, fanning herself with her hand. "Great thing to have on your mind when your brother comes looking for you," she murmured. But she pressed her lips together, and imagined she could still taste him, and the last, hungry kiss he had pressed to her mouth. Wickedly, she hoped he was still tasting her as well.

Glancing around the terminal, she looked for Mike, eager to see him and his new wife, Lori, who had become such a good friend.

* * * * *

O'Malley glanced at his watch one more time before studying the throng of people. His eyes caught on a cute brunette with big green eyes and a sexy smile curving her mouth, lingered just a moment, before he continued to look for his best friend's little sister Of course, thinking of Allie as his best friend's little sister was no longer the easiest way to think of her.

Even if he did force himself to think that way.

He wanted to think of her the way he had seen her that night—her long brown hair wrapped around his fist as he fucked her tight, sweet vagina, the firm curve of her ass, the hot stab of her nipples burning into his chest. His mouth started to water and his cock swelled just thinking of it.

Allie. Remember that? Little Allie? You and Mike taught her how to ride her bike?

So now I can teach her to ride me...

FUCK!

Damn it to hell, he didn't want to be here.

He didn't want to see Allie, didn't want to remember that night. He had been such a fucking coward. He should have at least gone after her and made sure she was all right—apologized.

Fucked her again.

Shit.

No, he didn't want to be here. But how could he tell his best friend—who was worried about his pregnant wife—that he couldn't pick Allie up because he'd fucked her brains out, it was the best fuck of his life, and now he was scared to see her again?

Still no Allie.

Probably missed her flight.

From the corner of his eye, he could see the little brunette approaching, and he started to hope Allie had missed the flight. She looked vaguely familiar, especially those green eyes. If Allie had missed her flight, then he could flirt with this much safer brunette with the wide smile. He could push Allie out of his mind temporarily, talk this cute thing into grabbing a bite with him, and he would put dealing with Allie off again.

He'd been successfully doing just that for months.

"Alex?"

His head swung around, his eyes narrowed. He knew that voice. He'd often wondered why God had wasted such a soft, throaty voice on a woman like Alison Ryan. Half the time, she was even afraid to talk, and when she did, it was in stops and starts that made her sound breathless.

But it wasn't Alison standing in front of him.

This long, leggy brunette had sun-streaked brown hair that tumbled and curled around a sweet, elfin face and a laughing smile on her sexy mouth. This sexy thing had big green eyes that met his head on while Allie preferred to stare past his shoulder, at her feet, or at his butt when she thought he wasn't looking.

Long slim legs outlined by form fitting jeans, a beat up pair of Nikes. Slim hips, the glimpse of a tight ass. He dragged his eyes back up the amazing pair of legs, over the mint green sweater tank that molded itself to her sweet little tits — not Allie. Couldn't be.

This cute thing had round, mouthwatering little breasts…just like Allie's. A smooth, slim white neck, a pink mouth…just like Allie's.

Oh, hell.

She arched an eyebrow and her luscious mouth opened again. "Have you seen Mike?"

"Allie?"

She grinned, and Alex blinked his eyes, certain sleep deprivation was playing a dirty trick on him.

"Long time, no see," she said, even though he could tell she was snickering inside.

"Uh, he, Mike asked me if I could pick you up. Lori had to go to the doctor, some kind of stomach bug." Drawing his sunglasses from his pocket, he slid them on, wanting to study her a little closer, without her grinning at him like that.

Like she knew he had been hit across the head with a two-by-four.

"Is she okay?" Allie asked, catching her carry-on before the strap could slide down her arm. "Is the baby okay?"

Automatically, he reached out and took it, his fingers brushing against her bare arm as he drew the strap down. "I'll carry it," he said gruffly. Clearing his throat, he answered her question. "Yeah. Some kind of stomach flu or something. Are you...are you ready?"

Once on the automatic sidewalk, he fell behind her so they could walk around the people standing still. From behind the shield of his dark glasses, he studied her, still unable to believe his eyes. This couldn't possibly be the girl he had seen fighting in an alley back in February. The girl he'd woken up fucking, his dick buried inside her sweet, *sweet* body. The girl he had watched ride away in a cab in the middle of the night while he stood there, too fucking embarrassed and afraid to go after her.

But it was. On the back of her right arm, she had a small scar, one he knew she had gotten when she was eight. And on the back of her left shoulder, revealed by her sweater tank, she had a small heart-shaped birthmark.

But the rest of her...her tight little butt curved into her jeans—jeans that hugged long curvy legs. Had she always been that tall? Most likely. She just always seemed smaller, the way she carried herself. But she stood five-eight in her sneakers and most of it looked like leg. The sleeveless sweater she wore revealed toned, tanned arms and smooth slim shoulders.

She hadn't always looked like that, he knew. Skinny. That was what Allie had been. There still wasn't much to her, but everything was rounded and curved exactly where it should be. God, that sweet, round little ass...

Swallowing, he had to clear his throat again as he followed her off the moving sidewalk and around the corner. Her long, leggy stride was eating up the ground and she chattered easily.

"Once," he answered when she asked if he had ever been to Ireland. "I was eleven or twelve."

Allie smiled slightly. "Oh, yeah I remember that. You complained to Mike about it for a month before you left. And when you came back, you didn't say a thing."

"It was beautiful," he said, remembering the green hills, the ocean, the colorful villages Mom and Dad had taken him. He hadn't been back since, and now he had to wonder why. "I didn't know you had gone on vacation."

Her smooth shoulders lifted in an absent shrug and she said, "I finished up my courses at Spalding, and decided to reward myself."

"Courses?" he repeated.

"RN courses. I'm a registered nurse now. I work at University, on the med-surg floor, but next week, I move down to the ER."

Dark brown brows rose at that. "You sure you can handle trauma?" he asked. As a cop, he knew what kind of cases you could see in the ER, and he couldn't quite get a picture of Allie handling them. Gun shots, stab wounds, motor vehicle accidents. Blood, brutality, death.

"It's what I've always wanted to do," she said. One hand drifted up, toying with a gold charm at her throat, drawing Alex's eyes as they neared the baggage claim.

A Celtic knot, he thought, eyeing it. That dreamy smile was back on her face and her green eyes had gone misty and soft. The look a woman got on her face only when she was thinking of a man.

The punch of jealousy in his gut knocked him off guard and he took a step back, running a shaky hand through his hair, tearing his eyes away from her butt and closing them.

Good heaven, this was Alison, the girl he had known since she was a toddler.

The girl he had rescued from a mugger high on heroin and so strung out he couldn't even remember his own name. But that wasn't exactly so. She had knocked the mugger down and had done a damn fine job of protecting herself.

This was the girl who had cried herself to sleep in his arms, only to wake up with him shoving his stiff cock inside her tight body. The girl he had allowed to leave his place—alone.

Alone—only hours after she had nearly been killed. He'd figured out that night that she wasn't the gutless mouse he had always pegged her as.

Alone—after what he suspected was her first time. If he had been a decent guy, hell, if it had been somebody besides Allie, he would have gone after her. But he had been floored.

He still couldn't get over that night, still couldn't forget how good it had felt to slide his cock inside her slick wet tissues, the way her eyes darkened with mingled fear and excitement as he spanked her sweet little butt, the taste of her mouth under his. And he couldn't forget how badly he had wanted to go after her and fuck her again, repeatedly.

He had almost driven over there, to the little house she had on River Road over in Jeffersonville, but he had been too embarrassed. And too worried. How had she affected him like that? Allie, of all women.

And he had turned down the invitations to Mike's barbecue on Derby Day and Independence Day, just so he wouldn't have to see her.

A hand, soft and cool, came to rest on his forearm. Opening his eyes, he stared through the tinted lenses down into the concerned green eyes peering up at him. "Are you okay, Alex?"

Other than a sudden urge to press his hand against hers, to press her tight sexy body up against the wall, to cover her mouth with his? Well, other than that, and this unreal sensation coursing through his body, hell, he was fine.

He moved his shoulders in a stiff shrug and said, "Late night." And then, unable to resist, he reached out, slipped a finger under the slim gold chain around her neck, pretending to study the intricate knot. "A gift?"

That smile came back—that little feline, totally *female* smile a woman gets that will drive a man out of his mind—and she said, "Yes. A friend." Reaching up, she patted his cheek and turned away. "Let's get my bags so we can get you home. You look exhausted."

Irritation flooded him at the gesture, the kind a schoolteacher gives a small boy. Or that of a woman petting her dog. He clamped down the urge to seize her hand back and jerk her up against him, and he wondered what the hell was wrong with him. This is Allie—maybe she looked a little different, hell, a lot different, but underneath that sassy smile, she was still the same girl she had always been.

He shifted on the tiled floor as she strolled up and down beside the conveyor belt, searching for her bags. Alex's eyes narrowed behind his tinted lenses as a suit clad man flashed her a long look, followed by a slow smile. Alex's eyes widened as Allie smiled back.

Dear God in Heaven, he thought. Allie was flirting.

His feet started moving without him even being aware, and soon he was close enough to hear Allie say, "I've got a ride, but thank you." She made an absent motion in his direction with one hand while the other brushed a stray lock of hair back away from her face.

"How about a phone number?"

Allie grinned, tucked her head a little bit, reminding him of the Allie he knew. The tension in his back started to loosen as he waited for her to stammer out some sort of 'no,' but instead, she recited a phone number and held out her hand. "I'm Alison," she told him as he took her hand.

"Gray. Gray Douglass." And he repeated the number, tapping his temple while he did it.

Somebody called out Gray's name and he turned, held up a hand, before turning back to Allie. He flashed a bright, charming smile and said, "Maybe we can do lunch or something."

"Maybe. It was nice meeting you," she answered.

As Alex stuffed his hands deep into his pockets, Gray turned away, his gaze sliding over Alex before he headed out of the baggage claim area.

"I don't suppose I should mention how utterly stupid it is to give out your number to total strangers," Alex growled.

Allie jumped, spinning around to stare at Alex. "Oh, I didn't hear you come up." Then she gave a negligent shrug of her shoulders. "I gave him the number to my cell." She turned her eyes back to the conveyor belt and started forward. "Finally. I've only got two more, those two black suitcases coming down now."

He bit off his reply before brushing past her, taking the two cases and turning back to her. "I didn't realize that somehow in the past few months you had lost your common sense," he finally said, stalking away from the conveyor belt.

"Common sense?" Allie repeated, her voice soft.

Something in her tone stopped him and he turned to stare at her. A sad smile curved her mouth upward and he realized with a jolt—that wide, sexy mouth was the same. Her smile had always been the same; it hadn't changed. It was just so rare that he saw it, so rare that she used it.

"Common sense," she repeated in a murmur. She moved a few steps closer, crossing her arms over her chest. "I've used my common sense my whole life, Alex. And I've been miserable," she said quietly.

Miserable?

Her eyes moved away from his, studying the crowds flowing around them. "Something dawned on me not too long ago, Alex. I hated my life. Hated who I was. I had always used my common sense and what had it gotten me? I had a job that broke my heart, almost no friends, and a date a year, if I was lucky. I spent every night at home alone. The highlight of my week was on Tuesday, when the new books came out at the book store."

"I wasn't happy. I am now. If you think I'm foolish, then go ahead and think that." Her wide green eyes turned back to his, glittering and bright. Her voice almost shaking with intensity, she whispered, "I'm happy, Alex. *Happy.* Happy for the first time in my life. That's what matters. And you know what? If Gray Douglass turns out to be a mass murderer who kills me tomorrow night while I sleep, at least I'll die knowing what it's like to have really lived. At least a little."

Then she moved past him, her long legs eating up the ground.

Behind her, Alex dropped one of the suitcases, reached up, shoved his sunglasses up and pressed his fingers to his eyes. "Aw, shit," he muttered.

What in the hell was wrong with him? How many women had he seen that he got a phone number and a hell of a lot more from them within five minutes of meeting them? He grabbed the suitcase, and took off after her, watching the pale green of her top as she wove through the crowds. He caught up with her at the drop-off area and caught her elbow, pulling her to a stop as he set the suitcases down.

"I'm sorry, okay?"

She tugged her arm away, gently but firmly, lowering her own suitcase as well.

Alex's eyes narrowed but he resisted the urge to pull her back. "I am sorry, Allie. But I'm a cop and I can't help but worry."

She turned her head, staring at him with blank eyes. "I'm a cop's sister, Alex. I know all about being careful," she said flatly. "And it's none of your business who I give my number to."

Alex bit back the sigh, bit back the urge to argue, and held up one hand in a gesture of truce. Even if what he wanted to do was paddle her ass...*damn it what in the hell was wrong with him*? He had no right to feel so fucking possessive of her. "No, it's not. And I said I was sorry."

"Apology accepted," she said, turning away and grabbing the handle of her suitcase.

"You want to go get a bite to eat?" Alex asked cautiously, unsure of her attitude just now. "I haven't eaten much and I'm getting pretty hungry."

She started to say no, but glanced at her watch. It was just now four. And she hadn't eaten on the plane. Now her belly was rumbling. "Sure. Why not?" she said—still stinging some from his comment.

Alex resisted the urge to breathe a sigh of relief. Instead, he guided her out to his truck, sliding her suitcases in the back of the cab before turning to help her in. "By the way," Alex said quietly, waiting until she turned her face to him. Reaching up, he stroked one finger down the curve of her cheek, feeling the soft, silky skin. "You look great."

By the time he had circled the truck and climbed in, Allie had wiped the foolish grin off her face.

* * * * *

The little old cafe had been in Jeffersonville for as long as people could remember. If the inside looked as disreputable as the outside, then there was no way she was venturing in.

Enough people ate there to keep the place going so maybe some people didn't worry about things like food poisoning or health hazards.

Apparently Alex didn't. Allie sat in the scarred booth, absently rubbing a finger over an ancient scratch on the cheap vinyl tabletop while she studied the menu.

Quirking an eyebrow, she glanced up at Alex and whispered, "You're sure it's safe to eat here?"

Alex looked at her with a grin and said, "This from a woman who gives out her phone number to total strangers?"

Glancing around the dim interior that smelled of smoke and liquor, Allie said, "I want to live, enjoy life, experience life.

Not experience food poisoning." Some misguided soul had attempted to brighten the atmosphere by stringing white lights from the ceiling. The man who stood behind the bar polishing glasses scowled their way and hollered, "Annie, you got customers."

Somebody, Annie, Allie presumed, shouted out an irritable, "Wait one damned minute."

Alex reached over, plucked the menu from Allie's fingers and asked, "Do you trust me?"

"With my life, absolutely. With my stomach lining? I'll have to think about that."

As Annie stalked out of the kitchen, she shot the bartender a sour look before turning toward Alex and Allie. She brightened and called out, "Well, hey, handsome. Why didn't you tell me it was you?" Eyeing Allie, she studied her, and then winked at Alex. "Your taste is improving."

Allie blushed and studied the table as the brassy blonde flirted with Alex. And Alex, of course, flirted shamelessly back before ordering burgers for both of them. After the waitress had sauntered off, Allie looked up and said, "I take it you come here often."

With a shrug, he leaned back in the torn vinyl booth. "I was in and out of here for a while, trying to get a lead on a case last summer. Never panned out. But I found the best burgers in all of Kentucky and Indiana."

"I guess I could always order a drink and hope the alcohol kills any of the bacteria lurking in here," she said, reaching up to toy with her necklace. Her fingers stilled as Alex's eyes drifted down and locked on the movement of her hand. Slowly, she lowered her hands and locked them in her lap.

Alex's mouth curved up in a smile. "Don't worry, Allie-cat," he said, calling her by an old nickname. "Nobody has died here yet."

Her eyes widened, then rolled and she dryly said, "How very reassuring."

"What did you do to your hair?" he asked, reaching out and catching a sun-streaked lock. The booth was too tiny for her to be able to draw back, which she wanted to do—Alex could tell by the look in her eyes.

Her lashes drooped and when she looked back at him, the nervous look in her eyes was gone, replaced by an easy laughing one. "Cut it off," she replied succinctly. "It was so damn long I could sit on it. You have no idea how heavy long hair is until it's all gone."

With a playful tug, he let it go. "I like it. Contacts?"

"For now. I'm having the lasik procedure done in a few months."

Automatically, he flinched, thinking of those pretty green eyes being operated on. "You sure you wanna do that?" he asked. "Is it safe?"

"Oh, the doctor says it's at least fifty percent effective. He's only had three or four people go blind," she replied, accepting her soft drink from the waitress and taking a sip.

The bland look on her face cracked as Alex went pale and repeated, "Buh-blind?"

She stopped biting her lip to keep it from trembling and just started laughing. "Geez, Alex. I didn't think cops were that gullible." As his deep brown eyes narrowed on hers, she giggled again, wiping a tear from her face. "Quit glaring at me. I can't stop laughing while you're looking at me like that."

His scowl faded and only by sheer strength of will did he avoid looking the way he felt. He'd known her for more than twenty years and seriously doubted he had ever heard her laugh like that. And he knew she had never looked as laidback, as happy, as she looked right now. He'd always thought of her as a friend.

Some friend he was, he thought, twirling his straw in his glass. He had never even begun to guess how unhappy she was.

He doubted anybody had—not even her brother.

"So when did you quit your job at the nursing home?" he asked, resolving to worry about the rest later.

One of the few customers at the bar ambled over to the old jukebox and moments later, Hank Williams came pouring out. Allie's eyes drifted that way, a smile lurking in her eyes before she turned back to Alex. "Same time everything else happened. Six months ago."

He was starting to understand. "He really scared you, didn't he?"

"Yes," she said baldly. "And this is really going to sound weird, but I think it was the best thing that ever happened to me. If that hadn't happened...well, I may never have realized just how much I was missing." She frowned, twisting the thin paper napkin between her fingers. "I worked at the home another two weeks. It wasn't that I was unhappy with the job. I loved those little old people, and I still go see them on my weekends off.

"But I get too close to people. And the people I took care of were old and sick, anyway. I couldn't keep saying good-bye. It was tearing me apart inside."

"Is that why you quit?"

A quick laugh escaped and she shook her head. Taking a sip of her coke, she said, "No. I quit because somebody asked me to work another nurse's shift. Well, he didn't ask. He told me, and I was getting tired of being told what to do."

At his confused look, she gave a brief explanation. "That was it. I was tired of being taken advantage of—tired of people walking all over me—tired of people lying to me and thinking I was too dumb or too scared to do anything."

"Here we go, two burgers and fries," the waitress called out, coming through the door.

"Thanks, Annie," Alex said. He nipped a French fry before she had even set the platters down and seized Annie's hand once it was free. "My undying gratitude if you get me some—"

"Ketchup," Annie finished up for him, pulling a bottle from one of the pockets on her apron. "Here you go. Dig in, enjoy."

She nodded at Allie before walking away, the tray tucked under her skinny arm. Moments later, she and the bartender were embroiled in an argument.

"Sounds like they enjoy arguing," Allie commented as she eyed the messy burger in front of her. French fries were always safe, she figured, snagging one and popping it into her mouth.

Spreading a napkin on her lap, she picked up the burger, and took a hesitant bite. The flavor of it exploded on her tongue, and she closed her eyes. "Oh, man. That's good," she mumbled around a mouthful.

Alex had already finished off a third of his. "Told you," was all he said as he took a drink. "Are you happier where you are now?"

Swallowing another bite of burger, she nodded. "Yes. I am. I had to force myself to start actually talking to people. And I told myself to stop thinking I was a pushover. But nobody there has tried to take advantage of me."

"That's because you made up your mind it wouldn't happen," Alex said with a shrug. "It's a case of mind over matter. It's the people without any self-confidence that get walked on." Alex lowered his eyes back to his food, scowling as he realized how often he had walked on others, taken advantage of others when it made his way a little easier. Had he done that with Allie?

Yes. He had. Any other woman would have made him pay for how callously he had treated her that night. With any other woman, he would have tried to make amends.

Looking up, he saw her watching him with calm eyes.

Even as he opened his mouth to speak, unsure of what he would say, Allie's mouth curved up and she said, "Don't worry about it, Alex."

"Alison—"

"Don't. Just let it go, okay?" she asked softly.

Silence fell between them, broken by the occasional shout from the bartender. Allie finished off about half of the burger before giving up and sitting back. "I think that's more than I usually eat in a day," she said, one hand resting on the flat of her belly. "Good thing I decided to pass on the airplane food."

Alex smiled, feeling unbelievably tired as he pushed his plate away. "They've got great mushrooms here, too. We can come back sometime."

Allie murmured a noncommittal sound as she arched her back, stretching her hands high overhead. "Man, I need a nap," she muttered, yawning. "Jet lag."

The long line of her arched back drew his eyes and he stared at her up-thrust breasts, his eyes locked on the points of her nipples, lids drooping as he remembered. His mouth started to water and he wanted to reach across the table, pull her up and spread her out before him and feast…

Damnation, he thought, as his cock hardened. *Not again.* It had taken *weeks* for him to sleep without dreaming of her, and he still couldn't go more than a week without it happening.

Casually, he slid from the booth, tossing a twenty on the table as he waited for Allie to stand up. Curving his hand around her elbow, he said, "Come on. Let's get you home. Are you going to go see Lori and Mike?"

She shrugged. "I'll give them a call. If Lori's not feeling well, I doubt she's going to want company." she said, blinking and squinting as they left the dim cafe, stepping out into the bright, late summer afternoon.

"I'll take you on home then." Before he just decided to go ahead and take.

* * * * *

Later that night, Allie's eyes opened and she looked around groggily. She was lying flat on her back on the couch. "Oh, man," she muttered, slowly sitting up, her stiff body aching with every move. "That was not smart."

Stumbling into the shower—shedding her clothes as she went—she turned on the hot water full blast and stepped under the dual shower heads. A blissful sigh of relief escaped her as the hot water started to pummel her tired muscles.

She showered and washed her hair and then just stood under the powerful jet, letting it pound her muscles until they relaxed. Climbing out and dragging a towel over her hair, she reached for her body oil.

A few minutes later, her oil slicked hands slid over her body, her damp hair hanging in a tangle past her shoulders. A ghost of a grin curved her mouth upward as her mind started drifting, reliving the dream she had been having before waking up on the couch. She had been lying in a meadow in Ireland, her belly full of a picnic dinner, her body warm from the sun. Strong hands had glided over her body, fisted in her hair. And his mouth...

Her eyes opened and she stared at her reflection in the mirror. It had been Alex. Every dream she had ever had had been centered on Alex—from the time she was ten years old. Once upon a time, the dreams had been sweet and childish, the kind a girl would dream. But as she grew older, the dreams got hotter and earthier.

The dreams, and one brief encounter on the floor, were likely all she'd ever have.

Staring at her trim, narrow body, Allie relived the shock she had seen in his eyes when he had seen her, recognized her, at the airport. It might have been wishful thinking, but she thought she'd seen some serious appreciation in his eyes. Is this all it would have taken? For him to finally notice her?

Idly, she spun a scenario around in her mind—of calling him, asking him if he wanted to get some dinner, catch a movie.

And then she stopped herself.

Pulling her robe on, she left the bathroom, combing her fingers through her hair as she headed for the den. Taking a fat picture album from the desk, she headed for the armchair, curled her body up, and opened it. Towards the back were pictures from the previous summer, at Mike and Lori's barbecue.

And there she was, clad in jeans and a baggy T-shirt, her mousy brown hair pulled back from her face with a headband. Although she might look different, although she took better care of her appearance and thought more of herself, inside, Allie knew she was still basically the same.

She liked to read, liked to watch movies, liked to go fishing. She loved sleeping in on rainy days, loved to go camping, and she loved kids. She had dreams of sweaty sex with Alex—always had, always would. Dreams where he loved her as much as she loved him.

Nothing about her had changed.

And she hadn't been enough to catch his attention then. Hadn't been enough to make him linger and kiss and cuddle her that night on the floor.

"You don't want it now," she told herself quietly. She had been in love with him for years, but she deserved somebody who could appreciate her—all of her—not just the surface changes.

With a sigh, she closed the album and stood up.

After returning it to her desk, she dismissed Alex from her mind and left the room.

Chapter Five

❧

"Don't," Alex told himself as he drove down the road to Allie's cute little house on the river. But he kept seeing how she would toy with that necklace, that dreamy little smile, the hot, satisfied look that would drift over her face from time to time. "Fuck."

"She's not your type," he muttered as he parked and stared up at the silent house. He liked sex, liked lots of it — liked it rough. And Mike would gut him, understandably, if he knew what Alex wanted to do to his baby sister.

Fuck. Mike knew just how Alex liked his sex — they had been sharing tales of their exploits for years. And double fuck — before Mike had fallen for Lori, they had shared *her*. Mike knew in fine detail just how rough and hard Alex could get and that was all fine and dandy.

But if it involved his one and only baby sister...

So if Mike had any inkling that Alex was eyeing Allie, it was all over.

He had no business getting out of his car, striding up to her door and pounding on it until she let him in.

But he was standing there, brooding. And waiting.

When the door swung open, she stood there wearing a thin, short robe, her hair wet, her skin soft and gleaming under the bright porch light. He could smell the scent of her skin, fresh out of the bath — peaches, mingled with vanilla now — and he was ravenous.

"Alex?"

He moved past her without answering, his eyes dark, his heart pounding slow and heavy as he waited for her to close the door and turn.

"Are you going to hate me forever for what happened that night?" he asked roughly, his hands curled into loose fists to keep from reaching for her.

Allie blinked. Once, slowly, like a sleepy little cat, he thought. She reached up and ran a hand through her tangled wet hair, an action that lifted her short robe even higher. Her body was still damp and when the robe rode higher, it clung and gaped, hinting at the naked body beneath it, revealing the slope of one breast, the edge of a soft, pink nipple. "I don't hate you, Alex," she said, shaking her head slightly. "I'm sorry if I've given you that impression."

"I've been avoiding your brother for a while, because I didn't want to risk running into you. I felt like an ass," he said gruffly, wanting to close the distance between them and kiss her, to see if her mouth was still as soft and sweet as he remembered. "I hurt you, and I'm sorry for it. That was your first time, wasn't it?"

Her cheeks flushed and her lashes lowered, followed by a soft, quiet sigh. "Yes. Alex, look—"

"Shh," he murmured, moving a little closer, pressing one finger to her lips.

He knew women well enough to understand what he was seeing in her eyes. Embarrassment and self-doubt—that was something he hadn't thought of until it was too late, and he should have, especially with Allie. He decided to risk closing that distance and he backed her up against the wall as he told her, "Do you know I dreamed of that night for weeks? Months?" He reached up, carefully, slowly—giving her every chance in the world to pull away—as he threaded one hand through her damp hair. "The best little fuck I've ever had…and it was Allie Ryan." He slid the tip of his thumb between her parted lips, opening her mouth just before he covered it with his.

And he still moved slowly.

Alex was all too aware that he was taking a big fucking risk here. He knew she was attracted to him, had known that for a while—years—and it used to make him uncomfortable. Then it amused him. That night six months ago, it made him burn.

But now, he was worried. After the way he had acted, no matter how attracted to him she might have been, he could have killed that. Sliding his tongue across her lower lip, he groaned in pleasure at her taste. She was so sweet, he thought as he parted her robe with his hand before cupping it around her slim hip and palming the smooth flesh. Alex stroked the taut muscles of her ass before sliding his fingers through her wet cleft as he tore his mouth away from hers to kiss his way down her neck and collarbone. He boosted her up, lifting her so that he could feast on her sweet little nipples while his fingers tested her wet depths again.

Shifting his position, Alex stared down the length of her slim, pale body, her perfectly rounded little breasts, topped with dark pinkish-red nipples, her slender torso and narrow waist, slim hips, and the sweet scent of her sex as he screwed his fingers deep inside her pussy. She cried out and rocked her hips against his hand, his name falling from her lips as her nails bit into his nape.

She was hot, wet, tight around his fingers, the sweet clasp of her pussy reminding him of how good it had felt to drive his cock inside her until he was buried inside her to his balls—and how she had mewled and sobbed beneath him.

He cursed himself for being a fucking idiot. Six months of this. He could have had six months of it. The golden brown curls at her mound were wet with her cream and Alex groaned raggedly. Lowering her to the floor, he took her down, arranging her so that her thighs were spread wide as he pulled her clinging cotton robe open, baring her body completely as he lay between her thighs—spreading the lips of her sex and staring at the dark pink, gleaming wet folds with hot, hungry eyes.

Dragging his gaze over the length of her flushed, quivering body, he met her dazed eyes with his own dark, hungry gaze, his hair falling over his forehead as he stared at her through the veil of his lashes. "I didn't come here tonight to fuck you," he whispered roughly, lowering his head to nuzzle her wet cleft. He drew his tongue up the creamy slit just once before taking his mouth away and resting his chin lightly on her pubic bone. "You didn't exactly get a fair shake that first night, did you?" he asked, as he slid two fingers deep inside her, twisting his wrist at the last second, so that he was stroking her G-spot, watching as her body arched up.

"I'd like to even it out a little. And maybe start over," he murmured, unsure exactly where he was heading with this. But he was pretty certain of one thing. The fucking necklace she kept playing with came from another man. That sweet, sexy look in her eyes when she thought about that man burned his ass and made him furious. And he didn't like it. Not at fucking all.

She cried out softly when he lowered his head and caught her clit between his teeth before sucking it greedily into his mouth, while using his hand to fuck her into completion.

She flooded his hand when she came, the musky scent of her climax perfuming the air around them as she sobbed, her nails biting into his shoulders through his shirt. He waited—cock aching and stiff—until her breathing slowed before he carried her into her room and lay her on the bed. Pulling the quilt over her body, he tugged his shirt off and kicked off his shoes, then climbed in behind her and cuddled her against him.

"Alex, what are you doing here?" she finally asked, long after he had thought she had drifted off to sleep. He had been trying to puzzle that out himself.

"Who gave you the necklace?" he asked.

"I asked you first," she said sleepily, reaching up to touch it.

"I can't stop thinking about you," he said, sighing, brushing her damp hair back. "Not just today. But for six fucking months.

I thought at first I just felt guilty. But I'm not going to feel guilty and still fantasize about getting my cock inside you again. Now who gave you the damn necklace?"

She sighed and snuggled deeper into her pillow. "Niall. I met him in Ireland."

Alex felt his jaw clench even though he had known it was from a man. "Did you sleep with him?"

"Yes," she said softly.

Alex clenched his jaw, closed his eyes. "It wasn't just a one night thing, was it?"

"No. He spent almost ten days with me," she said, drifting closer and closer to sleep, completely unaware of Alex's jealousy.

"And you were lovers?"

"Hmm," she replied, more asleep than not. "Yeah, oh, yeah." And she had a pleased little smile on her face.

She slid completely into the net of sleep while Alex lay behind her, a snarl on his face, his hand resting on her hip. He had to keep reminding himself he was an officer of the law. He wasn't allowed to take the necklace and go throw it in the river. That wasn't just stealing. It was also destruction of property.

Chapter Six

❧

He couldn't bring himself to leave her that night.

He finally slept though, keeping his jeans on in the name of self-defense. Alex had decided he was going to get Allie Ryan, and not just to sleep with. He had already done that.

He had fucked up, and badly. He hadn't been a lover to Allie, and he hadn't given her any reason to smile over him the way she had smiled over that Irish fucker…who'd be dead right now if Alex could be in two places at once.

He had given Allie something first, something Alex wouldn't be able to take away or change, and that infuriated him beyond all reason.

Alex was going to be the one who put that sleepy satisfied look in her eyes, and he was going to make up for the six empty months he had spent without her. He would have had a better start if he hadn't let her go home alone that night. If he had handled it better. A guy was entitled to a little bit of shock, but he had not handled it well.

He was going to show her he knew how to be a lover, not just a taker, and he was going to be the one who put that pleased little female look in her eyes.

Maybe it would soothe the burning jealousy gnawing at his gut eventually. But he doubted it.

➤ * * * *

She woke with a smile that quickly turned to a blush when she saw him propped up on his elbow watching her—his dark brown eyes heavy with sleep, a half smile curving his mouth, morning stubble darkening his chin and upper lip. "Why are you still here?" she asked as she stifled a yawn, stretching her arms high before she realized she was naked.

His eyes slid down to appreciate the view and his mouth followed, closing over one morning soft nipple that quickly hardened under his tongue. Her startled gasp had him smiling against her breast as he pulled away. "Wanted to talk to you," he murmured, smoothing her tousled hair down. "Why don't we take a shower" — he grinned as her blush deepened to rose — "separately and then we can go walk downtown and get a bite at the café?"

She rolled from the bed quicker than he could blink, wrapping the sheet around her toga style, and was gone before he could say another word. Alex lay back, laughing softly under his breath. No, Allie Ryan wasn't exactly his type, but she was just the sweetest damn thing. Maybe that was it. His kind weren't *sweet*. He didn't like sweet women, because he liked rough, hard sex. Liked knowing he could tie a woman up and fuck her any which way he damn well pleased and that she would enjoy it. Enjoy, hell. He liked making them *crave* it. Chances were, if Allie knew what he really liked, she would run away screaming.

Hell, it wasn't that it had to be rough all the time. Or even most of the time. But he wanted to know that when he needed it that way, he could have it without worrying the woman was going to freak out and run away crying *'rape'*. It had happened to a friend of his. And he knew damned good and well Jake hadn't raped anybody, but the girl had woken up the next morning and her conscience started telling her "*Nice little girls don't have that kind of sex.*" So she had to place the blame elsewhere.

If a woman was open enough to admit what she liked, and how she liked it, that would not happen.

But Alex wasn't seeing that as being a problem with Allie. Hell, he was fully aware that he had probably already pushed her as far as she could be pushed. Now, he'd just enjoy it while it lasted, and make sure it ended well. He'd show her that he could give her the sweeter side to sex, show her he could make love to her, as well as fuck her brains out, and then they'd drift apart.

He knew he couldn't put up with any more of the awkward distance he had forced between himself and Mike, so he had to get past the guilt he felt for what he had done to Michael Ryan's kid sister. And he had to accept the fact that he wanted a little more. So he would enjoy this—and her—for a while, and then drift away. They could go back to the polite friendly distance they had always shared.

If he was lucky, she would figure it out on her own—that he wasn't the right guy for her—and she'd pull away before he had to do it. Chances were, there wouldn't be too many easy movies, no more dragging her out or ribbing her into a bike ride…at least for a while.

If he was unlucky—Alex winced. What in the hell was he doing?

That easy, light friendship was going to fade away once this was over.

He ignored the funny little voice in his head that kept saying, *That girl ain't going anywhere.*

Yeah, she would. This was just for a little while.

He found the books a few minutes after he heard the water in the sink start—to cover up the sound of the toilet flushing. *Oh, have mercy*, he thought wickedly. *The girl has to pee?* He thought about knocking on the door to tease her, but decided not to. He was pushing his luck as it was.

He saw his watch on the bedside table and reached for it, only to knock over the glass of water while he was doing it because he turned to grin at the door when Mellencamp started to blare. Allie listened to Mellencamp while she showered? When he looked back, the water was soaking the table, a paperback, his watch, and seeping into the drawer through a hairline crack.

He grabbed his discarded T-shirt to mop up the water and opened the drawer. His eyes widened at what he saw lying there. *The Book of O*. A vibrator. A silver bullet. His eyes narrowed and he slid a look toward the bathroom. Shower going, music blaring. Crouching down in front of the drawer, he riffled through it carefully. But hey, he was a cop. He knew how to search for evidence without really disturbing anything.

Three more books—one pure erotica, the other two were romances, but looked to be a little heavier on the sex than what he would have guessed. A pair of padded handcuffs.

Alex's eyes widened and his heart kicked up as a slow, hot smile spread across his mouth. He was gonna die of a fucking heart attack. A butt plug. More restraints, unused—like she had bought them, wanting to use them—and either hadn't gotten around to it, or just never had the chance. Lubricant.

Damn it, he could see it, see *her*, tied to her bed, or kneeling down with that heart-shaped little ass in the air, her hands cuffed behind her back while he forced that plug inside her virgin ass.

She'd whimper and moan and when he got his cock inside her, her pussy would be so snug and tight and wet…

Alex groaned. And then he couldn't help it as a surprised, pleased laugh escaped him.

Allie was into bondage games.

Allie was into *his* kind of games.

He heard the shower stop and he quickly put things back the way he had found them, his heart pounding, his blood coursing hotly through both his head and his cock. When the door opened, he was sitting on the bed, staring into nothingness, all innocence. As he rose and walked by her, he brushed his fingers down her cheek and couldn't help but think, *Allie?*

She stood in the doorway, bundled into a heavy robe that covered a hell of a lot more than the one she had worn last night. "You could have used the other shower," she told him, looking disconcerted to see him still there.

He smiled at her. Allie felt her heart bump against her ribs at that smile—slow, sleepy, satisfied. And hot. "No rush," he murmured as he stopped in front of her and caught the lapels of the robe and pulled her against him, kissing her, sliding his tongue inside her mouth, touching her as his hands left her robe to slide down and cup her ass, lifting her against him. He ground his cock against her belly, but when she started to rock against him he lowered her back to the ground and walked into the bathroom. She half-turned, watching him, her tongue sliding out to taste him on her lips.

Her nipples tingled, her sex already ached, and she was wet.

Her cheeks went hot when he shoved his jeans down and off without even closing the door. That hard, muscled butt was taut and smooth, as darkly tanned as the rest of him, and Allie had to fight back the urge to walk up behind him and kneel down so she could sink her teeth into the firm flesh. She was still staring at him when he stepped into the shower. He turned, facing her, while he started the water, moving just a little away from the spray, adjusting it, down and back. And the jerk didn't bother to close the curtain all the way. She'd like to pretend she was pissed about the water that was puddling on her tiled floor but—

Oh, man.

She swallowed the spit that was pooling in her mouth when he closed his hand over his cock and started to pump, slowly at first and then faster, his fist closing over the thick, ruddy head before sliding back down that long length, up again, back down...while her cleft went hot and wet.

"I never would have guessed that you liked to watch, Allie," he purred roughly, chuckling as her face flushed. "I've done this more in the past six months than I've ever done it before—unless you count high school."

A rough groan rumbled out of him and he said, "Every time I'd wake up, I'd see you, feel you around me again. It's gonna happen again, darlin'."

His breathing sounded more ragged over the soft hiss of the shower and his head fell back, his wavy dark hair damp from the pelting water that hit the side of his body, one hip, his thighs and legs while he continued to stroke his cock for his audience of one.

Is he serious? she wondered. *Or is he playing with me?* If he was playing with her, she figured she was just going to kill him. She knew a thing or two about forensics. She just might get away with it.

But if he wasn't—

Nervously, her fingers undid the tie to her robe and she pushed it off, walked across the now damp floor, stepped into the shower and knelt in front of him, her body hot and tight, her cheeks flushed, her chest heaving with ragged breaths. Hesitantly, she touched his pumping hand and it froze. She felt his eyes on her. She was too scared to look up at him. Too scared to look at anything. She hadn't done this before—ever—and she wasn't certain she wanted to now.

Wrapping her fingers around the base, she slid them up and down slowly, watching the play of her hand on him as she leaned closer. His breathing grew ragged and he arched toward her.

The dark, ruddy head was flared, thick, smoothly rounded. The shaft of his cock was veined and thick, hot against her hand as she slid it down and leaned in closer to him.

Slowly, she slid her tongue around the head of his cock, finding it warm and smooth, salty. She felt Alex's hand thread through her wet hair and urge her on. Allie started to move shallowly on him, following his rhythm until she was able to find one of her own. With her hand around the base of his cock, she started to massage, mimicking the motion he had been taunting her with and she smiled inside when it made his long, powerful body start to rock against her.

Alex stared down at the tousled damp head in front of him. She was keeping her head low and he couldn't see her face, just the top of her head, the smooth line of her slender back, the rounded curves of her ass. Her wet, hot mouth closed over his cock like fiery satin, sliding up and down slowly, carefully, intent on driving him to the brink before he was ready.

His sac went tight and he shuddered when she swirled her tongue around the head of his penis before sliding slowly back down, while every muscle in his body tensed. He tightened his grip in her hair and forced her head up, just slightly, as his climax started.

"Look at me," he ordered roughly. "Watch me." He shuddered as her eyes met his and he pushed his cock a little farther between her sweet, full lips. He groaned and swore as his cock hardened even more right before he exploded—coming inside her mouth, riding it to the end—before he dropped to his knees, looping his arms around her and tugging her closer while the shower splattered all around them.

"You're making a mess," she said a few minutes later, a soft little giggle falling from her lips.

"I'll clean it up," he murmured, nuzzling her neck. "You promise you'll do that again sometime and I'll do anything you want."

Allie pressed her head against his chest, feeling the water that pelted them while he ran one hand up and down her spine in a slow, stroking motion. She'd like to promise him she'd do whatever he wanted her to do, whenever, and for however long he wanted it. But she was learning that she had to put her pride in front of her heart, especially when it came to Alexander O'Malley. When it came to him, she'd worn her heart on her sleeve for years and it had led to that disastrous night.

And *that* was not happening ever again.

True to his word, Alex bundled her back into bed and cleaned up the water. She tried to bring him some towels and he had resorted to tickling her, so in the name of self-preservation and jet lag, she had lain in bed, still half asleep. Allie was an excellent planner. And thanks to her excellent planning, she didn't have to worry about going to work for a few more days yet.

Her shift was three twelve-hour days a week, Wednesday, Thursday and Friday. Thanks to the way some people preferred to work, she only worked weekends once a month, and when she worked hers, she had the previous Thursday and Friday off. She had come back on a Friday, which gave her a couple of days to acclimate, unpack and just rest.

A warm, calloused hand on her calf had her lids drifting slowly open. She heaved a sigh and rolled her head towards Alex, who had knelt down and had his chin resting on the bed, on a level with hers now that he knew she wasn't sleeping. "Why are you here, Alex? You can't possibly be interested in me," she said softly, staring into his dark chocolate eyes.

He pressed one finger to her mouth, stroking her lower lip as he asked, "After what happened six months ago, what happened last night, and this morning, you're telling me I can't be interested in you?"

"Six months ago, we were both more asleep than anything else. And when you realized what was going on, and who you were with, you were disgusted," she said, closing her eyes and turning her head away.

"What?"

"There's never been anything wrong with my mind or my hearing, Alex. I saw the look on your face and I heard you clear as day. *I don't believe this,* you said. I didn't ask to be a pity fuck and you can—"

His hand caught her chin and his dark eyes glittered angrily as he growled, "I don't do pity fucks. And I wasn't disgusted with anybody but myself. You're my best friend's baby sister, and you damn near got yourself killed and what the hell did I do?"

Allie opened her mouth but whatever she was going to say died when he covered her mouth with his just as he drove one thick finger deep inside her, slowly working it past her initial resistance as his thumb started to circle around her clit.

He nipped her lip and swallowed the startled cry that followed before kissing his way down her neck and capturing a stiff swollen nipple in his mouth while he added a second finger and rubbed her tauntingly before driving back into her — stroking her slick, wet inner walls, going deep inside to find the sensitized nerve endings — as he kissed his way back up to nip the long slender line of her throat.

When he had her shuddering, when he had her lifting her hips to meet him, he lifted his mouth and whispered savagely against her ear, "And what I couldn't believe was this —"as he screwed his wrist and slid his fingers back inside. "This sweet, wet, little pussy that hugged me so tightly, that felt so impossibly good, belonged to somebody I still thought of as a kid." He pulled his hand away and mounted her roughly — watching her face for any sign of fear or reservation — but as he drove into her, reaching for her hands and taking both of them in his, holding her down, her pretty green eyes darkened with hot excitement.

He held still once he had burrowed completely inside her and waited until she was staring up at him with wide, hungry eyes before he lifted his wet fingers to his mouth and slowly licked the cream away, shuddering in pleasure at the taste. "I wanted more. I wanted all of it." Lowering his head, he rasped against her ear, "I wanted to tie you to my bed and fuck you while you screamed my name and I wanted to lick that sweet little pussy dry."

"I wanted things that would have made you run away screaming, little girl," he purred, rotating his hips against her.

He'd held her hands down that first time, he remembered. And slapped her sweet little ass a time or two, and she had squeezed so tightly around him. He pulled out and surged slowly back inside her, watching as her spine arched, lifting her pretty, softly rounded breasts up, the dark pink nipples drawn tight and puckered.

"But you let me hold you down, and you let me spank you, didn't you?" he wondered, driving back inside. "What else are you willing to try?"

Her breathy reply had him narrowing his eyes. She may be curious, but she was still a beginner, and she was still Allie, and shy.

"Anything…"

Lifting up, he stared down into her eyes and said, "Anything?" His cock was screaming at him, *she said anything so fuck her damn it!* But the tightness in his chest was rather insistent he be sure. Damn it, if he scared Allie, he didn't know what he would do. "Be careful what you say," he warned her gruffly.

"Anything," she said, her voice stronger and louder. And she tightened the muscles in her pussy around him in a slow clinging caress.

"Would you let me tie you to my bed?" he asked, releasing her hands to catch her thighs and he opened her wide, watching the bliss that crossed over her face as he drove inside her, hard and slow. He stared down at where they joined, watching as he pushed his thick cock inside the snug entrance of her sex. He circled his thumb around the swollen, hard bud of her clit while he trailed his eyes up over the length of her slim body. "Let me fuck that little virgin ass?"

"I'm willing to try," she offered, her words ragged and hoarse, her cheeks pink.

A slow, hungry smile curled his mouth and he pulled his cock out, wet and shining from her cream, and lifted her slender body, that slight weight, shifting her and nudging her. "Get on your hands and knees, Allie-cat," he told her, moving behind her and staring down at her—her slim hips and the tiny little pucker of her anus. He licked his finger and pressed it against her, watching as she shuddered.

Then he slapped her ass and she moaned, a low, rough aroused sound that made his balls ache. Gathering more cream from her pussy, he started to probe her anus with a thick, blunt finger. She flinched and Alex whispered, "Push down for me, baby."

"It hurts," she said on a gasp.

"I know," he crooned. "Trust me on this. Push down." Alex slapped her ass with his other hand, while working past the initial resistance as she moaned and pushed down.

Moving around, he positioned her between his thighs and circled his fingers around her clit, keeping his lone finger inside the snug sheath of her ass "Hmm, that's nice," he whispered when she started to rock against his tormenting fingers, which caused her to move up and down on the finger he had buried in her ass.

"Do you like how that feels?" he asked as her head fell back. He kissed his way down the length of her neck, eyeing the thrust of her reddened nipples with greed. The fit of her ass felt like a hot silken glove around him—damn it, getting his cock inside there just might kill him.

He caught one hard nipple in his mouth as she whispered, "Yes," while she pushed down harder against both his hands. He started to plunge his finger shallowly in and out of her ass, and she arched up, sobbing. Alex pinched her clit roughly before he slid down and plunged two long fingers deep inside her soaked channel. She climaxed with a scream and a convulsive shudder of her body as cream flooded from her pussy to soak his hand.

She fell against his chest, gasping, and Alex nuzzled her crown as he lifted the fingers he had been stroking against her clit and slid them inside his mouth. "Yummy," he purred roughly. "Now it's my turn." He pushed her quivering body down to her hands and knees and drove inside her pussy, sliding his hands up her back to her shoulders, down the slender length of her arms until he could grasp her wrists, using his weight against her back to urge her torso down low as he guided her wrists back binding her, smiling with hot greed at how she looked. Her golden brown hair lay tousled around her flushed face, her pert little ass up, the dark pink pucker damp from his earlier penetration.

Allie cried out when he pinned her hands at the base of her spine. "Alex..." She'd dreamed of this, just this. Then his hand landed with burning force on her butt and she screamed, creaming around him and tightening with such unexpected force, it stole her breath.

Alex surged inside her again and slapped her ass, groaning as her tight sheath clenched around his cock and clung to him as he pulled out. Gripping one cheek of her ass, he opened her and stared down at the reddened pucker.

Angling his hips, he pushed the thick head of his cock over the bundled nerves buried inside her vagina. His hard, strong hands held her wrists firmly at the small of her back and, as he pushed back inside this time, he spanked her again. Under the painful little pleasure bite of that, and force of his cock driving inside her, Allie lost it, coming again and screaming breathlessly as she pushed back against him and squirmed and rocked around him, whimpering and sobbing while she rode it to the very end.

Alex held still, deep and tight within her until the shudders had stopped, and then he started to thrust hard, forcing his cock to the limits of her sheath, while she lay there, gasping with her face pressed into the mattress.

"Do it again," he whispered, slapping her ass lightly. "I want to feel it again." She was so fucking responsive, Alex thought, gritting his teeth against the need to come *now*. He reached around her hip, rubbed her swollen clit, feeling how tightly she was stretched around his cock as he pulled out and pushed back in. After gathering some of her cream, he smeared it around her narrow little rosette and started to probe with his free hand, pressing the pad of his thumb against the tight opening while thrusting his cock slow and deep inside her wet sheath.

She flinched at the initial pressure and he murmured reassuringly. "Push down, Allie. You took it just a few minutes ago and you loved it." She squirmed and tried to pull away. Tightening his hold on her hips, he pulled her close and bent over her body. "Trust me, Allie-cat. I know it hurts a little more now, but that's because I'm inside you, inside this sweet little pussy of yours.

"C'mon, baby. Just push down...this one time. If it still hurts, I'll stop."

"It already hurts..." He knew it burned and felt her shudder when his thumb slid past the ring of muscle to the first joint, where he stopped. Shifting the angle of his hips he rode her harder. She screamed when he pushed deeper, sending her headlong into climax, and this time she took him with her, her vaginal muscles clamping down around him and milking his cock until he ejaculated into her with a rough groan — pulling his thumb from her bottom and gripping her hips as he rode her into the soft mattress — setting his teeth into her shoulder and marking her as he filled her with his come.

Rolling onto his side, Alex wrapped one arm around her when she tried weakly to roll away.

"I wanted you," he whispered into her hair. "Part of me recognized you, even while I was still asleep. The way you smell...I didn't realize it was you when I first woke up, but once I woke up, I knew who you were and I still wanted you. If I hadn't wanted to get inside you, then I never would have touched you to start with."

Chapter Seven

ഇ

Alex called her three days later and asked to take her out Friday. She hesitated, using work as an excuse so he easily said he'd settle for Saturday and instead of them doing much, they'd walk to the river to one of the restaurants close to her house and just make it an early night.

She agreed hesitantly and hung up the phone and was walking away from it when he called back. "I'm taking an hour personal time—I'll be over in a few minutes," he said.

Allie glanced down at her shorts and frowned. Looked at the clock and frowned. Glanced at the door and frowned.

It was only six, granted. She had walked through the door not ten minutes before he called and had just changed out of her uniform. It wasn't like she had any plans, but she really hadn't expected to hear from him.

He was probably being nice. He was going to take her out Saturday and gently tell her that he'd had fun with her but she wasn't his type. Big news flash there, she thought sourly as she paced the floor nervously.

The heavy knock on the door startled her. A few minutes? As in two? She opened it and he loomed over her, tossing a duffel bag to the floor, and she hadn't even opened her mouth to say 'Hi' when he had his tongue in her mouth, his hands inside her shorts, on her ass while he kicked the door closed behind him.

Alex had been thinking about nothing but her. Unless his fucking job dictated otherwise, and sometimes even then. He clutched the firm little butt and lifted her up, turning to brace Allie against the wall, rocking against her and groaning as she pushed back. Her fingers slid through his hair as he tore his mouth from hers and kissed her chin, her neck as her fingers pressed against his head and urged him lower. "Tell me," he ordered roughly.

"Suck on me," she whispered shyly, her lashes fluttering closed.

He laved one nipple through the cotton of her shirt and bit it gently before pinning her against the wall and reaching for the offending material, pulling it up and off before tossing it aside, baring her naked breasts. He stepped back and jerked her shorts down in a quick motion so that she stood naked in front of him as he slowly knelt before her. Cupping her ass in his hands, he slid his tongue through her curls, separating the tender folds, gathering her cream and groaning with pleasure. "So damn sweet," he said. He slid a hot look up her body and asked, "What about here? What do you want me to do here?"

Allie shyly caught her lip between her teeth and just stared at him.

"Tell me," he told her. "I'll make it worth your while. I brought you something. Well, a couple of somethings. One's for bed, the other thing is for you to wear for me and one is just because I was thinking of you. But you've got to tell me."

She slowly reached out and curled her fingers in his hair, guiding his head back to her as she haltingly whispered, "I want you to lick me. And suck on me. And do more of what you did the last time."

He complied, and she ended up on the floor. Again. He shoved her thighs wide and feasted, driving his tongue deep inside, before moving to suck on her clit and fuck her with his fingers. The cream from her cleft dripped down and lubricated her anus and he smeared it around before he slid his fingers lower, making her shriek when he penetrated her there and started to thrust shallowly, slowly as he licked and nibbled and sucked on her.

Allie's head thrashed on the floor, a strangled scream dying in her throat as he spread the lips of her sex wide and drove his tongue deep inside, stiffening it and thrusting it in and out, echoing the motions of his fingers in her ass.

She buried her fingers in his hair and ground her hips against his mouth, sobbing. Alex pushed his fingers deeper inside her ass, stretching her, opening her as he slid his tongue from inside her pussy to circle around her clit. He caught it in his mouth and sucked on it as her back arched.

Allie whimpered as Alex stabbed at her sex with his hardened tongue, rocking up against his mouth for more. It drove the fingers he had penetrating her ass deeper and she gasped and squirmed against his hand "Oh!" she cried out. "Alex, oh, fuck, please…" Her voice trailed off into a sob as he fastened onto her clit and started to suck, drawing it into his mouth.

Alex felt the tight, smooth walls of her anal sheath around his fingers and fantasized about sliding his cock inside that tight little hole. Not tonight, but soon. Her fingers tightened in his hair just as he shifted and thrust inside her with his hardened tongue and she climaxed against his mouth while he greedily drank the essence of it down before standing and carrying her into the bedroom.

Something told him he was going to go a little over the personal hour he had taken. He hoped nothing major came up. Well, besides the major hard-on he had. He laid Allie on the bed and went back to get his duffel bag.

He had bought a wand and a different butt plug, some padded cuffs and some lubricant. He knew Allie had the stuff they needed to open her sweet little tail up, but he suspected she was too damn shy just yet, and he also suspected he was going to have to move things at his pace, and not hers. She didn't trust him and if they moved at hers…he would have never gotten back inside her.

There was also a gift box. He had seen the little golden kitten a long time ago. Actually a year ago, at a jewelry store, exquisite detail, tiny emerald chips for eyes. The charm was beautiful. His then-current girlfriend had ooh-ed and ah-ed.

Alex had thought of Allie and had outright ignored Megan's not so subtle hints that he buy it for her. The thought niggled at his mind and made him a little more disconcerted than he cared to think about.

A year ago. He had seen the charm a year ago, and thought of Allie, before he had ever sunk his dick inside her welcoming body — nope, he wasn't going to think about that.

The other box was lingerie. With a wicked grin, he wished he had time to see it on her tonight, but he would. Soon.

She was just opening her sleepy eyes when he started to strip. He left the boxes in the bag but pulled out the rest and let her see it as he put it on the table. "You said I could tie you," he reminded her, kneeling beside the bed, taking her face in his large hands and then he tangling his fingers in her hair, pausing to devour her mouth hungrily. Three days. He'd gone three days. Why did it feel like three years?

"I didn't forget," she said when he pulled away, taking the hands she had crossed over her breasts and tugging them down so he could stare at her.

"I'm going to. And I'm going to put something a little larger inside your sweet little ass tonight," he said. He stood and she casually covered herself again. Narrowing his eyes, Alex said, "Don't do that. I want to see you." He knelt again and took her hands, staring at her breasts blatantly. "Pretty," he murmured, nuzzling the soft valley between before kissing each nipple. "Sit up for me."

She did so, slowly, her hands fluttering, as though she wanted to cover herself. Finally she let them fall to her lap and she sat there, staring at him with wide eyes, looking half-aroused, half-nervous.

Completely delicious.

He reached out without looking and caught the cuffs, binding her hands behind her. "I want to watch you suck on my cock Allie-cat," he told her as he threaded his hands through her hair. "Like this, with your hands behind your back, your eyes wide and a little nervous."

With his hold on her hair, he guided her closer, and shuddered as she slowly parted her lips and licked the broad head before sliding her mouth down half-way then retreating, falling into a shallow rhythm that had him breathing raggedly and rocking against her, forcing his length more deeply into her mouth. He felt the warning tingle in his balls and pulled away, lifting her up and off the bed. Alex guided her to her knees beside it and grabbed pillows to stuff under her to support her weight. "You make me lose my head, Allie-cat," he muttered, shaking his head as he reached for something. "I haven't been this fucking hot since I was a teenager."

Alex slicked the lubricant around her anus, then just inside. She jumped as his fingers began probing before being replaced by something rounded, smoother, longer. "Push down, kitten," he whispered. She held her breath and pushed down as he slid the wand into her, slowly, until it was completely inside.

"Hurt?" he asked as he stroked his hands possessively down the globes of her ass, eyeing the way the toy was nestled in her ass.

"A little," she whispered, shifting and squirming.

A smile curled his mouth and he said, "Want me to take it out?"

"No," she said sharply, rocking her hips, as if trying to ride the wand.

"Good," Alex said.

She gasped when he drove into her without saying or doing anything else, his thick width carving through her and not stopping until he was balls-deep inside. Each time he pulled out, the wand would start to slide out and when he drove back in his pelvis shoved the wand deep inside her ass so that she was being doubly penetrated.

Allie moaned with pleasure at every deep dig of his cock, with every stroke of the smooth wand inside her ass.

Alex stared down, watching the pale, flesh-colored wand penetrate her anus as he pushed back inside. Her small hands were clenched into tight little fists just at the base of her spine and she was whimpering and pleading mindlessly as he pumped himself into her.

The slick wet walls of her vagina hugged him tighter, more snugly with the wand in her ass. "Damn it, that's good," he said roughly, hunkering over her bound body and driving in deep. "You're tight, Allie, so little, so wet. Like it?"

"Umm," was her only response as he pulled out.

He chuckled. "I'm going to enjoy getting my cock inside this," he mused, emphasizing the point by lodging the wand deep and hard, listening to her shriek and wail as he drove deep inside her.

He spanked her lightly and laughed with shaky delight when she tightened around him and mewled, thrashing her head. He pushed the wand in harder, using his thumb to anchor it in place as he pushed her hips lower, filling her with short hard digs, reveling in the screams that started to fall from her lips, especially, "Alex, oh, please, Alex, again, damn it, please, Alex!"

He growled and slapped her ass harder and she came, vising around him, her sheath convulsing and spasming, while she screamed, a low, long, hoarse sound that echoed through the room.

The rhythmic clenching of her pussy tightened to the point of pain and Alex pulled his cock out before again driving in completely, holding there as he bellowed out her name, rocking his hips slightly against her ass, pushing the wand in and out as he pumped her full of his sperm, his cock jerking viciously inside the snug hold of her pussy.

Alex braced his hands on her hips and pulled out, rolling them onto their sides before he collapsed.

"You're going to kill me," he said hoarsely a few minutes later. "Gonna die of a fucking heart attack."

"You started it," she mumbled, shifting uncomfortably.

He frowned and reached around her, flicking the catch on the cuffs to free her, studying her face in the fading light. She looked…happy. Sated. Adorable. And the setting sun shone through the little window over her bed to wink on the Celtic knot at her neck. He bit back the snarl the charm instinctively caused and cuddled her against him.

"Did not," he replied affably.

"Did too. I was minding my own business when you called. I was going to read a book and go to bed early," she said.

He grunted, sighed and stood before taking her slight weight and depositing her on the bed. "Okay. You're on the bed. Your fault," he insisted, nuzzling her neck. "If you weren't so damn sweet —" and then he forced himself to pull away. "I better take a shower before I go back to work."

She was asleep before he was done.

He eyed her, a little nervously, but he knew if he saw her fingering that charm any more, he was going to lose it.

Just one more time, and he'd rip the thing off of her and stomp it into gold dust, then toss her down on top of it and fuck her senseless, fuck her until she forgot that Irish bastard's name.

So he took it off and replaced it with his. After leaving her a quick note, and gritting his teeth through the entire thing in order to not say anything about her wearing something from a man other than him, he left the other box on her dresser.

He was on his way out the door when he turned around and added an afterthought to the note.

Wear a dress tomorrow. No panties.

And he got hard again, wondering if she'd do it. He should have doubted it, but Allie was surprising him, more and more.

He got back to the department in just a couple of minutes, but at that point it didn't really matter. He'd already gone twenty minutes over the personal hour, but he was pretty sure nobody would give a damn He was gonna have to stay late to get some things wrapped up but he was off tomorrow so—

Oh fuck.

"Hey, man, what you been up to?" Sergeant Michael Ryan unfolded his five-eleven linebacker's frame from his desk and smiled at Alex. He took in the damp hair, the satisfied smile and put two and two together pretty damn quick. Hell, the guy wasn't a detective for nothing. "Well, somebody had a better lunch break than the rest of us."

"What are you doing here, Mike? This isn't your rotation," Alex said mildly. Sonuvabitch, he could feel blood creeping up the back of his neck. He was *not* going to blush because he was sleeping with a friend's sister. Hell, it wasn't the first time. But this was his best friend.

And Allie was—

Different. This was different. This was *Allie*.

"Something broke on a case and Dave and I came in to close it up. It was sweet. We have a material witness on the fencing op we've been trying to bust for the past month. Guy dumps his girlfriend, in exchange for her younger sister no less, and she comes straight here to give him up. And she has pictures, video, dates, times. She's been following him around and getting this stuff together for months. Dunno if she suspected something was up, or was just going to try to get a piece of the action, but hey, a woman scorned," Mike said, flashing a wide smile. "I'm babysitting the girlfriend to make sure she doesn't change her mind. Dave's out with a couple of uniforms to pick up the boyfriend."

Then he focused his green eyes on Alex and his smile turned from all cop to all male. Those eyes looked entirely too much like Allie's—more intense, more focused, meaner—but the same shade of deep green, the same shape, the same long spiky eyelashes that Alex had razzed him about growing up. "Now tell."

"Go away," Alex said, walking past him.

Mike laughed. "Aw, come on. You ain't gotta give me a name or anything, man. Just some sordid little details. I'm a married man now, I'm supposed to behave." He walked beside Alex up the stairs, ignoring the people who called his name in order to focus on ribbing Alex.

"Mike, no," Alex said roughly, closing his eyes briefly as he stomped into his office. *Of all the freaking luck. This case had to break, tonight.*

"Well, who is she?" Mike asked quizzically, eyeing the strained look on Alex's face. He'd seen that look on his friend before, just not over a woman.

"Don't worry about it," Alex told him.

"You're serious about her?"

Alex sighed and dropped into his chair, rubbing a hand over his face, suddenly overcome by exhaustion. *Serious? Over Allie?* "I don't know," he said quietly.

"How do you feel about her?" Mike asked.

Alex shook his head and said, "I'm not telling you how I feel about her before I tell her." But he decided to exercise a little caution and he added, "But I care about her. A lot. And I think I have for a very long time." Then he pinned Mike with his dark eyes, staring at him for a long moment before he cracked a smile and said, "Now will you get the hell out?"

* * * * *

Allie woke up a good hour before her alarm was ready to go off—wide awake, pleasantly sore and happy. Her fingers were absently stroking the charm when she registered it felt different.

Rolling from the bed, she flicked on the light and blinked, waiting until her eyes adjusted before she padded naked over to the mirror. She paused, catching sight of herself. *Damn.* Her mouth was still swollen from last night and her hair was tousled. She looked sexy. Like she had just spent the night with a man. Even though he had left hours before. She saw the note and tugged it down to read.

Hope you like it. I saw it a while back and it made me think of you.

I bought it last night with a few other things. The other stuff is more for me, but—

He'd started to write something else, then scratched it out, signed his name, then added at the bottom, *Wear a dress tomorrow. No panties.*

She snorted. Yeah, right.

And then leaned over and looked, brushing her hair aside.

A kitten, a tiny, adorable little gold kitten, paw drawn up like he was getting ready to bat at something, with his head just slightly turned, two tiny little emerald chips for eyes. She glanced down and saw the Celtic knot Niall had given her. Hmm. Her first piece of jewelry from a guy. She hadn't thought she'd want to take it off for a while, but she put it away without a blink, and smiled as she stroked the kitten at her neck.

* * * * *

Alex paused just as he planted his feet on the ground, staring at Allie. How in the hell had he been missing this?

She wore a long, smoky-gray dress, slit up the sides to the knee. Black leather boots that went up forever.

Her hair fell in soft wisps around her shoulders and she looked beautiful.

And her smile…shy, sweet, and hot, all at the same time.

He shook his head, clearing it, and headed up the walk to where she stood in the doorway.

She started to come outside when Alex climbed out but he shook his head. "Let's go back in for a few minutes," he told her, still eyeing the dress she wore. It was growing cooler out so the longer sleeves would keep her from getting cold on the walk. The neckline vee'd down in the front and the back and the clever little bra made the most of what little she had. She had found a pair of boots she had badly wanted, three-inch heels, but blocky, so walking wasn't a chore, but the boots went way up, past her knees. They were the entire reason she had tried on the dress, and the entire reason she had worked up the courage to go without panties.

She lifted a brow at Alex but turned around and went back inside, feeling the warmth of his hand at her back, his breath stirring her hair. He slid his hand up and stroked the bare skin of her upper back as he murmured, "You look fantastic." He closed the door and leaned back against it, taking her hips and pulling her against him, gathering fabric in his hands and lifting it slowly. "Are you wearing panties?"

She smiled, and hardly believing she was actually teasing Alex O'Malley, said, "Why don't you look and see?"

He knelt in front of her and his eyes heated as he ran a hand over her leather-covered calf. "Nice," he purred, sliding it higher. The leather stopped a little past mid-thigh and he followed it up, and found her naked cleft, petting the damp curls. He stood quickly and startled her when he pulled the dress over her head, staring at her black bra and sexy leather boots. "There's something I need to do before we go and we can't have you getting wrinkled," he teased as he draped it over the coat rack.

Allie's breath caught when he picked her up and carried her to her room. "Duh-dinner?"

"Oh, we're going out," he told her with a grin. "In a couple of minutes. Where are the things I left? Get them please."

He leaned against the door jamb and admired the picture she made, bending over the bedside table in the little black bra and her black boots, her slim ass naked. If all went well tonight, he was going to ride that tight little hole before the sun came up in the morning.

She turned, holding the butt plug, wand and lube to her belly, eyeing him nervously, still blushing. One hand started to cover her naked cleft and he lifted a brow at her. "Don't do that, Allie. I like looking at you, at your body. You're so pretty, pink, and soft. You keep covering yourself up like that and I'm gonna get testy about it."

One corner of her mouth curled up, but she dropped her hands and stared at him with arched brows, her cheeks pink, lips parted.

"Put them on the table. Have you got a vibrator?" he asked casually.

She nodded and turned back around, offering him another look at her butt as she pulled out the vibrator and the silver bullet he'd seen. "Which one do you like more?" She put the vibrator away and kept the silver bullet out. "Now get on your hands and knees and turn it on, use it," he told her roughly, kneeling down behind her and sliding his tongue inside her cleft just as she slid the bullet against her clit.

When she was riding the edge of orgasm, he lubed his fingers and her anus and started to probe gently, and then penetrate. The tight little ring opened more easily now and she pushed down and back on him, humming hungrily under her breath and riding his hand, rocking against him and moaning wildly.

The inner walls of her ass were hot and smooth and incredibly tight, Alex mused as he finger-fucked her there.

When she was riding his hand eagerly and panting for more, he withdrew and grabbed the butt plug, lubing it heavily and placing the rounded tip of the sex toy against her. "Push down, kitten," he said roughly, watching with hot eyes as the little pink hole stretched tight around the sex toy and opened, taking it in. She cried out but he continued to push, reaching around until he could find her clit with his fingers. She had dropped the bullet. Finding it, he pressed the madly vibrating egg against her and she shuddered and started to rock. "Push," he told her.

She shook her head and said plaintively, "It hurts." Lowering his head, he bit her shoulder and snapped, "Push!" He dropped the egg and drove his fingers deep inside her pussy. She was wet, tight, and so hot he thought she would burn him. She cried out, pushed and he drove the plug home, so that it was lodged completely inside her, the wide flared base holding it in place.

She was panting, moaning and rocking against his fingers. Flipping her onto her back, he shoved her leather-clad legs high and stared at her wet swollen sex. A little further down, the plug was nestled between the cheeks of her ass and he studied it for a minute before he breathed out a soft, "Sweet damnation," and started to feast, driving his tongue inside the slick, wet folds of her cleft, shuddering at the sweet, tangy taste of her. He plundered her with his tongue until she started to lift to meet him, until she was riding his mouth and then he moved up, replacing his tongue with his fingers so he could take her clit in his mouth.

When he caught the hard, swollen bud, she bucked and cried, buried her hands in his hair and mewled, rocking her hips against him and coming with a scream that left her breathless.

Thirty minutes later, his cock still heavy and stiff, he led her back into the living room and pulled her dress on. "What about the um, well," she mumbled, dragging her feet in her pretty black boots. Allie wasn't certain she'd ever wear them again without blushing, without thinking of Alex.

"The butt plug?" he supplied, grinning when she flushed. "We're leaving it, as long as it doesn't hurt you." He wrapped his arms around her and held her close, reveling in how good, how right she felt. "And when we come back, I'm going to take it out, and then I'm going put my cock in your sweet ass. It's going to be good, Allie-cat. I'm going to make you burn."

She shuddered and whispered, "You're already doing that." But her eyes narrowed and she slid him a glittering look and said, "I'm not going out with this in me."

"Why not?" he asked, cupping her backside and rocking her against him.

"I just can't," she said, shaking her head. The flush spread from her face, downward, even as the idea started to make her breath catch in her throat. "I can't possibly—"

He was sure it didn't hurt, not any more. It was stretching her, it was probably making her sore, but it was the good kind of sore. However, she was apparently *not* going outside with it in. Even if she was tempted.

"Sure you can," he told her, pulling back before he was tempted to lift that long, slim fitting skirt and drive his cock inside her. She'd be narrower, tighter. Damn it, his eyes crossed just thinking of it. Tugging her hand, he led her outside, and when she started to resist, he slid her a taunting grin. "Dare you. C'mon, Allie-cat. Nobody's going to know, besides me. And I want to know," he purred, backing her up against the overhang of her shaded porch, out of sight. "I want to know that toy is inside you, stretching you, opening you so I can take you there without hurting you. Nobody but me knows you're all but naked under this pretty dress, that your sweet little pussy is wet and aching. Nobody but me knows you're getting yourself ready to let me fuck that sweet little ass—damn it, I want this." The lust inside him shifted and turned to something tender as he stared down at her familiar, elfin face, eyes misted with need and desire, hot and sleepy with satisfaction.

'You're so pretty," he murmured. "So sweet...so hot..."

Allie's eyes closed as his hands cupped her face and his mouth found hers in a soft, sweet kiss that had her heart flipping over in her chest. Alex. Her fingers curled into his sport coat, and she rose on her toes, pressing against him.

"I can't stop thinking about you," he murmured against her hair a few moments later. "You're in my head. All the damn time. Ever since that night, when you knocked that little punk down. You should have been terrified and screaming and you were fighting and mad. And when you started crying, you broke my heart." His big hands rubbed her back as he continued to whisper, "And then, when we fell asleep, and I woke up, driving inside you, it was the sweetest damn thing I've ever felt in my life. I wanted to run after you, but I figured you were too mad, too scared. But damn it, I wanted you again. I can't stop wanting you."

Her eyes opened slowly and she stared up into his strong, familiar face, a slightly dazed smile on her lips. "You're certifiable, you know that, don't you?" she murmured, stroking down the lapels of the jacket she had wrinkled.

He laughed. "Let's go," he said, and urged her off the porch before she decided to start arguing with him again.

They ended up at a small café downtown instead of one of the larger more popular restaurants on the river. Alex waved the waiter away and guided her into her seat in the little alcove before sliding in next to her, sitting close enough that the long line of his thigh was pressed against hers through the thin material of her skirt.

She jumped when she felt his hand on her lower back but all he did was rub slowly in soothing circles as he perused the wine list and ordered a red for both of them before turning his attention to the menu. Shortly after the waiter left, Alex's attention focused on her. "Lift up," and she did and almost wished she hadn't because he lifted the bottom of her skirt and then fiddled a little, so that when he urged her back down, she was sitting on fabric, but not her skirt. "Mine," she felt him whisper against her hair. "A handkerchief."

"Why?" she asked, her eyes wide and nervous. He wasn't going to—

He grinned hotly and Allie gulped.

Her heart was beating too fast, Allie thought. And it felt too big for her chest, and too heavy, and too light, all at the same time. If he really meant what he had been saying, "Huh…What?"

He laughed and lowered his head back to her ear, and whispered again, "If I promise that next time we do whatever you want, can I have whatever I want tonight?"

Her breath caught in her throat. He had turned his back to the room, shielding her from view and was sliding one hand up under her skirt, to stroke her naked folds. Licking her lips, she tried to speak and found she couldn't.

"Do you want to know what I want?" Alex whispered as he slid one finger inside her. He could see, just enough, from the corner of his eye, and would know when somebody approached the table, which was why he had requested this table. "When we get home, I want you to keep the boots on, and the bra. Then I'm gonna put you on the bed, and I want to cuff you, one wrist to each corner, one ankle to each bed post, some pillows under you to help keep you up. This okay so far?" he teased.

She nodded, half closing her eyes as he drove his fingers further inside and circled his thumb around her clit. Licking her lips, she realized she had found her voice and whispered, "What else?"

Then his hand was gone. She couldn't think at first and was startled to realize she was rocking very slightly back and forth—the minute movement sending the toy she had in her ass into motion—and she shuddered. Alex slid his arm around her shoulder, tightly, pulling her far too close, and then she heard the waiter.

Her ears were roaring, her face hot, as he ordered for them. Was she embarrassed? But when his hand slid back up her thigh and her legs parted, she realized she was *hot*, she slid a little closer to the edge and rode his hand, hearing Alex's muffled curse, but it didn't register. She was too focused on biting her lip and keeping it quiet as she shuddered her way through the orgasm.

He groaned into her hair as she finished and pulled her back against him. "Damn it, playing with you is like playing with fire," he muttered, pulling his hand from under her skirt and watching her as he licked his index finger clean.

Smiling, she whispered huskily, "You started it."

He laughed. "I'm going to tie you on your belly," he said, taking up where he left off. "And I'm going to watch while you suck my cock for a while. It's a pretty thing, seeing your mouth full of my cock. Then I'll ride you for a while, slowly, make sure you're hot and burning, then we'll take the plug out and we'll see if you can take my cock."

She was panting and squirming by the time he was done. Her sex was soaked and she was glad the bastard had pulled her skirt up, otherwise it too would have been soaked through with her cream.

She took a sip of her wine, followed by another, wishing to cool her heated body. Sliding him a look, she asked hesitantly, "So let me get this right. You get tonight, then I get to pick mine?"

* * * * *

Alex studied his handiwork.

She was tied up, stretched out, open, her pert little ass in the air, the leather boots hugging her legs closely. He'd decided to lose the bra after all, but was glad he'd stuck with the boots. He ran one hand up her inner leg, slowly, and ran one hand down the front of his fly absently. He'd left his clothes on, hoping if he kept them on, he'd be forced to move at least a little slower.

He paused at her butt, and climbed up on the four poster, using both hands to spread the cheeks of her ass, admiring the plug nestled there. "Hurt?"

"No," she whispered. She cried out when he moved his fingers lower and plunged them deep inside her wet cleft, massaging briefly before withdrawing. She had to be nearly mindless before he started to work his cock inside the tiny hole of her ass, otherwise it would hurt too much. If he had the patience or any sense at all, he'd wait a little longer.

He shucked his khakis and tossed them aside before kneeling in front of her and sliding a few extra pillows under her, holding her head and guiding her mouth to his cock. The hot little gleam in her eyes — would it ever stop surprising him? She liked this, loved it, and his gut told him she was going to eventually turn the tables on him. Allie's swollen lips opened up and she flicked her tongue against the head before sliding slowly down, taking him inside. He waited until he could tell it was too much and then he started to pump his hips, watching as his flesh slid in and out, as her eyes slid up his body and locked with his.

Her body flexed and arched and she pushed against him, and he groaned when she took him further, the hot silk of her mouth caressing his length. He pumped harder and faster until he erupted inside her mouth, coming down her throat in a series of rhythmic waves that left him gasping.

Allie was gasping slightly, but when he pulled away, she slid him a cat's smile, smug and female, and he wondered who in the hell was teasing whom as he moved around her body to kneel between her spread thighs. He cupped his balls in one palm as he started to thrust two thick fingers in and out of her wet, clinging sheath, listening to her moans and cries.

He freed her ankles and lifted her hips just slightly in his hands, then he delved into her pussy with his tongue, listening to her squeal and feeling her squirm. She was so wet the cream was sliding down from her cleft to soak her thighs. He licked it off before he moved back and grasped her hips and he drove in, still hard, still hungry. Urgency filled him, and confused him, but Alex figured he'd worry about it later. He worked his cock inside her tight sheath, narrower with the plug that was still inside her. He had put her silver bullet under the pillow and now he went for it, flicking it on with one hand and baring his teeth in triumph when she wailed with pleasure as he pressed it against her engorged clit.

One hand holding the bullet, he held her still with the other and drove into her, hard and deep, until she was sobbing and crying and begging. When he felt the orgasm starting to build, he pulled out, jerked her to her knees and slowly, steadily pulled out the plug. The lubricant was under the pillow and he grabbed it, slathering his cock and her gleaming rosette while she whimpered and pushed back and begged, "Please, damn it, don't stop."

The folds of her sweet little cleft were red, swollen, dripping with cream. Her slim little ass quivering and taut as Alex gripped her hips and pressed against her rosette with his cock, reaching around and over to jerk her free from the cuffs. When her arms came back to reach for him, he simply brushed them aside, and wrapped them around her so that she hugged herself, one hand between her thighs, the other at her own breasts. He pushed the bullet into her hand and said, "Use it," before he hunkered over her and started to possess her ass.

"It's going to hurt, isn't it?" Allie asked shakily. She voice sounded tremulous and her body shivered.

Allie gasped as Alex's fingers returned and pushed the bullet against her sensitive clit. "It will hurt at first, then it's done," he said gruffly. "Use the bullet. Be still. If you fight it, it'll be worse." He rocked against her slowly, maddeningly, just the first two inches inside, and she cried out with pleasure. The ridge of his cock just barely penetrating her, Allie started to move and slide hesitantly on him, searching for the bliss he held just out of reach.

Hungry little whimpers fell from her lips and Alex started to push further inside, groaning when she started to rock back against him as her body accommodated him, relaxing just the tiniest bit to let him slide back and forth so he could thrust in tiny shallow movements without worrying about hurting her. Splaying his hands wide across her back, he pushed her a little lower and started to work his cock in a little deeper, groaning as three more inches of his cock were wrapped in satin slicked heat. Allie's body was quivering and she was keening and arching and rocking against him, seeking more, driving him insane. He pulled back a little and she pushed back with him, trying to take more, and he said sharply, desperately, "Damn it, Allie, you're going to hurt yourself."

"Alex, please, oh, please, I can't take it, please," she chanted, pushing her sweet little butt against him and he lost it, staring down at her puckered anus stretched so tight, while she pushed herself hungrily back against him.

"Push down," he rasped and he pulled out before driving back in, jack hammering his hips against hers as one sharp scream after another fell from her lips. He could hear the pain in those screams and he told himself to stop, he was hurting her, and she was too fucking small, and too tight, and damn it, she felt so good—

"Alex!" she screamed and came, her hands coming up and her nails setting into his arms, squeezing down while she screamed.

"Allie, sweet, oh, fuck, Allie—" he groaned against her hair, while he rode her ass harder, his whole body quaking from the hot, molten pleasure, as he helplessly drove his hips again into the sweet, tight glove of her ass. "Tell me I'm not hurting you, please...oh, hell."

Breathily, she whimpered, "More, Alex. You're not hurting me." She pushed back, trying to take more while he shoved her hard back down to push the bullet against her clit. The engorged flesh was hot and throbbing, swollen against his fingers. Her nipples were tight and swollen, throbbing in time with the pulsing in her clit and groin as she writhed wildly against him. He pulled out and she pushed back, opening up to take him in. She shuddered as he drove deep. "Good, it's so damn, good," she moaned.

Pushing back and away, Alex shuddered and surged back inside, watching how the tight little opening stretched around him, and his long powerful body bucked when he felt the phantom light touch of her fingers against his balls. "Oh, baby, don't do that," he muttered surging back inside her narrow little passage before withdrawing and doing it again "I'm not going to last too long anyway You're so sweet, so hot."

She started rocking back against him again, squirming and riding his cock hungrily. The bullet buzzed roughly against her clit while she started to plunge her fingers inside her cleft. Alex could feel her fingers through the thin wall of tissue that separated them.

His hand smacked her butt and she cried out, going still, her hand falling away from her body, the bullet dropping to the bed. He laughed roughly and did it again, while driving into her harder, and harder. She started to come, clamping down and convulsing madly as he rode her, and the slap of his hand the third time sent her over the edge. A low keening cry built in her throat and broke loose the fourth and final time he spanked her, just as he came, flooding the tight hot depths of her ass with his seed.

He eased her down and curled around her, loathe to pull out. She didn't seem in any hurry, so he lingered but finally withdrew, still semi-erect and already hungry for her again. He angled her head around and kissed her softly before forcing her to look at him, studying her face. Allie's eyes were like windows, always wide open and so easy to see through. "Did I hurt you?" he asked urgently, rolling her onto her back and cupping her face in his hands, propping his weight on his elbows.

She smiled sleepily, turned her face into his hand just a little to kiss his palm. "A little, at first. Maybe a little too much," she admitted, growing aware of the burning, sore pain. "But I liked it. All if it." Her sweet, elfin face flushed and her eyes twinkled as she whispered, "I've always had dreams about ah, hmmm…well, kinky stuff. Especially things like that. I wanted to do it. And I loved every second of it."

He sighed, his long body loosening in relief as he lowered his head to kiss her. "Damn it, you're something," he muttered as he pulled away. "Come on. We need a shower."

She sulked. "I wanna sleep."

"And I'm gonna wanna fuck you the second I wake up, which means shower, now," he said softly, carefully lifting her in his arms, watching her face and seeing her wince. "Damn it, I'm crazy about you." He paused by the bed, just to kiss her and when she sighed and smiled against him Alex's whole world felt more complete.

Chapter Eight

છા

He was working his way down her slim body when she woke up. Her fingers curled in his hair and she tugged. He glanced up at her and grinned, "D' ya mind? I'm having a snack."

"You said I could have something my way," she said, poking her lip out.

His cock went hard and she knew he wondered exactly what she had in mind. Was she going to try cuffing him to the bed?

"I want you to cuff me again. Standing up, with my arms overhead," she said.

Alex grinned at her, shaking his head. "You're really into bondage, aren't you, baby?" he teased, reaching for the padded cuffs they'd never gotten around to putting up.

She shook her head, jerking her hand away. "Wrong cuffs. *Your* cuffs. And I want it rough," she said. She slowly scooted away from him and sat up, watching as his gaze fell and landed on her naked breasts. Alex maybe hadn't realized she had discovered her backbone. And she was figuring out just how important her own wishes and needs were.

She had fantasies, damn it. And if Alex was just going to be around for a little while, why not go ahead and make a few of them come true? If he was actually, *please, please, please,* interested in her, seriously, then he'd want to, wouldn't he?

Allie shifted onto her knees and crawled over to him, staring at him while she whispered, "Hard. Fast. Anyway you want to do it—you can make me suck your cock again, spank me, anything you want, however you want, if you want, as long as it ends with me standing up, cuffed with my arms over my head, while you fuck me hard and rough." She knew she was blushing—couldn't stop that. She wasn't sure how sexy a woman could look if she was blushing from her crown to her nipples, but she also knew a year ago, she couldn't have done this. "That's how you like it... isn't it?"

Hot need flashed in his narrowed eyes, but he lashed it down, staring into her eyes. She looked straight at him, even though she was nervous and embarrassed and afraid. "You sure about that? You're so little, Allie. I don't want to hurt you," he said, groaning silently as she straightened up, her slight body uncurling on the bed, putting her breasts on level with his mouth.

"But I do. I want it." She slid one hand down her torso and touched her clit with her finger, stroking it rapidly, until her eyes glazed and her head fell back. "You wanna hear the truth, Alex? I've been dreaming about *you* for years, and I've been wanting you to do just that. So, yes, I'm sure. I want it hard enough, rough enough, that you hurt me. I think I'd like it. I know I would," she said and she cried out when he knocked her hand away and drove two thick, long fingers inside her aching sex.

He didn't know she had woken up late that night and had lain there, staring at him. She loved him, not with a crush, but seriously, completely. And she needed to tell him. If he couldn't love her, then this needed to be over with. But damn it, she'd have her dream first.

He slowly drew away and climbed from the bed, his eyes wild and glassy with hunger. "All right," he rumbled, his voice deep and rough with need. He snagged his jeans and jerked them on, then his T-shirt and belt. His cuffs were on the table along with his gun and shoulder harness. He left the gun but put the harness on as he slid the cuffs on his belt. He rummaged through her drawers until he found what he was looking for, jeans shorts, a button down top, demi-bra, thong panties. He turned to her and grinned, a naughty grin that made Allie feel like she'd been caught playing with herself in church.

"Indulge *me* a little, kitten," he whispered, dressing her. "You want me to play rough. Right? How rough?"

Taking a deep breath, Allie decided to lay it out. "As long as it's with you, Alex, as rough as you wanna get. I'd sooner die than let anybody else know this, but I've had all sorts of dreams about you, everything from candlelight and romance to rape fantasies. Today I want the rape fantasy—"

The words no more than left her mouth when he grabbed her, whirled her around and had her pinned against one of the posts of the bed, kissing her brutally, jerking the shirt he had just buttoned open and palming her breasts roughly with his wide, calloused hands. She ached already.

Did I really tell him that? she asked herself frantically. But there was no time left to think. Alex snaked one hand inside her shorts and jerked the thong up so that it bit into her still sore ass and her cleft and she shuddered. He lifted her up and bit her nipple roughly, sucking it deep into his mouth as he ground his cock against her before moving away, staring at her with hot eyes. "There's something dangerous about fantasies, Allie. Sometimes you forget what's real and what's not. You willing to risk that? You willing to play rough?" he purred against her ear.

She stared at him, half frightened, but so hot, so eager for him, she'd beg if that was what it took.

"Yes," she said shakily.

He smiled, a slow, rather cruel twist of his lips that had shivers running down her spine. He licked a long wet trail along her neck and rasped into her ear, "You asked for it, kitten."

He fell back a little and stared at her, looming over her even though two or three feet separated them.

"Run," he whispered as he cupped his cock through his jeans.

She ran.

He caught up with her by the stairs and she screamed, a little panicked when he shoved her to her knees and jerked his pants open, taking his swollen cock in hand and dragging her head closer, one hand fisted tightly in her hair. "Your mouth," he ordered roughly. "On me, now."

When she hesitated, wondering if she had gotten in over her head, he moved around behind her, pushed her onto her hands and knees and slapped her ass, hard and rough—then he pushed his cock against her rump and growled roughly in warning when she automatically tried to reach for him. He spanked her butt again, harder, and she shuddered. "You wanted it my way, we're doing it my way, Allie-cat," he rasped, slid his fingers through the cream soaking through her shorts. "Now when I tell you to put your mouth on my cock, are you going to do it?"

"Yes," she whimpered. He slid two fingers up the leg of her shorts and plunged inside her, twice, shallowly, before he withdrew. Then he spanked her again, harder and harder until she cried out, the pain mingling with the pleasure.

When he moved back in front of her, taking his imposing cock in his hand, he growled, "Take my cock in your mouth, Allie. Now." His dark eyes glittered with a feral light and his smile, usually so easy and mellow, was menacing, almost mean. "Now, Allie," he repeated roughly.

She complied and wondered if she was going to come just with that. He shoved himself into her mouth, roughly, fast, hard until she was fighting not to gag. "Be still," he ordered when she tried to pull away. He buried both hands in her hair and did something with his thumbs that forced her mouth open wider around his cock as he shuttled in and out and she felt him grow larger, felt the cream pooling in her panties and wondered if she was going to die before he touched her again.

He drove himself further inside than she had ever taken him and her lungs burned as her air was cut off but she took it while he growled and said, "Swallow it, baby, open your mouth for me, and swallow," and she did as he drove deep and pumped harder and faster. She tried to pull away and he barked, "Take it, damn it," so she took it and she loved it and wanted more and heard him groan as he came. Then he was jerking her to her feet and pinning her against the staircase and growling in her ear about how he was going to fuck her, and spank her, and Allie felt faint as she stared up at him.

He loomed over her, crowding her against the stairwell as he roughly said, "I'm gonna fuck you hard and rough. I'm gonna spank your sweet, naked little ass, and I'm gonna listen to you moan and scream and *beg* me for more."

Alex couldn't believe he was doing this, couldn't believe Allie wanted it. *This* was exactly how rough he liked to get, but he had never imagined taking it so far with her. He could see the half terrified, half desperate arousal on her face as he jerked her hands high over her head, until her spine was arched and it had to be uncomfortable but he cuffed them around one of the banisters, and smiled, a little evilly, as it lifted her breasts.

He paused, pushing the cups of the demi-bra down so that her breasts were lifted and exposed, her nipples hard and ripe and swollen. Alex pinched each one, then licked each one in turn and she moaned, a low rough sound that went straight to his rock hard cock. He left her torn shirt in place as he knelt in front of her and jerked her shorts down to her ankles, but not completely off, leaving the thong in place. He forced her to turn around and admired her ass, the way the black lace rode the sweet crevice, the long slim lines of her legs. He moved against her rump and pumped his cock against her as he reached around and cupped her breasts, pinching the nipples hard enough to make her arch and whimper before he moved away and to the side — then he spanked her. Five times, each one a little harder until her ass was pink and flushed and she was crying and gasping out.

He whirled her back around and kissed her, biting her lip, sucking on it. His cock brushed against her lace covered cleft and she arched against him. Alex moved away, wrapping his hand around his cock and pumping slowly while he stared at her. His eyes glittered with a hot, hungry light, his hair spilling over his forehead. His muscled chest was bared by the shirt he had jerked open, the flat line of his belly tanned and carved and hard. His cock jerked in his hand as he stroked it, staring at her hungrily, watching her with a wolf's stare

"I almost wish I had waited," he said softly, clucking his tongue. "If I had waited until now…hmmm, shoving my cock inside your ass right now would be the sweetest damn thing I've ever felt. Watch your tail, Allie-cat. When it ain't so fucking sore…" His voice trailed off and he gave her a slightly evil smile.

Her pale, pretty body was naked except for the black lace of her thong, the shreds of her shirt and the pushed down cups of her bra. Her nipples were red, tight and swollen, the breasts framed by the wire of the demi-bra. And her face was glowing, her sweet green eyes hot and half blind with arousal.

He had never seen a more beautiful sight in his life.

Alex went back to her, grasping the black lace and pulling it aside as he grabbed her hips and lifted her legs—opening her wet folds, draping her thighs on his shoulders, letting enough of her weight hang on her hands that she was a little uncomfortable but not too much—as he feasted on her sweet, intoxicating cream. Her clit was swollen, hard and when he caught it in his teeth, she screamed and came in a geyser against his mouth. He drank it down greedily and drove his tongue inside her passage, alternating between stabbing at her clit and biting it and then thrusting into her with his hardened tongue until she came again and again.

By the third climax she was moaning and telling him to stop. He looked up at her and growled roughly, "Shut up, Allie. My way, remember?" Going back to her, adding his fingers and screwing them in and out of her—he then stopped and left her there, moaning and panting, arms stretched overhead while he went to get her vibrator. Returning, he knelt in front of her and drove it inside roughly, quickly, waiting until she was rocking against it and sobbing before he went back to suckling her clit.

"Damn it, Alex, I *can't* —" she shrieked as he forced her into a fourth.

"You will," he growled, pulling the vibrator down, then driving it back up inside. She climaxed around it with a sob and went limp. He slid the vibrator from her with a wet, sucking sound and tossed it over his shoulder as he studied her swollen tissues before looking up at her.

She looked exhausted.

He smiled, a hot, feral grin that made his eyes gleam. Then he leaned in and licked her lightly to test her. Almost there. He wanted her tight and swollen and sensitive. When he finally pulled his face from her soaking pussy, he touched her lightly, just a ghost touch of his index finger on her clit, and it made her scream.

Allie looked too drained for anything else. He hadn't done what she had asked yet, but he touched her clit lightly, with just his fingers, and she jerked as though struck by a lightning bolt. She stared down at him warily as he looked up at her with dark, unreadable eyes.

He continued to kneel at her feet, his face wet and gleaming from her cream, as he slid his shoulder holster and shirt off with slow methodical motions. "You're tighter now than you've ever been," he mused. "Swollen, and wet, and sore...you're going to feel so tight around me. And it's going to feel like I'm driving clear up to your throat." Wrapping his hand around his cock as he knelt by her feet, he said, "I'm going to like this, Allie. I hope you know just how much."

Slowly, he pushed to his feet, his thick cock throbbing against his flat belly as he reached for her hips and moved slowly, waiting until she was staring at him. "My way," he whispered darkly before driving ruthlessly inside her tight body, working his cock deep inside while she shuddered and twisted and moaned. He drove completely in, fighting the tight, swollen clasp of her body and when he had his thick ten-inch cock completely inside her, he buried one hand in her hair and made her look at him. "Tell me again...how do you want me to fuck you?" he purred roughly.

"...your way..." she sobbed, twisting weakly against him.

"My way," he agreed and he jerked her thighs high, wide-open, and gave her exactly what she had asked for—a rough, hard fuck. He shoved her breast high, catching one nipple in his mouth and biting down, while she screamed out his name.

Her legs were wrapped around his waist and she was rocking against him, riding him as surely as he rode her. He reached behind him with a snarl and unlocked her legs, catching her behind the knees and pushing her open, letting her weight rest on his forearms and from the cuffs that still held her. Staring into her eyes, he pulled out and drove in, hard. "Fuck you, hard and rough, remember?" he purred, moving around until he could pinch her nipple roughly. "In your rape fantasies, did you fuck me back, or was it just me fucking you?"

"Just you..." she whimpered, crying out as he surged back inside her.

"I like these fantasies of yours, Allie-cat," he growled, gripping the soft underside of her knees with bruising pressure while he used all the power in his thighs and back and hips to drive his cock inside her swollen, tight sheath. Her tissues clung to him, silken and wet. "Too much. Later, you fuck me, but now—" He drove back inside, loving her slick, wet pussy, the way she sobbed his name, how she looked, cuffed and open and begging for him.

Her shirt still hung in a tangle around her shoulders, the demi-bra pushing her round little breasts up, framing them. Her nipples were tight, hard and swollen, rising and falling raggedly as she struggled to breathe. Her green eyes were wild and frightened and hungry, driving him on as he rode her harder, the sound of her moans sending little thrills of sensation down his spine to tighten his balls to the point of pain.

Her sheath held him tightly, too tightly, resisting each deep, brutal thrust and he loved it Catching her mouth, he kissed her savagely as he drove deep and hard, ramming his cock against her womb.

She screamed and shuddered and started to chant his name, "Yes, please, Alex, more, please, Alex, more, more, please, more, damn it, more, Alex, Alex, Alex, Alex, Alex!" With each deep driving thrust of his hips, she screamed his name and shuddered.

* * * * *

The car stopped in front of the house and Mike got out, helping Lori out with a slight frown on his face as he spotted the black truck. What was Alex doing here? He and Allie had been at odds for months. Mike was aggravated about it, yeah, but he wasn't going to lose sleep over it. Allie was so quiet, said so little about anything, it wasn't like it was going to cause any problems. Lori had barely noticed the black truck. As he opened the gate, Mike heard the moaning and a woman's hoarse cries.

And he knew he should have turned around.

There was a burning low in his gut. His eyes narrowed and he recalled the odd exchange back at the station a few days ago, how Alex wouldn't say a damn thing beyond she's different, how well...*nervous*, he had acted.

No.

No fucking way.

He used his own key to open the door instead of knocking, smiling absently at Lori, who had finally registered something was going on. She locked her fingers on his arm and pulled as he started to barrel in. "Mike, let's go, *now*," his wife was snapping but he hardly heard her.

His baby sister was cuffed to a banister and couldn't get away and—

* * * * *

The ecstasy shuddered through Allie and exploded with an intensity she couldn't fight as it came from her in a series of ragged screams that Alex echoed against her mouth as he fell into her, stroking his hands up her legs to grip her tightly against him while he came inside her.

Cool air against their overheated bodies was the first sign something was wrong.

The soft, urgent, "Damn it, Michael Ryan, this doesn't concern you," was the second.

"Oh, fuck," Alex muttered.

Mike's pregnant wife wasn't an idiot. Nor was she fragile or slow. So she did what any sensible woman would do. She planted herself in front of her husband and wrapped her arms around Mike, giving Alex time to uncuff Allie while she said, "Mike, this is none of our business. Let's go outside—"

"My business, all right," he disagreed affably, glaring at Alex as he shielded Allie while she quickly clothed herself. "It looked to me like rape."

Lori laughed and said, "Save me from older brothers. Thank you, God, for not giving me any." She caught his arm, batted her lashes at him, and held on like crazy as he tried again to move past her. He couldn't exactly do much with her attached, could he?

Allie stomped out from behind Alex who tried to grab her arm and she said, "Excuse me? Rape?"

He couldn't look at her. Not without seeing somebody other than his baby sister. So he glared at the man responsible. "Outside. Now."

"I'm not fighting you over this, man," Alex said, even though he had a bad feeling he didn't have much choice.

"The fuck you ain't," Mike growled, taking a menacing step in his direction. "I thought you were my friend, but you go and treat my baby sister like that? The fuck with you! We're done! Now outside! Or do I kill you in here?"

"He's here because I want him here, Mike," Allie said, forcing herself into Mike's face.

"Allie, go to your room," Mike said.

"My room?" she gasped, her eyes going wide. "I'm not twelve. And this is my fucking house. Alex is here, with *me*, because *I* want him here."

"Well, *I* don't," Mike snarled, dragging his eyes from his sister's face, ignoring the woman he saw standing there, focusing on the kid he remembered. He glared at Alex. "Ready?"

Allie grabbed Mike's arm and hauled him back around when he tried to stomp outside. The strength in her small hands shocked him, everyone could see that, but what was more surprising was the fire in her eyes, and the guts it took to face him down. Lori had seen the changes months ago, but Mike hadn't.

"No," she said fiercely. "Not over me. Not like this. Rape doesn't usually end with, *Yes, please, Alex, more, please, Alex, more, more, please, more, damn it, more, Alex, Alex, Alex, Alex, Alex!*" She mimicked the breathy scream with an accuracy that had blood rushing to Mike's face, and to more southern regions of Alex's physique. He moved closer to Allie, eyeing Mike warily as he wrapped his hands around her arms, and eased her back. "Come on, Allie-cat." He waited until he had guided her a few feet back before he whispered, "Don't rub it in, okay, kitten?"

She glared at Mike, furious and shaking with it. "This is *my* house, Alex. He doesn't seem to remember that. And I'm grown up. I can do whatever I want." And then, nastily, she added, "Or whom. But if he doesn't like it, he can pretend I'm still the baby, still the awkward little brat who can't take care of herself. And he thinks he can say you raped me so he feels better about what he saw?"

Mike's face flushed and he looked away. "Don't, Allie. Just don't." He glared at Alex and snarled, "Now."

Alex smoothed one hand down Allie's arm and said, "Wait in here, kitten. It's gonna happen, might as well be now."

Alex walked outside and took the punch that came flying without even trying to dodge it. He landed on his ass and sat there, running his tongue over his teeth before lifting his eyes to stare at Mike. "I'll let you have that one. She's your baby sister and it had to hurt seeing what you saw."

He waited until Mike's furious eyes met his before he went on. "But I told you the other night, and I meant it." he said quietly. He pushed to his feet. When Mike moved at him, he moved away. "You got one Move at me again, and we're going a round. I care about her, and that's really all you need to know," Alex said.

"Oh, fuck off," Mike snarled, moving into Alex's face and shoving him. It would be easier to hate him, to fight him and pound him into the dust if he wouldn't be so, well, understanding about it. And so fucking sincere. But damn it, he knew what kind of women Alex dated, and Allie wasn't among them. Damn it, she was afraid of her own shadow. "What's the deal? You get bored with your whores? You think you can make my sister one?"

Alex decked him and felt the blow clear up into his shoulder. "That's *Allie* you're talking about. *Alison.* You think I could do that to her? I adore her—I always have and you fucking know it!" he shouted, shoving Mike up against the porch when the shorter man tried to move around him.

"And that's what I saw? You were showing your worship?" Mike panted, lashing out, knocking Alex's legs out and they ended up on the ground, Alex catching Mike's elbow in his gut before he returned the favor by clipping Mike in the chin. "Handcuffed? And you've ignored the—ouch, you motherfucker—crush she's had on you for years, because you adore her."

Alex was briefly, and humiliatingly, pinned by the shorter, broader cop before he knocked him off. He rolled to his feet and braced himself, staring at Mike with angry eyes. "You stupid fuck, if you had fucking called, or knocked—shit." Alex's words trailed off and he wondered exactly what he was supposed to say. Quietly, keeping his voice down, he said, "I'm not using her for sex. And I'd kill any man who treated her like a whore. I care about her. I already told you."

"You want me to believe that crap?" Mike's voice was *not* quiet. It was loud, rude and mocking, meant to deliberately hurt. "About Allie? Skinny, underfed, little rab—

Alex delivered an uppercut that knocked Mike off his feet. He rubbed his knuckles and would have gone for him again, just because Mike would have said something that could have hurt Allie, but then both of them got doused with cold water. He tossed the little brat responsible a dirty look and she smiled angelically.

"Cool off, Mike. Grow up, figure out that *I* have, and cool off," she suggested. "And don't forget something. Alex is your best friend. He always has been. Seeing him with me shouldn't change that. Especially since he was doing something *I* asked him to do."

Alex watched as she turned around walked into the house.

Chapter Nine

ഌ

The low lying pile of cinderblocks didn't look like much of a bar. It lacked space, ambience, and locale, but the owner didn't mind. It was right behind the station and it was exactly what the retired cop had planned — a cop shop. A few locals drifted in and out to watch sports, but it was too quiet a neighborhood for party goers, and the cops who came in after shift weren't looking for dates or to get laid so there wasn't much trolling going on either.

Alex squinted through the smoke and saw Mike shooting pool — focused, determined — ignoring any and all talk going on around him. Allie had tried to offer him an easy way out but it wouldn't have worked. No matter what, even if Mike had walked in on the candlelight and romance fantasy, he still would have seen his best friend fucking his baby sister — the shy little girl both of them had spent most of their boyhoods looking after.

Mike glanced at him from the corner of his eyes and grunted, "Got nothing to say to you. Get out."

"I love her," Alex said simply, tossing the players at the other table a bland look. They all glanced around, shrugged and wandered off as Alex leaned against the vacated table.

Mike snorted and took a long drink from his beer before taking his cue stick again and going back to his solitary game. "She's a kid, Alex. And she's not your type. I don't know how in the fuck you talked her into —"

"I didn't talk her into anything," Alex said flatly. "That's one thing we're setting straight here and now. I moved on her when she came back from Ireland, and maybe I moved a little too quickly, but I didn't talk her into anything. Your sister isn't a kid. She's a woman, and believe it or not, she's a woman who knows what she wants."

Mike's face went hard and tight—a flat, cool look of dismissal there. He couldn't see it, didn't want to see it. Didn't want to acknowledge his little sister had grown up. "And you think it's you," Mike drawled. "Hate to tell you this, pal, but Allie's playing around. She came home from Ireland all aglow, lost her virginity there and now she's ready to try out some new games."

Alex blew out a ragged breath and rubbed his hands over his face.

Mike mistook the action for disbelief and laughed meanly. "Don't believe me? She found herself a guy over there as soon as she was away from people who were just trying to look out for her and she spent the entire two weeks getting fucked every which way."

No, Alex thought, shoving the gut-burning anger down. *Not every which way.* He was going to be rational about this. He had known there had been somebody in Ireland. He had known. He wasn't going to lose his cool.

Mike continued to taunt him. "Change your mind, old buddy? Knowing she went from fucking one man—and she is still so new at it—to you in just a week or two?" Mike said evilly. *Why in the hell am I saying this? Why am I so fucking pissed?* Too much to drink, too little sleep, Lori was mad at him, Allie wouldn't talk to him, and he knew he was wrong. Why else? "Just think, if you had moved just a little quicker, you could have been the first."

Alex dropped his hands and lifted his head. "I was the first," he said levelly.

Mike was in the middle of lifting his beer to his smirking mouth when he froze. Staring at Alex with narrowed eyes, he slowly lowered the bottle and asked, "When?"

Heaving a sigh, Alex said, "While you were on your honeymoon. The night that punk tried to mug her." He moved back when Mike took a menacing step in his direction. "Don't. We've already done that. After we get through this, if you want to pound on each other some more, fine. But this first. You can't say or do anything I've not wanted to do to myself. You think I'm proud of it?"

"I'd suggest you get through whatever you think you need to get through. Because I really need to kill you," Mike growled, hurling his cue stick down and stomping away. Why the fuck had he quit smoking?

He didn't realize he was looking for a cigarette until Alex laughed and reminded him, "Lori? The baby?"

Right. Lori. The baby. That was why he had quit smoking. Not a good example. And that was a good reason why he shouldn't kill Alex. He couldn't be a good dad if he was in jail, now could he? And cops didn't tend to do well in jail. "Why, Alex? Can you tell me that?"

"Why that night?" Alex shrugged. No. He didn't know why that night. He had been exhausted. She had been there, warm, soft, and everything he hadn't realized he wanted. "Or why ever? I love her, Mike. And here's the bitch of it all—I think I've always loved her. And I'll be damned if I let you, or anybody else, fuck this up for me."

Mike plowed his fingers through his hair and glared at Alex. "She's not your type, Alex. Damn it, you and me, we aren't the kind of guys who are going to settle for regular, average sex. For crying out loud, I shared my fucking wife with you, more than once."

"She wasn't your wife, then. And I won't ever touch her again. I don't ever want to," Alex said. *And I'd really rather Allie not know anything about that.* He winced at the thought and wondered if Lori and Allie were close.

"I don't recall inviting you to," Mike snarled. "But that's not the point. How long do you think Allie is going to keep you satisfied, damn it?"

A slow, hot smile curved Alex's mouth and he replied honestly, "Forever." He pushed off the table and met Mike's eyes. "We can go pound each other now, if that's what you want."

Mike glared at him and grabbed his cue stick and went back to his game.

* * * * *

When Allie walked into the candlelight, she stopped dead in her tracks. Her eyes ran over the living room, the familiar furniture, the staircase that led to the two bedrooms upstairs. Yes. It was her house.

But there were candles everywhere, and rose petals on the floor and the heart-breaking sound of Enya in the background. Alex moved around the doorway from the hall and smiled at her slowly, sweetly, and she felt her heart stop. "You're still in one piece, looks like," she said, pleased her voice was level. And feeling a little underdressed. She had just left the gym and her spandex and sports bra weren't exactly as classy as the silk shirt and black trousers he was wearing.

He smiled slowly and glanced down. "Looks like," he agreed. He eyed her clothes and the duffel. "Gym? I was wondering where that nifty little body was coming from," he mused, running one finger down her bicep.

Goosebumps flared under his touch and she shivered.

"Come on," he said, taking her arm and guiding her into the bedroom. "I think I timed this about right. You said you'd be home by five or so..." he pushed the door to her bathroom open and Allie blinked and felt her heart melt. More candles, music playing just a little louder, a bath all ready for her in the deep sunken tub, more rose petals floating in the water.

"Are you, um, feeling all right, Alex?" she asked conversationally. "Mike didn't crack your head open and cause some mysterious head injury that resulted in this, right?"

He grinned as he tugged the band from her ponytail down. "Fine. Nervous, but fine." He bent over and kissed her lightly. "Take your bath." He brushed his fingers over one nipple and said, "I'd love to help, but I can only handle so much."

Alex waited until he heard her settle into the water before he walked out of the bedroom. He moved away before he could change his mind about joining her and met the boy at the back door and paid him an extra twenty to set the meal up.

A guy usually only planned on proposing once. He was going to do this right.

Especially since Allie had so kindly provided the candlelight suggestion. Alex wasn't big on romance, but anything that put that soft look in her eyes was enough for him. After the kid left, he went back to pacing. He figured if he got it all out of his system now, he wouldn't look nervous in front of her.

He didn't know if she loved him or not.

And he didn't know if she'd believe he loved her, not after the fiasco their first night had been.

He heard her moving around after about fifteen minutes, and grinned. He had reckoned on her being too curious to wait for long. He met her in the bathroom, her body wet and gleaming from the oils he'd found while rummaging through her cabinets. She smelled like vanilla and lavender and sex, Alex thought, moving closer and taking the towel from her, rubbing her dry, turning her to face the mirror so she could watch with him.

He settled her down on the chair in front of the mirror and pulled the clip from her hair, watching the shoulder length locks spill down before he started to brush it out. Once it was gleaming, he took her hand and led her into the bedroom and took the gown he had laid out for her — white silk, v-necked, cut like a slip. He pulled it over her head, leaving her oiled, smooth flesh naked underneath and then kissed her hand.

"Let's go eat," he said. And he wondered why in the flying fuck he had even bothered with dinner.

Romance, buddy. Romance.

He'd drawn all the curtains, blocking the sunlight, turned off all the lights, and the candles were all glowing softly.

She had been smiling and staring into nothing when he came to take the plate away. He returned and pulled the chair out but kept her from rising, just turned her so that she was facing him as he dropped to his knees in front of her. "You look delicious, smell delicious, taste delicious," he whispered roughly, stroking one finger over her cheek. His hands slid up her calves to her knees, gathering the silk and taking it higher. "Mind if I have some?"

Alex lifted her and laid her on the cleared table, drawing the night gown off and studying her with hot eyes as he pulled her to the edge. Leaning over, he kissed her mouth gently and whispered, "I'm in love with you, Allie Ryan," as he started to circle one finger around her entrance.

Her eyes flew open and she stared up at him, the dark green of her eyes glittering and wide, her mouth trembling. Slowly, he kissed her again as he slid two fingers inside her pussy, while she helplessly lifted her hips against his hand, her wet tissues tight and silky, the hard little bud of her clit swollen against his thumb. He drove his tongue inside her mouth, loving her taste, the weak hungry moan she made, how her hands clutched at his nape and held tight. Her tongue met his and he retreated, sucking hers into his mouth and shuddering when she came eagerly, tasting him, catching his lip between her teeth and nibbling before seeking his tongue out again greedily.

He drew away and pressed a kiss to her chin as her head fell back, her neck arched, and he kissed the rabbiting pulse he found there. He worked his way down to her breasts while he continued to screw his fingers in and out of her creamy, wet cleft. His mouth closed over one swollen, peaked nipple as she cried out, "Alex, I love you, I've always loved you."

Well, fuck. Alex lashed the sudden biting need to drive inside when he heard her speak. The words seemed to cause an explosion inside him and his cock swelled to the point of pain and all he wanted to do was mount her and fuck her until they collapsed. Instead, he settled on his knees between her thighs and licked her—torturing himself with the sweet taste of her cream as he stabbed inside her entrance with his stiffened tongue—until she was lifting her hips to meet him, riding his mouth, and calling out his name raggedly. He slid his hands under her butt, used his fingers to torment her by spreading her ass open a little and letting her cream dribble down to coat her anus.

He moved up and took her clit in his mouth and she screamed, arching up. He bit down gently and her body shuddered. He sucked and she came, screaming hoarsely, while lifting herself up and begging, "Alex, oh please fuck me, Alex!"

He rose and stood staring down at her as he slowly removed his shirt and trousers, his face gleaming wetly from her cream in the dancing candlelight. He waited until she was staring at him, panting and reaching for him before he moved to mount her. "Say it again, ALie-cat," he said gruffly.

With a ragged grin, she asked, "What, fuck me?"

He shifted to the side and smacked her burning pussy lightly. "No, and you know it, brat," he admonished before covering her again, taking her thighs and pushing them to her chest, so that she was open. He stared into her eyes and waited.

She smiled sweetly and said, "I love you, Alex. I'm surprised you didn't know that."

He shuddered and looked down at her body. Her position opened her red, dripping folds, exposed the swollen bud of her clit. He watched as he leaned in and pushed the head of his cock inside, lashing down the hot, burning need to drive repeatedly inside, and never leave this sweet wet haven again.

"A—lex," she groaned as he continued to push so slowly inside. Tightening her inner muscles, she grinned up at him when he glared at her and shoved a little harder inside her.

She did it again, and again—then his control snapped as she looped her arms around his neck and whispered, "I love you so much." He slammed into her, hard and fast, bringing a startled cry to her lips.

He came into her again, deep, tight and full, again and again, his cock rubbing against the sensitized nerve endings near the mouth of her womb as she pushed down on his hard, thick, hot shaft. Against her ear, he whispered, "Love you, Allie, damn it, love you so much," while she pushed up against him, and pushed down inside, as he caressed her there again and nudged against her cervix, reveling in the sweet, hot feel of her.

His mouth covered hers and his tongue was in her mouth, thrusting deep as his cock was thrusting in her cleft. He slid one hand up her thigh to circle over her anus, then he was probing and pushing inside and Allie was screaming and coming in a hot geyser that stole her breath.

Alex saw her eyes flutter closed as he pummeled her hips, his come jetting into her wet welcoming sheath, as she slowly went slack around him. He pushed a little deeper and rode it to the very end then collapsed against her and rested briefly on her body before pulling out and rolling off to catch his breath.

He had to stifle a laugh when he looked over at her and saw that she was still out. He hadn't ever fucked a woman into unconsciousness before. He sat up and got off the table—thankful the solid oak had held up—then he picked up Allie's limp body and carried her into the bedroom.

She was on her belly when she came to and her hands were behind her back. She had to smile, but then she groaned. "Alex, honey, I really don't think I'm up for anything right now," she said, tugging on the cuffs.

He nudged her with his cock as he tugged her up onto her knees and stuffed some pillows under her, supporting her weight. "That's okay, kitten. I'm up." he said, and pushed against her to prove it. "It's been a fucking week since I touched you You wouldn't let me come over until today and you hardly talked to me on the phone so you should have been expecting this."

She whimpered in pleasure when he pressed a cool slick finger against her anus. "All better here?" he asked, pushing inside and groaning as she took him easily. "Yeah, looks like. We're going to try something else then." He took her vibrator, and moved to the side, working it inside her body, thrusting it deep, alternating between fucking her with it and stopping to spark her, until she was moaning and swearing at him.

When she was crying out her need, Alex moved behind her, leaving the vibrating toy buried deep inside her sex, watching as she squirmed around it and rode it, trying to find the orgasm on her own as he lubricated his cock. The vibrator had one of those external extensions that vibrated and stimulated her clit and she kept rocking against it, moaning and whimpering hungrily.

Alex smeared the lubricant on her anus, and then inside it, stroking his shaft as she pushed back eagerly against him. He pressed against her, staring at her — her long slim back, the hands still cuffed at her spine, her face turned to the side, golden brown hair tousled over the pillow — as he started to push inside. "You're so tight," he said with hot rough pleasure, lifting his hand and smacking her ass when she started to pull away instinctively from the double penetration. "Push down for me, kitten, come on."

She sobbed, bit her lip, but did it, and then she quivered with pleasure. She was stretched, invaded, tight, as he drove completely inside her ass, pulling out and driving back in as she pushed back to meet him. He spanked her again and she mewled, shivered and bucked against him as the vibrator teased her clit. "Tell me you love me, Allie," he ordered, burrowing back inside the tight sheath, pulling out, and watching as she shoved back greedily on him like she couldn't stand not having his cock inside her.

"Love you," she sobbed, and she screamed and creamed around the vibrator as he spanked her again and fucked her ass harder and harder, pushing her into the mattress and covering her bound body with his as he rode her ass with hard, brutal strokes that had her coming and screaming. Thrusting to the hilt he groaned and shot her sweet little hole full of hot creamy seed. "I love you," he whispered raggedly, trying to catch his breath.

When he could breathe again, he rolled from the bed and climbed out, reaching for the last thing he had brought with him. She wriggled and jingled the cuffs. "Forget something?" she mumbled.

"No." He had meant to do this a little earlier, and he'd be damned if he tried to go back to candlelight and romance again. Alex wasn't even sure if he could remember how to write his name just yet.

He picked up the box and took out the ring, sliding it on her ring finger before he undid the cuffs. Then he watched as she rolled over and sat up, staring at it. Her eyes were wide and wet with tears as he cupped her face and whispered, "Wanna marry me, Allie-cat? I may not do the candlelight and romance part as often, but I can do it. And I can't think of anything I'd rather do than spend the rest of my life making every fantasy you have a reality."

She launched herself at him, laughing and crying. He took that as a 'Yes.'

Also by Shiloh Walker

෨

A Wish, A Kiss, A Dream *(anthology)*
Back from Hell
Coming In Last
Ellora's Cavemen: Legendary Tails II *(anthology)*
Ellora's Cavemen: Tales from the Temple IV *(anthology)*
Every Last Fantasy
Firewalkers: Dreamer
Her Best Friend's Lover
Her Wildest Dreams
His Christmas Cara
His Every Desire
Hot Spell *(anthology)*
Make Me Believe
Myth-Behavin' *(anthology)*
Mythe: Mythe & Magick
Mythe: Vampire
Once Upon a Midnight Blue
Sage
Silk Scarves and Seduction
Telling Tales
The Dragon's Warrior
The Dragon's Woman
The Hunters: Ben and Shadoe
The Hunters: Byron and Kit
The Hunters: Delcan and Tori
The Hunters: Eli and Sarel

About the Author

ഇറ

Shiloh was born in Kentucky and has been reading avidly since she was six. At twelve, she discovered how much fun it was to write when she took a book that didn't end the way she had wanted it to and rewrote the ending. She's been writing ever since.

Shiloh now lives in southern Indiana with her husband and two children. Between her job, her two adorable and demanding children, and equally adorable and demanding husband, she crams writing in between studying and reading and sleeps when time allows.

Shiloh welcomes comments from readers. You can find her website and email address on her author bio page at www.elloracave.com.

COWBOY & THE CAPTIVE
ഉ

Trademarks Acknowledgement

ဢ

The author acknowledges the trademarked status and trademark owners of the following wordmarks mentioned in this work of fiction:

Stetson: John B. Stetson
Jeep: DaimlerChrysler Corporation

Prologue

સ

The enemy's promises were made to be broken.

From Aesop's Fable. The Wolf and the Nurse.

Luc Jardin knew Miss Maria Catarina Angeles was going to be trouble the minute she stepped into the small hangar where he and his friend and partner, Jack Riley, were waiting to see if they could pick up a last minute job flying out of the small South American airport.

This job was looking too good to be true. He never did like the ones that were too much of a good thing, and this woman could be described no other way.

She was slender and graceful, her skin a bit pale, but otherwise appearing as soft as satin. Her green eyes were vacant, but he had recognized her right off the bat. A spoiled little rich girl with too much time and money on her hands. It wasn't exactly the demeanor Luc had glimpsed the few times he had been forced into the social circles she moved in, but it wasn't the first time he had been wrong about a beautiful woman. He was sure it wouldn't be the last.

He and Jack had always been suckers for redheads, though, and Maria Catarina Angeles was a true redhead. And she had the one thing they needed desperately to keep their floundering air delivery service off the ground. Money. Lots of money and a name that should be trustworthy.

The American businessman, Jonathon Angeles, was considered one of the richest men in the nation and Maria Catarina was heralded as an angel of mercy and light. What could it hurt to help her out?

"I'll give you a hundred thousand dollars and a night you'll never forget," she purred sweetly as she stepped up to Luc, rubbing her lithe little body against his harder one.

His cock liked that. The feel of her moving against him almost made him forget the little niggle of worry that tapped at his brain. The one that warned him there could be more to this than delivering a simple little crate filled with supplies being returned to the charity's home office. But damn if it wasn't hard to think about danger when slender fingers were loosening his belt and undoing his jeans. All he could think about was sex and the lack of it in the past few months.

Luc glanced at his partner as the slender socialite went to her knees and released the hard flesh. She had no shame — but hell, neither did his dick. He grinned over at Jack as slender fingers stroked his straining cock. This could turn out to be fun.

"Consider this a down payment," she murmured.

His cock was thick and insistent, and as he watched lustfully she sucked the thick head into a mouth that would have put the most experienced whores to shame. Hot and snug, her mouth covered his cock, her tongue flickering over the hard shaft as she drew the mushroomed tip to her throat. The move was blatantly sexual and would have been hotter than hell if it weren't so practiced.

Damn. Now there was a woman who knew exactly what to do with a man's body — she was experienced, sensual. Her moans echoed in the sultry air around him as she began to suck him to a rhythm that had his body tensing in pleasure.

Luc's hands went to her hair. Thick, dark red curls wrapped around his fingers as he pushed in deep, determined to enjoy every second of her hungry mouth as she moaned around his erection.

Jack watched the scene with heated intensity, his cock free as he stroked it slowly. There was just something about a good head job that Luc could never resist. Hell, he doubted any man could. And this woman was a pro. She worked his cock like a delicate instrument, drawing a hard, ragged groan from his throat as she worked her red lips over it her mouth sucking him deep, making him tense with the need to spill his release down her throat.

Hell, it had been months since he'd had sex, and this was prime sensation. The fingers of one hand cupped his balls, the pleasure causing the fleshy sac to tighten and tingle as he began to fuck her mouth harder.

He held her still, his fingers clenched in her hair as he felt the impending climax boiling in his nuts. Oh yes, this was going to be good.

She moaned around the shallow thrusts, her throat relaxing as the head of his cock entered it, her tongue stroking as he exited, wrapping around the bulging head a second before he thrust in again and let her have her way with him.

"Yeah, suck it, baby," he groaned as her lips tightened on him, her mouth and tongue creating a friction determined to drive him insane. "Suck it deep and tight."

"Damn, she's good, Jack." Luc groaned, knowing the other man was about to go crazy watching the scene. "I think she might be the best to ever wrap her lips around my cock."

She moaned again, the sound vibrating on his sensitized flesh as his hips flexed, driving his cock deeper. He could feel the warning tingle of release building at the bottom of his spine, as good as it was, he couldn't make it last much longer.

"Fuck. I'm going to come." He couldn't hold out against her for long. She was devouring his dick, moaning heatedly, drawing the come from the depths of his loins as he shoved in hard, held her still and let her consume every thick, creamy spurt of his semen.

When she finished, he tucked his flesh back in his pants and watched as she went to Jack. She did the same to the other man, making him cry out hoarsely with pleasure as he filled her as well. And she never broke a sweat.

Luc narrowed his eyes, seeing a complete lack of excitement about her. She could use that mouth like a weapon, but it meant no more to her than a means to achieve exactly what she wanted.

When she finished Jack off, leaving him damp with sweat but satisfied, she rose to her feet, wiped her mouth delicately then looked back to Luc.

"Do we have a deal then?"

A hundred thousand dollars plus a night of screwing her silly. He wondered if she was as cool and disinterested during the fuck. But hell, it was an easy enough job. Transport her and the crate of supplies back home from the South American jungle before the rebels could figure out she was there. It was a short flight. She had the crate sitting outside and it wasn't as though they were overbooked. She could have gotten a much better deal if she had bargained for it.

"Where do you need to go?" Jack was all for it.

"A small private airfield just over the American border." She smiled sweetly. "My friends will be meeting me there to take the crate, and the neighboring town has the cutest little motel we can spend the night in."

Easy enough. So why were his guts sending out warning signals? Luc shook his head at his own suspicions. He was getting too cynical. Maria Angeles was known for her flights of mercy over international borders. The fact that she was flying supplies into America raised a question, but not enough of one to have him cutting his nose off for the answers. He wanted the money. He could survive without the fuck, but he needed that money to finance the cargo operation he had started the year before.

"Get ready to fly." Luc shrugged. "We'll load the crate."

The small South American airfield where they were cooling their heels waiting for a chance to hire out wasn't the busiest in the country. They were unlikely to get a better deal. Hell, they hadn't had a better deal in the year they had been running the plane anyway.

The flight from the airfield to the small California border town was uneventful, but then, most flights were. The fact that she directed them to a nearly deserted, dusty field to land in should have been his first warning.

"This doesn't feel good, Jack," he said softly into the headset he used to communicate with his buddy in the co-pilot's seat.

Maybe it was time to return to the ranch, Luc thought. The plane wasn't turning a profit and some of the jobs they were offered were less than legal. Some were downright life-threatening. And this one was just plain making him nervous.

"There you go, letting the good things slide by you again, man." Jack laughed as he pushed a wave of long blond hair back from his face. "Go with the flow. What could happen?"

But Luc was worried enough that he checked the gun he carried at his hip before landing the plane. As Miss Angeles had predicted, there was a truck waiting at the end of the airfield, as well as several of her friends

"We're right on time," she announced happily from behind him as he and Jack rose from their seats and headed to the back of the plane.

Luc watched closely as she picked her purse up from the seat. He pushed the box down the small ramp Jack was lowering and watched as it slid to the ground. Several of the "friends" were moving closer. Luc liked to think he wasn't an overly suspicious guy, but the bulges under those coats were starting to mess with his nerves.

"Thank you for the rice, Mr. Jardin." Maria's voice was unusually high, her pupils dilated.

Luc stared at her closely then glanced to the cargo area, thinking about the crate. His uneasy suspicions were getting worse and screaming that crate held more than just supplies for the various charities the woman worked for. Drugs. He knew it.

Son of a bitch. He kept his expression impassive as he watched her move into the cargo area, her hips swaying with a sensuality that hadn't been present before. She was too relaxed now, smiling too sweetly as she kissed Jack on the jaw before moving down the ramp.

"My friends will take care of your fee." She giggled like a young girl as she turned back. "But I don't think they'll let me fuck you after all. My boyfriend gets pretty possessive." She watched them closely now as she stepped to the ground. "The money should be enough, though."

Luc glanced at Jack in concern. This job was about to go from sugar to shit real fast. Shock lined the other man's expression as he saw the men who came to a stop at the ramp. Several grabbed the crate and hauled it away as Luc quickly estimated their chances of surviving. They weren't good considering three of them had their hands disappearing beneath their jackets.

"Get back!" he yelled to Jack as he hit the control button for the ramp and threw himself at the other man.

Maria's scream echoed around him as she jumped from the plane and turned to look back into the interior. Luc pushed Jack into the recessed frame and prayed for a miracle as the ramp began to rise slowly. Too damned slowly.

"Come on! Cockpit," he yelled at Jack as he caught sight of the automatic weapons her friends were aiming into the plane, glee reflecting on their faces as their fingers tightened on the triggers.

Gunfire ripped through the plane as he ducked and jerked Jack back, nearly falling as the other man stumbled against him, a stain of red blooming over Jack's chest. Luc threw him into the co-pilot's seat before taking his own and accelerating the plane back down the runway.

"Son of a bitch," Jack wheezed as he gripped his shoulder. "Dammit to hell, Luc, this shit hurts."

Bullets pinged against the hull of the plane as Luc sped down the runway, fury enveloping him as he realized Jack hadn't been the only one hit. His leg was bleeding profusely and the ranch was over an hour away. He prayed harder. But amid the prayers was a fury that surged hot and sweet through his brain. Angel of mercy, his ass. That bitch would pay, he swore. And he would make certain she paid well.

Chapter One

ഇ

Family obligations shouldn't involve life or death, Melina Catarina Angeles thought as she faced her parents across the brightly lit living room. The sun shone through the large arched windows at the side of the room, reflecting back from the highly polished hardwood floors and lending an air of comfort and warmth to the expensively decorated room.

Antiques were her mother's passion, and the living room reflected her love for them. Surrounded by everything her parents had worked for in their lifetime should have comforted Melina. Instead, it left her cold as she stared back at them, fighting to hide her shock.

She was one of two daughters, the younger of a set of twins. The quiet, studious one. The one who had always stepped in to save her parents the humiliation of what her older twin had wrought. But she couldn't do it any longer.

They had rarely associated with her in two years. Not since the last fiasco her sister, Maria, had managed to cause. With that one, she had nearly killed two innocent men, and through her selfishness, had almost caused Melina's death months later. She had sworn then that she would never step in to play Maria's part ever again. Her parents had retaliated by cutting her out of their lives. Until now. Until Maria had once again gotten herself into a mess she couldn't get out of.

"This isn't my fight." Melina faced her estranged parents in the family room of her father's mansion and finally put her foot down. "Maria has gone too far this time, Papa. I refuse to cover for her."

She held back the pain that they would even ask it of her. Her twin sister was once again in a scrape that even their money couldn't buy her out of without the proper presentation. They needed Melina for the presentation. After the last time, there wasn't a chance in hell. She had spent a week in jail, during which time her father had been out of town and supposedly had not received her messages.

Thankfully, the police had already fingerprinted Maria and she had been saved the horrifying knowledge that her fingerprints were on file as a criminal. A drug addict. A thief. Good God, her sister was deteriorating rapidly. And now this. Arrested for smuggling drugs into the country. Again. It was a certain prison term and Melina was sick of paying for her sister's crimes. There was no way in hell she was going to take a chance on going to prison for her sister. Not after the last debacle.

A man had nearly died the last time. When Lucas Jardin had arrived on her father's steps two years before, furious because his friend had nearly died, her father had almost broken the man financially as well as personally. If Jardin hadn't been a highly respected rancher and businessman, then her father would have. All because of the addiction that was growing closer to destroying not just her sister, but her family as well.

"Melina, Maria needs all our help right now. She can't fight this addiction alone," her father argued passionately. "It's little enough to do."

Melina turned from the pleading eyes of the man who had sired her to glance at her mother's miserable, tear-filled eyes. Margaret Angeles loved all her children, but her eldest twin daughter was destroying all their lives.

"No, Papa," she repeated gently. "It was enough that I spent a week in jail for her and you ignored the messages I left both here and on your answering service. I told you then, I won't ever make the same mistake."

She remembered the look in Luc Jardin's eyes when he entered the house and saw her standing with her parents. He had thought she was Maria, and Melina had been too shocked to deny it. After learning the reason for his fury, she had wanted to kill her sister. Jardin was a man unlike any Melina had known in her life. Not just tall and broad, but rough enough around the edges to make her long to attempt to smooth them. He was untamed, and she was woman enough to want to tame him.

He was man enough to despise her, though, when her parents introduced her as Maria. It was then she began to suspect the position she had allowed her parents to place her in. The week spent in jail had only cemented it. She had sworn then she would never lift a finger to get her twin out of trouble again.

Convincing her father to cease the crusade of vengeance against the pilot hadn't been easy. He had flatly refused until the day after Melina had been released from the hospital. She had walked into the lawyer's office and threatened to publicly side with Jardin, had it not ceased. She had moved out of the family house the next week. But she had never forgotten Lucas Jardin or her reaction to him.

"Melina, your sister could go to prison," her mother sobbed then, tears spilling from her eyes. "I cannot imagine one of my babies in prison."

One of her babies? Melina stared at her mother in bitter realization. Her parents barely acknowledged any child but Maria. They had other children when they needed help getting Maria out of trouble. Period.

"Momma, you said that when it was a jail sentence," she argued furiously. "Maria didn't spend any time in jail, but I did. It didn't overly affect you then." And she hadn't forgotten it. She still had nightmares about it.

"It was a mistake, Melina" her father exclaimed fiercely. "You were supposed to get probation. The lawyer assured us that was all. He even said everything was fine when we called."

"The point is, you left." She crossed her arms over her chest as the remembered horror and fear swept over her. "You weren't in the courtroom, you weren't there to make certain I was protected and on top of it, you knew that lawyer would lie for her. They were sleeping together, for God's sake."

Jonathon Angeles flinched. "I was wrong. It won't happen again."

"I won't do it." Her heart clenched as her mother's weeping grew louder. "Papa, you have to make Maria accept the consequences. She's going to kill herself at this rate if you don't."

"I promise. We'll put her in a clinic," Jonathon swore.

"You promised that last time." She stared back at him, hating the bitterness that filled her, the cold, objective realization that these weren't her parents. They were Maria's.

"There is such a thing as loyalty to the family, Melina," her father snapped. "Your sister will never convince the judge she had no idea what was happening. You know she can't."

"You have to have a family to be loyal to first," she said bitterly. "And Maria is actually a very good liar. Maybe she can pull it off. I wish her luck, but I won't help her."

Silence met her harsh words. Her father placed his arms around her mother's shaking shoulders and tried to comfort her weeping, and though Melina didn't shed a tear, inside her heart was breaking. It was a reenactment of the last crisis her sister had caused. Only then, Melina had given in. She had sworn she never would again.

She turned from her parents and paced over to the large window that looked out over the private lake of her parents' home. She had grown up here. Had learned to swim in the lake and had realized as she grew up that she would never measure up, in her parents' eyes, to Maria. Somehow, her twin had drawn complete loyalty from them, whereas Melina had drawn only their distant affection.

"Melina, I cannot believe you would see your sister suffer in such a way," her father accused. "This would be no hardship for you."

"This is a federal offense with a mandatory prison term if convicted." She turned back to her parents, unemotional, uncaring. "With Maria's record she's certain to get time, no matter how great the argument. I will not go to prison for someone who stood aside as her criminal friends nearly slaughtered two men. It's bad enough she has no loyalty to her family, but she has no respect for life, either.

"I'm sorry, Papa, but spending time in prison would be considered a major hardship for me." She shook her head, fighting the memory of a week in jail. It had been horrible, locked into that tiny block room, at the mercy of the guards as well as the other prisoners.

She had been without protection. The required bribes to the guards that would have ensured her protection hadn't been paid and Melina hadn't been strong enough to defend herself.

"You will not go to prison." Her father surged to his feet, his portly body shaking with anger. "I have told you, I will not allow it."

Bitter amusement filled her as she watched her handsome father, his face lined worry as his eyes glittered with his rage. He was furious with her of course, and for the first time, she really didn't give a damn. She was no longer willing to do whatever it took to please her parents, to ease them or to make up for Maria's faults.

"I'm sorry, Papa." She wasn't really, but she didn't know what else to say at this point. "I can't do this for you. You know as well as I do that all the pleading and good behavior in the world is not going to save Maria this time. You would be better to petition the courts or the prosecutor for a plea bargain. They would look more favorably on that than they would a sweet little protest of innocence. Surely even your lawyer has told you that."

"He has assured me this will work." His hand sliced through the air furiously as her mother's sobs filled the background. "I am asking you for nothing. Nothing. This matter is so slight it will take only a single afternoon of your week."

Melina pushed her shaking hands into the pockets of her jeans and lowered her head to hide the misery in her eyes. How many times had they argued just like that? That it would take so little for her to take her sister's punishments. All her life she had been standing in front of Maria, taking the blame and the punishment in her name. She wasn't willing to do so anymore. Maria had turned into a vapid, heartless conniver. All that mattered were the drugs. Nothing more. Not family or friends or even personal honor held any meaning to her.

"No. Please don't make me keep saying it, Papa. I won't do this. Not ever again."

She was too sensitive. She had known that all her life. Her parents' happiness and her family's success had always meant more to her than her own happiness. At least it had until she faced Lucas Jardin and the knowledge of how far Maria would go to save her own skin and escape punishment. She hadn't slept for months after her brother had finally managed to get her released from jail and even now, two years later, the nightmares plagued her.

"I cannot believe you would say no." His voice clearly reflected his surprise. "I cannot believe you would allow your sister—your twin, for God's sake—to suffer so horribly."

"My sister isn't an innocent here." Melina's head raised as her own anger came to the fore. "She uses you to get her out of trouble and then goes on with business as usual when it's all over. She's getting worse, Papa. You know it and I know it. I won't suffer her punishment for her."

"What punishment?" He threw his hands into the air a second before he clenched his thick silver and brown hair in frustration. "There will be none if you just do as the lawyer directs you."

"I won't take that chance again," she snapped. "Papa, they beat me—more than once—and almost raped me. You know this. You know what I suffered in that jail, and still you ask this of me? How could you?"

Melina couldn't understand her parents' complete loyalty to her sister. It made no sense. They were trading the daughter who loved them unconditionally for the daughter who loved only their ability to get her out of trouble. Was it pride? Or were they truly unable to see how corrupt Maria had become?

"Almost," he blustered, his face paling as it had the first time she had told him. "I will not let it happen again."

"No, Papa. *I* won't let it happen again," she said gently, trying desperately to hold back her own fury. "I had enough two years ago, you know this. I won't let her ruin my life."

Her mother was wailing now. Deep, pain-filled sobs interspersed with ragged prayers for her "baby." Her "sweet Maria." Melina wanted to crawl into a hole and cry herself. She gazed back at her father's disappointed face, his helplessness reflected in his deep brown eyes.

"I cannot believe you would do this," he whispered. "Go, Melina. Leave this house and never return. I will tell your sister of your refusal and pray it does not break her as it has broken us."

Melina blinked back at him in shock. "You're disowning me?" she whispered, her voice bleak, filled with disbelief. "Papa? You would disown me for this?"

His gaze was hard, remote. "I do not know you. You are not the child of my heart as I believed, Melina. Until you can aid your sister as you should, then you are of no consequence to me."

He turned from her and went to her mother, enclosing her in his arms and letting her weep against his chest. Later, he would hold Maria the same way. Console her, pat her back and whisper his love to her. He hadn't held Melina like that in years. Even when he arrived at the jail to learn she had been beaten and nearly raped, her face bruised and horribly swollen, he hadn't comforted her. It had been her brother, Joe, who had picked her up from the gurney, whispering senseless phrases of grief as he carried her from the jailhouse.

It had always been her brother who had eased her fears, her tears. But even he was gone now. He had left the family and the business before Melina had, his own disgust at his parents' foolishness where Maria was concerned had gone too deep for him to stay. She wasn't ever certain where he was now.

Sighing deeply, holding back her tears, she did as her Papa ordered and turned and left the house. The butler was silent as he held the door open for her, his expression impassive. She knew there was little sympathy to be found there. All loyalties were given to Maria exclusively. Melina had never understood it, but she accepted it.

Night had fallen, casting hazy shadows over the Pennsylvania countryside and wrapping around Melina with trailing fingers of warmth. On nights like this, she thought of Jardin. Wondered if his friend had survived his wounds, if he had ever realized the young woman he had cursed so vehemently had been the wrong woman. She shook her head mockingly. Her parents accepted praise for the work Melina used to do as Maria's successes. The charities had been in Maria's name, the work attributed to her until that day. They had all fallen apart when Melina left. Just as the rest of the family was falling apart.

She turned the key in the ignition of her car and pulled out of her parents' driveway. She fought back the tears and the regrets and thought about trying to contact her brother before too long. She knew a few of his old friends who might know where to find him. Joey had always seemed to care about her and seen past her likeness to Maria. He would understand the grief tightening in her chest even if she didn't.

She should have answered his messages those first few months after her release from the hospital, she thought regretfully. Facing him hadn't been easy, though. He knew what had happened to her and every time she thought of the pity she had seen in his face, and heard in his voice, she had cringed. It was time to put it behind her, time to make the final break with her parents and her sister. Joe knew how to do that and, hopefully, he would now teach her how. Because she would be damned if she knew.

Chapter Two

🙵

Luc narrowed his eyes against the darkness of the apartment and waited. He was a patient man. He had planned this night down to the last detail and he wasn't going to rush it. He had watched the parking lot carefully for her car to drive in. He didn't want her surprising him by coming in unannounced.

He knew she had been visiting her parents, likely pleading for help after the last scrape she had managed to get into. The woman was heading on a path of self-destruction and he was more than willing to help her along. After he got his pound of flesh.

She had made her parents relent in their war against him, but she had started the war to begin with. She had paid for Jack's medical bills and recovery then called and turned ole Jack's heart with her tears and her apologies. But Jack was well known for his soft spot and his love for a pretty woman. Especially one who could suck cock like a dream and swallow without a grimace.

She had even called Luc.

Luc remembered the overwhelming rage and fury he had felt at the quiet dignity in her voice as she whispered her apology and offered to pay for the plane he had crashed upon landing that day. He had heard the thickness of tears in her voice, but she hadn't sniveled. She swore she hadn't known what would happen and had no idea what was in the crate. He didn't believe her. Hell, he knew better. But she spun a damn fine tale. He had to give her credit for that one.

He had waited two years for his chance for vengeance and, surprisingly, it had come from someone he least expected it to. It wasn't that he didn't have other things to do in that time—

vengeance hadn't consumed him. But seeing her face plastered all over the papers over another drug charge brought it all back. He could do society a real favor. Clean her up and teach her the value of a hard day's work, all with the permission of her family.

He smiled slowly. He knew his main problem was boredom rather than revenge. It had been too long since he had allowed himself to ride the edge of danger. The ranching was easy. Hell, some days, it was too damned easy. Jack took care of the business stuff when he wasn't running around the fool planet trying to sell the horses.

Luc took care of the actual ranch, oversaw the training and breeding of the prized Clydesdale horses and worked at making the ranch even more successful than it had become in the past two years. But he hadn't forgotten the blatant disregard Maria Angeles had shown with her decision to allow her drug running buddies to ambush them.

Boredom could do strange things to a man. Make him do things like accept her brother's suggestion that maybe his sister needed a place where she would have no choice but to clean up her act. Make him plot and plan and carry out a kidnapping that was sanctioned by her brother. There was no fear of legal reprisals and he had complete control of her. That was all that mattered to him.

Her bags were packed and stored in the trunk of the car, and a private plane was waiting at the nearby airfield. Before Miss Maria Catarina Angeles knew what hit her she would be on the road to recovery. He chuckled in amusement, imagining the coming battle. He thrived on a good fight, and teaching the spoiled little brat how to be a drug-free member of society was going to be a battle itself.

He shook his head at the thought. He never understood the attraction to drugs. The loss of control, the addiction and subsequent mistakes that came from it. He was still just pissed enough to have very little mercy for the young woman he was about to kidnap. He wouldn't hurt her, but he'd be damned if he wouldn't paddle her ass good if she didn't toe the line. He was starting to think that might well have been her problem all along. Her daddy should have spanked her more often.

As he hid in the shadows moments later, he heard the key turn in the lock. Stepping further into the darkness of the bedroom door he listened closely as the door opened and the sounds of entrance could be heard.

"Mason, Momma's home." Her voice struck Luc immediately. Husky, tear-filled and miserable. At the same time he watched in surprise as the dark lump on her bed moved. A black shadow rose and stretched into the form of a fat cat that glanced at Luc disdainfully and jumped from the bed.

Hell, what was he supposed to do about the cat? He'd have to call Joe and have him collect his sister's little *familiar*. He didn't like cats much anyway, black cats even worse.

"There's my baby," he heard her croon softly moments later. "Are you hungry yet or are you still pouting at me for leaving? I'll take you to the park tomorrow instead. How's that?"

Luc frowned at her voice. She didn't sound drugged. She sounded immeasurably saddened. Almost broken. That wasn't the voice he remembered, but he admitted the events of that day were so fuzzy now that he just couldn't be certain. He knew it was Maria, though. He had seen the car drive up and watched her step from the vehicle minutes before. He had the right woman. And it was just his luck she had a cat. A small smile tipped his lips. She didn't seem as hard as he remembered. She sounded softer, sadder. The Maria he remembered would never have bothered to look beyond herself long enough to worry about feeding a cat.

"Hungry little thing, aren't you?" she said from the other room. "Let's hope Momma can keep the goodies coming. If I don't get that job tomorrow we might be raiding trash bins." She didn't sound like she was joking. "Sucks when your parents hate you, Mason."

He lifted his brows. She had a strange definition of hatred. They had likely managed to buy her out of a damned drug smuggling charge. That didn't sound like hatred to him.

As he heard her moving around again, he slipped the chloroformed cloth from his jacket pocket and waited behind the bedroom door. She would have to come in here eventually and when she did, he would be waiting for her.

'Shower," he heard her mutter. "Damn if Papa can't make me feel like dirt after listening to his accusations. And I think he disowned me, Mason." She sounded lost. "Being cut of the family isn't nearly as bad as being disowned."

Luc ignored the funny little feeling in his chest, the one that warned him he was about to feel sorry for the waifish-sounding hellcat. If she had paid attention to her father's pleas years ago, maybe she wouldn't be in this mess now.

He remembered his visit to the mansion. She had been surprised at first when her father had introduced her to him. As though he had needed the introduction. Then resignation had filled her gaze. She hadn't even known who the hell he was. His cock had hardened, though, despite his fury, despite his need to beat some sense into her. He had been stone-hard aroused in ways he had never been before, even the day she had sucked his dick down her throat.

Hell, she had looked so innocent the day he had stormed into her parents house that he would have sworn she wouldn't know what to do with a cock if he did push it between her lips, let alone how she would react to having his semen filling her mouth. But the thought of it had fueled more than one hot daydream.

"Enjoy dinner, Mason. I'm going to shower and see if I can't get hold of Joey. Maybe he can help us."

Luc smirked. Joe had already taken care of her.

He palmed the damp cloth and prepared himself to place it over her nose and mouth. He heard her quiet footfalls, heard the cat meow, then she was walking into the room, flipping on the light and passing by him.

Luc moved. He had a second to glimpse her wide, terrified eyes before they closed and she slumped against him. Catching her in his arms Luc moved to the bed, lowered her on it and stared at the cat that jumped in after her. The beast stared at him with narrowed eyes.

"You're going to be a problem, aren't you, boy?" He sighed as the animal growled low in his throat. "I thought cats were supposed to be aloof, uncaring. You're a cat, not a dog."

He placed his hands on his hips and watched the confrontational animal.

"Hell, just what I need. An attack cat. I wonder if she has a carrier for you. Are your rabies shots up to date?"

He found the carrier. He received a brutal scratch for catching the animal by the thick fur of his neck and stuffing him in. He'd have to remind Joe that he wasn't a cat lover next time he talked to him. In explicit terms. And why the hell he was bothering, he couldn't be sure. But all he could hear was the emotion in her voice when she spoke to the animal, the caring. Things would be hard on her at the ranch, it wouldn't hurt, he excused himself, to allow her the cat.

"Well now, let's get you ready." He lifted her in his arms, caught the carrier with one hand and carried her quickly out of the apartment and to the service elevator by her room. It was a short trip to the car parked next to the elevator doors in the basement. Once there, he laid her in the backseat, quickly bound her hands and set the cat's carrier on the floorboard.

Mission accomplished. Well, partially anyway, he thought with a grunt. He still had to control her once she woke up. Thanks to the chloroform, it should be several hours, though. By then he would have her safely at the ranch and everything in place to teach her the error of her ways.

As he started the car and headed for the airport, his gut warned him it couldn't possibly be this easy. He grimaced at the thought.

Pulling the cell phone from the carrier on his belt he punched in Joe Angeles' number and waited for the other man to pick up.

"You have her, Jardin?" The other man sounded worried.

"I have her. We're headed to the airport. Is the plane ready?"

"Fueled and ready to go. Just pull into the hangar. The guard is waiting on you. Remember, it's a company airfield so you shouldn't have any problems. Did you get her cat?"

Luc frowned at the other man's tone of voice. He sounded as though he were almost afraid to ask.

"Yeah, I got the black bastard," Luc told him. "I'm still bleeding for my efforts, too."

Joe chuckled, suddenly sounding more relaxed. "Mason is a bit protective of her, but he's easy enough to get along with. Keep me updated and make sure you don't fall for any of her tricks. She's really a good kid, Luc. I know you don't believe that right now, but you'll see."

Luc shook his head. Her brother's belief in her was to be commended. Stupid, but commendable.

"Good kids don't turn a blind eye to murder, Joe. But I promise I won't hurt her. You know me better than that."

Joe had come to the ranch two years before, after Luc's trip to the Angeles mansion. For months, Luc had no idea who he was as the younger man worked with the horses and they formed a wary friendship. Finally, Joe had come to him with the truth, that he needed to know how far his parents were willing to go to protect Maria, so he could protect them. Luc had understood it, but damn if he hadn't been pissed for a while.

"Yeah." Joe sighed. "I know you won't hurt her, Luc. That's the reason you have her. You're the only one I can trust with her. I'll talk to you soon."

"I'll call you when we lift off," Luc promised. "Later."

He disconnected the phone and turned away from the apartment building, heading for the airport. Joe hadn't seemed quite this fond of his sister during the long talks they had shared through the past two years.

The brotherly concern he was showing now didn't sit well with Luc. Not that he thought Joe was lying. It was just a bit odd considering the other man's reticence in discussing his family, or his sister. That boy hated lies, but something wasn't right. He shook his head and sighed wearily. Whatever it was, Luc thought, he had no doubt it would rise up and bite him in the ass soon. When it did, then he would deal with it. Until then, he had vengeance to secure.

* * * * *

Joe hung up the phone and stared across his desk at the tall, slender figure of his father's butler. Johann held the same cool, aloof expression that Joe could remember he had always held. He had seen it crack once in the past thirty years. And only once. The week before when Johann had shown up late into the evening and informed Joe that his parents were going to attempt to convince Melina to once again stand in Maria's place.

He had known this was coming. Had planned for it. He couldn't let Melina put herself in danger again, couldn't take the chance that she would give in under the pressure of their parent's condemnation. Melina had fought for their love all her life, and the thought that she would give her life for it terrified him.

"Mr. Joe, if she walks into the courtroom as Maria, she might as well stick to it. Miss Maria is going to be locked up, one way or the other. I've already found that out. Her parents know it, but they won't accept it. If Melina stands in for her, they'll lock her away, and she's just not hard enough to survive that."

Johann had shed tears at the thought of it. His faded blue eyes had welled with moisture and they spilled down his cheeks as fear overcame his reserve.

"Miss Melina doesn't deserve this," he had sniffed. "She's a good girl, Mr. Joe. They'll hurt her worse next time she gets locked up."

Joe had been in shock. Not because of the tears, though those had contributed, but by the depth of his parents' ignorance. Maria slept with every lawyer they hired for her, and they would tell her parents whatever she wanted them to hear. And as usual, she wanted Melina to take the fall.

"What are the chances of her agreeing to it?" Joe had asked him

Johann had shaken his head. "You know Miss Melina. She'll rage and cry but when her Papa speaks sharply to her, he will gain her agreement. She dreams of their love, Mr. Joe. I'm terrified she'll agree to it."

Now, a week later, Joe was reasonably satisfied that Melina wouldn't be agreeing to anything their father wanted. Sending Luc after her thinking she was Maria didn't sit well with him, but he'd be damned if he would see her nearly broken, almost dead, as he had after taking her out of that jail two years before. Not that Maria had cared, even though it had been her fault her sister had endured it.

Rather than contacting their parents she had gone on a weeklong high and merrily allowed Melina to face a punishment she didn't deserve.

"He has her," he finally told Johann, watching the other man slump in his chair in relief. "Now where's Maria?"

"Your Papa has her confined to her rooms." He shook his head dismally. "You know how long that will last."

"How close are they to buying her out of it?" Joe asked, knowing his parents would spend any amount of money to do just that.

Johann sighed bleakly. "I heard them discussing information their investigators had that could embarrass the judge, as well as the prosecutor. They will blackmail her out of it just as they did the last time. They have paid one of the arresting officers off and are now attempting to do so with the other. But to be honest, I do not think they can do it. Even the investigators have warned them that chances are slim that such efforts will work."

Joe sighed wearily as he pinched the bridge of his nose, assuring himself he would not strangle his parents next time he saw them. "What are they asking for?"

"Complete dismissal. They have disowned Miss Melina, though. Poor child left crying. It was all I could do, Mr. Joe, not to cry with her." Johann shook his head compassionately. "Poor little thing feels so alone. It's not fair we had to do this to protect her."

One problem down, one to go. Maria. Joe fingered the file he had before him. The private clinic in Switzerland would cost him an arm and a leg once he delivered Maria to it, but it would be worth it to have Melina protected after all this was over. If Maria managed to escape justice, she wouldn't escape him.

"If they manage to pull this off, Johann, you let me know," he said. "I'll take care of Maria after this. Just keep me updated."

Johann rose wearily to his feet. "That Mr. Jardin won't hurt her, will he, Mr. Joe?" he asked softly. "He was a hard man. I wouldn't want her hurt."

"Luc won't hurt her, Johann. I give you my word." Joe was positive there would be no true danger to Melina. He wouldn't have contacted Luc if he thought there were. Luc was just the only man he could trust to do the job and not go to Maria's parents for more money to release her.

It was becoming harder to protect Melina than it was to keep up with their parents' attempts to protect Maria. They had always seen Melina as stronger, needing less love than Maria had. Joe wasn't certain why his parents had made a stronger bond with Maria, unless it had been the health problems that had nearly taken her life so many times as a newborn. Melina had been the healthy, strong baby, while Maria had required constant care.

Melina had always lain quietly, while Maria would scream for hours. Often it had been Joe who had picked up the newborn Melina, fed her, changed her, took care of her as her parents concerned themselves with the other, more demanding, sickly, twin.

When Maria had begun getting into trouble, his parents had learned that Melina had a natural innocence and inborn depth of honesty that could get their troublemaking daughter out of her messes. It had been then that they had begun using the younger twin, almost unconsciously, as though it was Melina's job to keep her sister from facing the consequences of her actions. Now, Maria had sunk to new levels, uncaring of the harm she created because she knew her parents would use Melina to get her out of it.

Joe had enough the day he learned Melina was in jail in Maria's stead. Melina had tried calling her parents for days with no success. If it hadn't been for Johann and Melina's call to Joe's secretary, he would have never known the danger Melina was in.

"I must return to Mr. Angeles then." Johann stood slowly to his feet, his expression weary and grief-stricken. "Each day, Mr. Joe, I think more often of retirement, hearing them disown that child…" He shook his head painfully.

"If you decide to do so let me know, Johann." Joe nodded respectfully. "I'll make certain there are no repercussions."

Johann drew in a hard, tired breath. "It is a shame, Mr. Joe. A shame. Once, your parents were good people. Good people. Now…" He tucked his hands in his pockets and moved for the door. "Now, I just don't know…"

And Joe agreed with him. Like Johann, he had no idea what had happened to his parents, but more to the point, he had given up on them ever returning to the caring, decent people they had once been. If they had ever existed.

Chapter Three

She had been kidnapped. Melina fought to hold back her terror as she awoke to realize her hands and feet were bound. She was lying on a surprisingly comfortable bed. Not that comfort meant anything. She was certain even serial killers could have comfortable beds. But she knew it wasn't a serial killer who had kidnapped her. Damn, the more she thought about it, the more she was beginning to fear that her chances would be better with a nutcase than they were with the man she had glimpsed in one blinding second the night before.

She fought to still the fear as she remembered the face of her kidnapper. For one heart-stopping moment she had stared up at him and realized that once again, despite all her efforts, she was going to pay for Maria's sins.

This was great. Like he would believe she wasn't Maria. How many people knew her parents had two daughters? She could count them all on ten fingers and have a few left over. Since she was a child, she had been content to be left alone with her dolls, her books, her various hobbies, rather than be the social butterfly her sister had started out as. And her parents had been willing to leave her behind. The fewer people who knew Maria had a twin, the easier it might be to get the older twin out of trouble later. That lesson had been learned early.

She opened her eyes, her senses groggy, her mind sluggish. She needed to think clearly, to clear the fog out of her head and figure out how to handle this one. There was no doubt Jardin was out for revenge. And she couldn't blame him. The surprising part was that he had let her live long enough to wake up.

"Awake, are you?" His voice sounded behind her.

His voice sent shivers up her spine. It was deep and rough, like the growl of a hungry predator. It sent a chill of dread through her and had her licking her dry lips in response to the nervousness suddenly flaring through her body.

The man most likely to kill you shouldn't sound so damned sexy seconds before doing so. Melina swallowed tightly. She should be more frightened and less aroused by that voice.

Her darkest fantasies had been filled with the image of him for two years. She had often awakened in the middle of the night, her hips lifting, reaching for the dream vision ready to impale her. She was as sick as Maria, she thought in disgust. The way she lusted after him made no sense.

"I assume you are at least reasonably clear-headed," he drawled mockingly. "Pretending to sleep won't save your ass, little girl."

Melina winced at the pet name. She wasn't a little girl, dammit.

She breathed out in resignation. She had to use the bathroom and her mouth felt like cotton. She might as well give in and get it the hell over with. Jardin hadn't seemed like a man who would easily be sidetracked or sweet-talked. Not that she had ever been very good with the sweet talk anyway.

That didn't mean she had to like the unusual response to him. Why, of all the men in the world, did she have to be so attracted to this one? She was certain he would just as soon kill her than look at her. And knowing that, why was her pussy heating, her breasts tingling, her body so sensitized in response to his voice?

Drawing in a deep breath she prepared herself to face him. The sooner she did so, the sooner she could possibly find some peace.

"Do you think you could untie me long enough to use the bathroom before you begin tormenting me?" she asked him coolly.

She wasn't about to roll over and make the pain in her shoulders worse by lying on her back, bound as she was. It was damned uncomfortable with her hands tied behind her. She also felt too vulnerable, too helpless. She was at his mercy, and being in such a position was much too arousing.

Arousing? It should be terrifying, not arousing.

Melina trembled as he moved. She felt cold steel slide between her bare ankles, slicing through the ropes, then between her wrists. Flexing her hands she eased into a sitting position, placing her feet tentatively on the floor. Glancing through her lashes she saw the lean, strong legs that moved into her line of vision.

She raised her eyes as her heart stopped in her chest. He was releasing his belt. Oh God. She gasped for breath as his fingers, calloused and very male, began unbuttoning his jeans.

She wasn't going to whimper, she assured herself. She would not show her shock and arousal by actually letting that helpless little sound free. But as he pulled his thick, hard cock from the depth of his jeans she knew the sound squeaked from her throat as his broad hand stroked over the dark flesh suggestively.

"Come on, Maria," he whispered darkly. "Open wide, baby, and let me have that tight throat again."

Her gaze flew to his. He was watching her with a deep vein of amusement and lust, his handsome face taut with arousal and demand. Melina wanted to laugh. She almost did. She wouldn't know what to do with it even if she did consider "opening wide" as he suggested.

"Uhh, I really need to go," she whispered faintly, trying desperately not to gaze at the hard cock only inches from her mouth. "Really bad."

His lips quirked mockingly, his dark gray eyes darkening further. "Then pay the price," he suggested softly. "Come on, Maria it's not like it's the first time."

It wasn't? It was the first time for her, she thought with disbelief. Surely he didn't think she really would? Melina never had, but she was well aware of the fact that Maria would do it and had done it.

He moved his arm, his hand lifting, fingers threading her hair, the touch sending tingles of sensation to her scalp as he held her still and moved closer. Her gaze dropped nervously, her vision filled with the dark, pulsing flesh of the head of his cock.

He really thought she was going to? Thought she could?

The broad, purpled head touched her lips, throbbed, then spilled a soft pearl of semen against her lower curve.

Before Melina could stop herself, she jerked back, a cry of outrage escaping her mouth as she rolled clumsily across the bed. Shaking with nerves, she fell over the side and scrambled to her feet before staring at him across the mattress.

"No," she snapped out, though her response was rather late, she thought as she watched him redoing his jeans with a quizzical frown. He appeared both amused and bemused by her reaction.

"That's all you had to say, Maria." He shrugged. "I don't remember you being so hesitant last time."

Last time? She wasn't hesitant? She was going to kill Maria. Seriously. Honestly. First chance she had her parents were being cut down to one daughter in truth instead of just in wishes.

Would he believe she wasn't Maria? Melina clenched her teeth in fury, weighing her options carefully. He didn't seem determined to kill her at this point. He was lazily amused, perhaps a little sarcastic and mocking, but he didn't appear murderous.

"Look," she finally said, fighting to keep her voice steady as she heard the betraying quiver in the words. "You've made a terrible mistake here. Really. I'm sure you'll find it quite funny…"

He frowned. The look sent fear rioting through her system. Thick black brows and stormy gray eyes darkened, his lips flattened, the high cheekbones standing out prominently. The look was a warning and sent Melina's heart pounding in her chest.

"Really?" he drawled. "I never imagined for a moment that there wouldn't be a good explanation." He crossed his arms over his chest and watched her through narrowed eyes. "I think I should tell you right up front, Maria, that there's no getting out of what I have planned for you. You may as well forget any excuses, lies or tricks. This is hell, baby, and I'm your warden. So get used to it now."

Melina's eyes widened "What do you mean, you're my warden?"

He smiled. The hard curve of his lips sent a pulse of warning through her nervous system.

"Exactly what I said, sugar. You're here to finish crying out and clean your act up. And I know just how to ensure that. You, sweet thing, are getting ready to learn how the other half lives. No drugs, no servants, no booze, no pampering. Now get showered. I'll be up to get you in half an hour. Be dressed and ready or face the consequences." He watched her intently, his eyes dark and steady, frightening. "And I promise, the consequences won't be pleasant."

Melina gaped at her captor in shock as she blinked just to be certain she was awake and not having some horrible nightmare. He was actually threatening her. Had set himself up as judge, jury and executioner and thought she would go along with it. She would laugh if he didn't look so damned serious about it.

"You're joking." She couldn't stem the horror that she knew reflected in her voice.

"Nope." He crossed his arms over his chest arrogantly, staring back at her with cold, mocking eyes. "No joke, sugarplum. You play, you pay. If the courts can't do anything with you, then I can sure as hell try. Consider it punishment for the little crimes you've escaped in the past years. All rolled into one." His smile wasn't comforting.

Melina drew a hard, deep breath. Patience was a virtue, she reminded herself. Only cool, calm heads solved extreme problems. She had faced the wrath of her parents, been disowned and turned down for the last three jobs she interviewed for. She could handle this. She hadn't killed anyone yet. She really didn't have to start with this ignorant cowboy.

"What in the hell makes you think I'm going to go along with this?" she asked him incredulously. "Do I have 'stupid' written across my forehead? 'Wimp'? 'Go ahead and step on me because I'm too stupid to live and I enjoy abuse'?" She threw her hands up in frustration as she faced him in disbelief.

He looked at her closely. "Hmm. Not that one could see. But I'll reserve judgment. You never know what may show up after a good hot shower."

She was going to lose her mind. Right there, in a strange bedroom, facing the sexiest, most aggravating, arrogant man she had ever laid her eyes on. She was going to commit murder. Namely, on him.

"Look, Mr. Jardin." She tried for a smile that held none of the fury she was beginning to feel build up within her. "I'm sure you think what you're doing is right. I'm certain you're even convinced you have the right person to punish. But you're not and you don't. I am not Maria. I'm her sister, Melina. Her twin sister."

He smirked at her. Melina bit her tongue as her eyes narrowed on his smug expression and her fists clenched at her side as she fought not to jump across the bed and claw his eyes out.

"Sweetheart, I'm sure you wish you had a sister who could get you out of this," he said complacently. "But since we both know you don't, you can stop with the innocent act because I'm not buying it."

Melina drew in a deep breath. If she could get her hands on Maria she would strangle her now, she thought. As though the past twenty-two years and all the times she had willingly tried to save her sister wasn't enough. Now, Mr. Hardass, who thought he could reform the wrong damned woman, had kidnapped her. It was too much. Even for her.

"That's fine," she gritted out. "Because I'm not trying to sell a damned thing. I assumed you were a reasonably intelligent person…"

"Just like you assumed you could let your buddies kill me and Jack when we helped you deliver that crate of drugs?" he asked snidely. "Or how you assumed your parents could ruin the names of two good men when charges were brought against you? How about the assumption that your parents' money can get you out of anything? This is the end of the line, little girl. You might as well buckle down and save the lies for someone willing to believe them."

Melina could feel the fury brewing in her chest. Vivid and hot, it flared in front of her eyes like a matador's cape.

"Or save the truth for someone with enough brains to see what's right in front of his face," she snapped back heatedly. "Get real, Mr. Jardin. Do I look like a drug addict to you?" She waved her hands to her side, indicating her body.

She expected him to look, she just didn't like the flare of arousal that lit his gaze when he did so. Nor did she like the way her nipples beaded as his gaze paused on them, or the heat that flared in her pussy when his eyes then moved to her thighs.

She could feel her skin sensitizing, her vagina dampening, and she didn't like the sensations in the least. It was bad enough she had done nothing but fantasize about him for the past two years, she didn't need to become aroused after he kidnapped her as well.

"Look, I know you're angry over what Maria did to you and your friend. But this is a mistake…"

"The mistake is yours." His sharp voice caused her to flinch in surprise. "Don't think for a minute you can lie to me again. Now get your ass in the shower and get ready to face the day or you can get on your knees and see if you can't convince me another way."

On her knees? Convince him? She blinked in outraged surprise at the suggestion. And she was ignoring the crazy flash of desire and hunger that seared her body at just the thought of accepting his cock into her mouth. The brief touch of it on her lips was enough of a temptation, thank you very much. She did not need to find herself lusting after this man anymore than she already did. As a matter of fact, she needed to be as far away from him as possible.

"You're crazy. I'm going home. Now."

She turned on her heel, heading quickly for the bedroom door. She'd had enough of this. Accepting Maria's punishment because of her own misplaced family loyalty was a far cry from accepting it because this man decided she would. She didn't think so. It didn't matter how big or how good-looking he was. It didn't matter that he deserved his pound of flesh. She wasn't about to let him take it out of her hide.

Her hand had just wrapped around the doorknob, her fingers tightening on it, when a broad palm smacked the wood above her head and a hard male body pressed her tightly against the wall.

A hard, hot, muscular body. One that surrounded her, his heat pouring off his flesh in waves and wrapping around her. A male presence that smelled of long sultry nights and forbidden desires. Melina swallowed, feeling the aura of danger that suddenly emanated from him.

"You don't want to piss me off, little girl," he warned her softly. "Especially not right now. That bullet you let your friends put in my leg hasn't been forgotten. Neither is the fact that they would have preferred it being my heart. Now shut the hell up, get your ass in the shower and get dressed. This is a ranch.

Everyone does his or her part here, and you're here to pitch in. Whether you want to or not.'

He moved then, one hand insinuating itself between the door and her body as he unwrapped her fingers from the knob and pushed her lightly toward the bathroom. She wasn't about to do a damned thing he ordered her to do.

Melina turned, staring back at him furiously, shaking with the need to smack the growing smirk off his face as she retreated.

'You're wrong," she informed him angrily, though she could tell he had no intention of believing her. "Won't you even check it out? I have a brother Joe Angeles. At least contact him. He'll tell you who I am. Better yet, try using your brains and the internet. I have a birth record, moron."

She didn't like the amusement that glinted in his eyes. "He wouldn't tell me anything new, little girl."

"I'm not a little girl." She felt like stamping her feet in fury. "And I'm not Maria. I have to go home. I have to take care of my cat. Who's going to take care of my cat?" That sudden, horrifying thought slipped into her mind. She had forgotten all about Mason. Her baby. What would happen to him?

He would be all alone. He would be frightened without her. Lonely. He'd been the only creature in the world who had stayed by her side all these years, and now she wasn't there to care for him?

"Don't worry about that mangy animal." Luc suddenly snarled. "He's in the barn with the other — "

"In the barn?" She practically screamed out in surprise and fury. 'You put my cat in the barn? My baby is in the barn?"

She stared at him, unable to believe the words that came from him. Who would be cruel enough to put sweet little Mason in a barn? He couldn't do this. Her fingers curled, flexed, as she ached to attack him.

There went his arms over his chest again. "So?"

"So. You can't put Mason in the barn." She propped her hands on her hips, fighting mad now. She would not allow him to abuse her cat. "You go get him now."

He frowned at the harsh demand in her voice.

"If I were you, I would worry about my own problems, not that black mouse chaser," he snorted.

Outrage flew through her. She felt fury vibrating violently through her body.

"Mason does not chase mice," she informed him coldly. "And Mason does not sleep in barns. He sleeps in my room, on my bed, next to me. I want my cat. Now."

He tilted his head, watching her with a sudden, inquisitive expression.

"How bad do you want that cat back, Maria?" he asked her softly.

She wanted to slap his smug face. He was going to blackmail her. She could see it in his eyes, in his expression. The son of a bitch was going to use her baby against her. She wanted to tell him to go straight to hell.

Instead, she gritted her teeth, counted to ten and said, "What do you want?"

Melina was aware there had to be something wrong with loving a black little ball of fluff that rarely gave her the time of day. Unless she cried. Then, he was all over her, comforting her, letting her hold him, even if it was with an air of supreme boredom. He had gotten her through the past two years when there had been no one else. She wasn't about to leave him in a dirty, dusty barn.

Luc stepped back to her, pulling her against his harder, taller body as she stared up at him in shock. She hated the awareness that flared in the pit of her stomach as his hard cock pressed into her. Hated the hunger she could feel welling within her.

Her lips parted as he stared down at her, his gaze flickering with heat as they settled on her lips. Melina trembled. She could feel her pussy heating, dampening, and cursed her response to him.

She braced her hands against his shoulders, resisting — not just Luc, but herself as well. He had the most kissable lips she had ever seen on a man. That fuller, lower curve fascinated her, made her want to eat him up. But he had set the boundaries with this kidnapping. There wasn't a chance in hell she was going to lay down and let him walk all over her. She was tired of being anyone's doormat.

"I thought you were my kidnapper, not my rapist," she snapped when she managed to find her voice. "Let me go, Mr. Jardin. I won't whore for my cat. But I'll be damned if I'll cooperate in any way without him."

His brows snapped into a frown as his arms tightened around her. Eyes narrowing, he gazed down at her thoughtfully for long seconds before slowly releasing her.

"Take your shower and get dressed. We'll discuss terms downstairs after you've managed to cool off and act decently. I might allow you the cat, if you can control yourself and follow the rules." With that said, he left the room, closing the door quietly behind him.

She was going to kill him, she assured herself. Then, she was going to kill Maria.

Chapter Four

ഇ

Twenty minutes later, freshly showered and dressed in a pair of jeans and white cotton shirt, Melina entered the large kitchen at the far end of the house. The two-story ranch house was laid out fairly simply so the kitchen wasn't hard to find. Of course, the banging of the cabinet doors might have helped a little.

Tucking a stray reddish-gold curl behind her ear, Melina checked the French braid she had arranged her hair into for neatness and stepped into the kitchen. She knew the second she walked into the room that she loved it. Too bad it belonged to the big arrogant cowboy frowning into the depths of a cabinet.

The stove was to die for. It was a modern cook's dream with a gas grill in the center, four large burners on the side and adequate ventilation above it. The floor was hardwood with an area rug beneath the six chairs and kitchen table that sat near a large picture window. The cabinets were cherry, though dusty and appearing dull in the light of the morning sun. But there were plenty of them. A large central island was located several feet from the sink, yet still near enough to the stove to make it handy.

It might have been a cook's dream but it was a housekeeper's nightmare.

Luc was turned just slightly away from her, giving her a clear view of his muscular back and the taut, well-rounded curves of his butt beneath his snug jeans. He had an ass to die for. The sight of it made her fingers itch with the need to touch. As though she would know what to do with it if she did touch, she told herself sarcastically. But still, she had always admired a nice male backside, and his had to be the best she had seen yet.

Drawing in a long, deep breath, she glanced away from the temptation.

"You need to fire your housekeeper," she told him expressionlessly as she stared around the room once again. "She's not doing her job."

The kitchen resembled the living room she had peeked into, as well as the dining room she had walked through. Dusty, unloved. As though the home wasn't really a home but merely a place to spend the night.

Luc turned to look at her, his brows lowered in a dark frown as she hunched her shoulders and tucked her hands into her jeans pockets. She was still dying to claw his eyes out. She figured it better to restrain her hands enough to where she would at least have a second to think before actually trying to do it. He was sure to make her madder before the hour was out.

She watched as he followed the move, a smirk tilting his lips as though he knew the reason behind it. Melina fought to keep her expression clear, the anger glowing in her chest from reflecting on her face. Damn him. She had never met a man more stubborn in her life.

Shoring her patience, she straightened her shoulders and met his look head on. She had resigned herself to the fact that he wasn't going to listen to reason, which meant she was going to have to try to find her own way out. She had a feeling that escaping Luc wouldn't be easy. But before she could even consider escape, she had to have Mason.

"I've showered, dressed and I've met you in the kitchen," she finally said with careful control. "Now where's my baby?"

Irritation flashed in his stormy gray eyes. It was obvious that there was something about her and her cat that he didn't like. Of course, it could just be Maria he hated, she thought with morbid amusement, which didn't bode well for her considering he thought she was Maria.

"How anyone can call that fat-assed black ball of fur a baby is beyond me," he growled. "That animal should be put down for its temper alone."

Melina's eyes widened in sudden fear at the sincere dislike in his tone and the implied threat to kill the little animal. Her baby. He thought Mason should be killed. And Mason did not have a temper. He was just a little spoiled, that was all. That was no excuse to be mean to him.

"You hurt Mason and I promise you, I'll make what Maria did to you look like a day at the park," she warned him, completely serious now.

He could punish her all he liked, and in a way she could even make some sort of twisted sense of it. But he wasn't going to hurt Mason. She had enough of Maria's thoughtless actions impacting her life in such painful ways. She blamed herself. She had allowed the trend to continue as they got older, but no more. She would not lose anything else due to her sister's selfishness and utter cruelty.

He crossed his arms over his chest. She was growing to heartily dislike that action. He was still frowning at her, the low cast of his brows giving his expression a dangerous appearance. Melina fought back her fear as she met his gaze silently.

"You're in no position to be giving out threats here, sugarplum," he told her softly, his voice almost too gentle to suit her. It reminded her of the eye of a violent storm. She would have been more frightened if it weren't for the fact that she was hopelessly in love with that stupid cat. Even she didn't understand it.

"Listen, Mister, I understand you think you have a problem with me. Really, I do," she assured him sincerely. "I can even, almost, understand the mistake you're making. But if you harm so much as a hair on Mason's body, then I promise, you're going to regret it. That's my cat. He adopted me when no one else wanted me and I'll be damned if I'll let you mistreat him."

"Baby, maybe more people would want you if you toed the line a little bit closer. You know. Give a little, get a little?" he suggested mockingly.

Melina flinched painfully at the cruel words. Give a little, get a little. She would have laughed at the thought if it weren't so ironic. She had given everything she had for so many years ..for nothing. All she had to show for it was a black cat that deigned to curl in her lap and shed on her whenever she became weak enough to cry. But the warmth of his fat little body and his soft purrs had kept her sane through the aftermath of her nightmares.

"I'm sure you think your opinion of me should matter," she said reasonably, stilling the furious words that rose to her lips instead. "I'll even pretend it does for as long as I have to. But not as long as my cat is in that barn suffering."

If she could go to jail for Maria, then she could stand up to one temperamental cowboy for her baby. She could think of few things as horrible as that week she had spent in jail for her sister.

"At least he's alive," he grunted hatefully. "Have I mentioned I hate cats?"

Melina pushed back the fear rising inside her. Maria had nearly caused the death of this man as well as his friend. Killing a cat he believed was hers would be small compared to her crimes. But it was Mason. He didn't belong to Maria. Maria couldn't care less and she wouldn't spend a second grieving for his loss. And she sure as hell wouldn't care about the pain Melina would suffer without him.

She bit her lip as she fought the fear that Luc would hurt him. She looked up at him silently, swallowing in dread. She had a feeling her need for comfort from her fears might well be her downfall.

"Please," she whispered. "I just want my cat."

Melina saw the interest that suddenly flared in his eyes, the knowledge that the animal could be leverage against her that he might not have considered before.

"In exchange for?" he asked, confirming her worse fears. There wasn't a lot she would say no to in her effort to save Mason.

"I already asked what you want." She tried to still the frustration thickening her voice as she attempted to reason with a man who had already proven himself to be unreasonable. "I'm willing to cooperate as much as possible," she said nervously. "Fine, you want to punish me for what Maria did, but don't hurt my cat."

If his frown could have grown darker it would have. She saw the anger that instantly flared in his gaze and knew she had just made a major tactical error.

"Admit to who you are, and we'll talk."

Admit to who she wasn't. A sense of resignation overcame her. The cost of one small comfort would be once again allowing herself to be mired in Maria's identity. She slid her hands from her jeans, linking them together, trying to still the tremors that wanted to rush through her body.

"I told you who I am," she said as desolation washed over her. "Don't make me lie to you. Please. Because I will, for this."

His arms uncrossed, his thumbs catching at the front of the waistband of his jeans. She shouldn't notice the tight, hard body that the action displayed, or the lean, muscular hips and below, the thick bulge of his cock. She shouldn't be wet, shouldn't be longing for things she knew she couldn't have.

His brow lifted mockingly. "You would lie for something so small?" he asked with sarcastic disbelief. "Don't make this any harder on yourself than it already is," he suggested easily. "Come on, tell me who you are and we'll go get the cat."

Melina drew in a tired breath.

"Catarina Angeles," she finally said, fighting to hold her temper back now. If she let her anger free, she would never see Mason again.

He shook his head slowly, destroying any hope she had that he would, by chance, let this go. "Nope. Come on, sugarplum, full name. Admit to who you are and we'll go get the cat. Otherwise, he takes his chances outside."

She met his gaze directly, holding back the screams that longed to pour from her throat. "Don't do this."

Could she survive without Mason? She shuddered at the thought of the nightmares that were sure to come without his comforting presence. How would she hold onto her sanity without something or someone to comfort her?

"Your name," he demanded again.

"Maria Catarina Angeles," she said coldly, distantly. It wasn't the first time she had done so, but at least this time it served her rather than someone else. "May I please have my cat now?"

* * * * *

He should have been satisfied. Luc stared at the expressionless face, the weary green eyes, and felt anything but satisfaction. He felt like a damned monster. She had spoken the words as her shoulders lowered marginally, as though the weight of the admission had placed an invisible burden on her that was too great to bear.

The admission, though given as he asked, was voiced with such a lack of emotion that it made him regret forcing the issue. And her eyes. If he had ever seen such weary resignation in a woman's eyes, he couldn't remember it. They darkened, turning so vulnerable, so filled with shadows and pain that something about it twisted his heart.

She had spoken the words mechanically, almost...rehearsed. He tilted his head, watching, as she stood silent and cool in front of him. Her fury from earlier that morning seemed extinguished and weariness had taken its place. He felt like a complete bastard and didn't even know why. Damn her. It wasn't his fault she wanted to play games.

He hated cats. What in the hell possessed him to consider letting that demon into his house? *He probably sheds*, Luc thought in disgust. Just what he needed. But he'd be damned if he could stand that look in those dark velvet-green eyes. They were haunted, filled with an inner pain that he couldn't quite describe. A pain he had caused.

He snarled silently, lifting his lips in self-derision as he grunted in irritation.

"Come on, let's go get the bastard. But if he scratches me again I'll feed him to my dogs. He'd make a hell of a snack."

The barn was within sight of the house, but still nearly an acre separated it from the main building. Melina moved quickly behind Luc as his long legs ate up the distance. She couldn't keep her eyes off his strongly curved ass, no matter how hard she tried, or the bunch and flex of his hard thighs beneath his jeans. He had the long-legged, gaited walk of a cowboy. That undefined, strolling strut that made a woman's mouth water and her fingers itch to clench into all that male strength moving so temptingly before her eyes.

His buttocks were lusciously curved for a man and the low riding jeans showed them off to perfection. His back was like granite beneath the T-shirt, each muscle defined by the cloth that had been tucked into his pants. The whole picture was irritatingly sexy. She didn't want to lust for him anymore. It was fine when he was just a distant figure she could drool over in private, but now? She snorted silently. He had to be the most aggravating, ill-tempered man she had laid eyes on in her life. But, good heavens, if he wasn't the most delicious looking man she had ever seen.

Melina grimaced in self-disgust. The man had literally forced her into lying about who she was. He had blackmailed her with poor Mason's helpless life, and she was lusting over him. Her cunt was weeping, not just wet, but *drooling* in hunger. Like a man starved and presented a banquet, only to be told he couldn't partake. It wasn't fair. It was the most unjust act of deprivation where sexuality was concerned that she could have envisioned.

Following close behind him, her head lowered, her gaze on the delicious curves of his male rear, she was completely unprepared for his abrupt stop.

"Omph." She smacked into his back, stumbling, her face flaming as he turned to her and shot her a frown.

"Are you okay?" His hand shot out, gripping her arm as she jumped back again and nearly fell flat on her ass. "Dammit, you can't be on anything I made sure there wasn't a pill in the house before I kidnapped you."

God, he would be perfect if he would just keep his damned mouth shut.

Jerking her arm back she flashed him a look, intending to convey the pure violence toward him that suddenly surged in her head. Too bad her body wasn't listening.

"Moron." she sniffed, moving around him to the open doors of the barn. "I assume this is where Mason is?"

As she spoke, a cat's plaintive wail filled the air, causing her eyes to widen at the lost, pitiful sound. She turned, shot Luc a look that promised retribution and moved quickly into the shadowed interior.

"Mason." She gasped in surprise at the bedraggled black ball of fur that cried out at her from a bed of straw.

He was pitiful. Dusty, his fur matted, his amazing blue eyes damp and miserable. He wailed again, a feline sound of misery that broke her heart as she went to her knees in front of him and pulled him gently into her arms.

"Oh, Mason." she whispered against his once soft coat, ignoring the bite of his claws into her arms as he cried out plaintively once again. "My poor baby. That's okay. I'll take care of you now." She turned back to Luc, ignoring his dark frown. "You have abused my cat. There's no excuse for that, Luc. I didn't think you could truly be cruel until now."

His brows lifted in surprise, his hands going automatically to his hips as he stared back at her incredulously. She realized she had used his given name rather than the insults she had been throwing at him. But this just shocked her. She couldn't believe he had mistreated her baby.

"Abuse? The little bastard was doing his best to take a bite out of me. All I did was shoot him a time or two with the water hose. Hell, he barely got wet."

Mason wailed again as Melina groaned silently. The water hose? Oh hell, Mason detested getting wet. He would never forgive Luc.

"He will hate you for life now." She sighed as she shook her head. This was not going to be a pleasant incarceration.

"This is supposed to bother me?" He arched a brow mockingly.

Melina smiled tightly. "Well, let's see, I paid your blackmail for him, which means he's now a resident in your home. Let's pray there's no leather furniture, shoes or boots you're particularly attached to. If so, they're his the minute he gets his chance."

His eyes narrowed. "I'll kill him."

"Tsk tsk, Luc." She shook her head with a knowing smile. "You gave your word, remember? I upheld my end, and I didn't tell you to abuse him, so..." She shrugged. "Unless your word means nothing, I guess you're just screwed."

"As long as it's by you," he murmured, his voice dropping, deepening to such a sensual pitch that chills chased over her flesh.

Melina swallowed nervously, her grip tightening on the bedraggled Mason as she fought back the panic welling in her chest. God, it was bad enough she ached for Luc. He did not have to make it worse.

"Only in your wildest dreams, cowboy," she snapped. "Now I need to feed Mason."

That brow arched again. That was never a good sign.

"Was feeding him part of the deal?" He surveyed the cat thoughtfully. "I don't remember that part, sweet pea."

"You've got all you're going to get from me, Jardin," she warned him quietly. "More than you know. If you want any cooperation from me at all, you'll let this go."

Her voice was quiet, her look direct. She could go so far, and only so far. She could see the way his mind was working and she would be damned if she would whore herself to feed her cat. She had, quite literally, had enough. Good looking was all fire and well, sexy as hell was even better, but there came a point when what came out of a man's mouth just overwhelmed any appeal he might have. Luc Jardin was easing into that shadowed area really fast

"Hmm." The rumbled sound skated over her spine with a sensation too close to anticipation to suit her. When combined with the drowsy sensuality in his gaze, it was potent. "Come on. I'll get you started in the house. Keep that mouse chaser away from my leather or your ass will hurt for it, not his. I'll outline your duties and we'll see how appreciative you can be of my generosity."

"If you had any generosity, I might appreciate it," she grunted as she turned back toward the house.

She could only imagine what her "duties" would entail. If he thought cleaning that nasty house was going to be much of a chore he was dead wrong. The house was a dream and it was a sin, the shape it was in.

"Careful, sweet pea," he said as she passed, his voice diabolical in its sexuality. "I just might show you exactly how generous I can be."

And if she remembered correctly, he had plenty of reason to threaten generosity. The memory of the head of his cock resting on her lips, the small pearl of seed catching on the lower curve, slammed into her. She could almost taste the heady male essence of him once again. And that wasn't a good thing. He didn't need more ammunition to use against her.

"As I said," she shrugged, feigning nonchalance with no small amount of effort, "only in your dreams, cowboy."

* * * * *

His dreams could get pretty vivid. Luc followed her closely, watching the smooth sway of her shapely hips as he listened to that damned cat cry. But he could handle the feline theatrics for the chance of watching that pert little ass bump and sway across his ranch yard. And he owed her. He was well aware of why she had walked into his back earlier.

He had felt the heat of her gaze on his ass as he walked in front of her. It had been a bit disconcerting, a sensation he wasn't used to. Never had he *felt* a woman watching him like that, knew beyond a shadow of a doubt where her look was directed. And he was fairly confident she was pleased with what she was watching. But no more than he was.

He smirked as he noticed her efforts to control the ultra feminine sway of her hips. Could she feel his gaze as well? Hell, yes she could, he thought a second later, refusing to believe he was the only one in torment. That would not be acceptable.

He couldn't remember Maria inspiring this hunger in him two years before. He had been amused. Hell, he had been willing to fuck the tempting little redhead, but he hadn't hungered for her. He hungered for her now. If he didn't trust Joe so damned much, he would half suspect she really wasn't the woman who had gone to her knees with an experience he couldn't imagine her possessing now.

Luc shook his head as they neared the porch of the ranch house. The cat wailed again. Dammit, that fat black excuse for a mouse chaser was going to be in his house, shedding on his furniture, likely eating his food and tormenting the hell out of him. And only God knew what his wolf-hybrid, Lobo, was going to think of the addition to the house. He only hoped his canine friend was as well trained as he had tried to teach him to be. Otherwise, that cat would be wolf chow and an unpleasant memory in a matter of hours.

Chapter Five

🙟

It wasn't that the punishment was onerous, it was that the situation was pissing her off, Melina thought as she prepared to sneak out of the house. Cleaning house was child's play, and cooking was one of her favorite hobbies. Not that she had let Mr. Neanderthal know that. She had stayed mulishly silent, procrastinated, shot him ill looks as he watched her and generally did her best to get out of whatever work he assigned her after the confrontation the day before. She could tell it was no more than he expected.

She loved the house. But it wasn't her house and she wasn't Maria, and she sure as hell didn't think much of his stubbornness and refusal to hear the truth. Furthermore, she wasn't going to calmly bow her head and accept his idea of punishment. She was finished with playing Maria the day she nearly died in that jail cell.

"Come on, Mason," she whispered as she lifted the fat cat and slid him carefully into the sling she had made of one of the pillowcases. She wasn't about to toss him down two stories. He would never forgive her, and it would be her luck that instead of landing on his feet he would probably end up landing on his oversized head.

The bed sheets were tied together and anchored to the heavy post of the bed, giving her just enough room to slide down to about a four-foot drop below the end of the sheet. Mr. Know-it-all had locked the door to her bedroom but he had forgotten about the windows, she snickered.

Mason sighed his little breath of boredom as she slid the sling to her back and crawled over the window ledge. Gripping the sheet she slid carefully down its length until she was forced to let go of the material and drop the final distance.

She landed easily and smiled in triumph. She had no idea where she was, but she would find out fast enough. There was a road that led to the house, and roads always ran into towns some damned place. It might take a while to walk out of there, but at least she was free. Free of Lucas Jardin's sexy drawl, the heat that emanated from his big body and his sexy smile. Free from the temptation those two years of sexual fantasies had caused.

Moving quickly she sprinted across the flat harsh terrain, keeping the road in sight but staying a careful distance from it. If he happened to check on her and find her gone, he would most likely start searching the road first. Melina assured herself she wouldn't be a stupid escapee. She was going to succeed.

* * * * *

Well, he had wondered how long it would take her to make her first escape attempt. Luc chuckled in amusement as he caught sight of the sheets tied together and leading out of the window to the ranch yard below. His little captive had sprung her cage, and rather than the fury he would have expected, he felt anticipation rising instead.

She intrigued him. Damned if she didn't. He hadn't expected to be touched, amused or intrigued by her, but he was. And damned if the thought of chasing her wasn't giving him a hard-on like no other he had ever had before.

Shaking his head at the phenomenon he moved back to his bedroom, collected his rifle and commanded Lobo to follow him. The wolf-hybrid would be a hell of a surprise when he managed to track her down. Lobo wouldn't eat her or the cat, but he would give her an idea of what could be waiting on her when she roamed the East Texas landscape alone.

The wolf followed at his heels as he moved through the house and out to the back yard. Using the small penlight he carried, he checked the tracks under the sheet and estimated she had a good thirty minutes head start on him. Not nearly enough to do her any good.

Shaking his head as he smothered his laughter, Luc cut a large strip of the sheet off and lowered it to Lobo to get a good sniff.

"Find our girl, Lobo," he said softly as he smiled in anticipation. "I'll be right behind you."

What was it about her? Luc shook his head as he set off after the animal. There wasn't a chance in hell that she wasn't Maria, but things weren't adding up. This was a drug-addicted, spoiled little rich girl he was holding captive. But there were no needle tracks on her arms, her skin was creamy and silky smooth, rather than sallow and pale as he remembered it two years before. And there were no signs of withdrawal.

Her eyes were a vivid, dark green, her body lush and graceful with the most intriguing scent of heat and woman that he had ever smelled. It made him wonder constantly how sweet her pussy would be. And all those lovely red-gold curls that fell around her pixie-like face... It was enough to make a man's mouth water. Not to mention what it did to his dick.

It wasn't long before Lobo's yips alerted Luc to the fact that he had found the little escapee. Luc picked up his pace, jogging in the direction of the wolf's excited sounds as he carefully herded Maria toward him. He chuckled when he finally heard her voice, thick with fear and bravado as Lobo snapped at her heels.

"You think I don't know he sent you?" she snapped at Lobo as he playfully pounced toward the sack she carried in front of her. Likely that damned cat. "And no, you cannot have Mason." Yep, it was that damned cat.

Mason's wail of fear could be heard inside the cloth prison.

"Go away, you flea bitten creature." He could hear the threat of tears in her voice as he watched her attempt to resume the direction she had been heading. Lobo wasn't to be denied, though. He nipped at her feet, causing a squeal of outrage to fill the desert night.

"You bite me and I promise you, your master will be bald next time I see him. Stupid cretin. Get away from me."

Lobo had the tail of her shirt in his mouth, dragging her back, ignoring her desperate swipes at his head as he pulled at her.

Luc stood back and watched. Damn, she was adorable. She called Lobo every nasty name in the book, but as each minute went by he could hear the shadow of laughter thickening in her voice as Lobo played with her.

Lobo growled as she pulled at her shirt, a deep, warning rumble that was nowhere as threatening as Luc would have expected it to be. The wolf normally took his duties a bit more seriously. He was supposed to frighten, not tease.

"I'm not going back there." She strained against the tugging animal. "Now let me go."

The shirt ripped, but Lobo wasn't about to be deterred. He grabbed at her pants leg instead and pulled back sharply, sending her to the ground, flat on that pretty ass. Luc expected her to be up, fighting, raging. Instead, he watched as she merely sighed wearily.

"Dammit. I'm going to kill Maria," he heard her mutter. "I swear to God, first chance I get, I'm killing her."

There was a deep sigh of resignation before she laid her head on her upraised knees. She was breathing roughly as Lobo watched her with canine curiosity before turning back to Luc for guidance.

Luc watched her curiously. She had to be aware he was there, but her whispered words still bothered him more than he wanted to admit. He knew Maria was slick. She had to have been to sweet-talk her way out of so much trouble over the years. The reports he had seen on her various court appearances were astounding. She could sway a judge better than the most accomplished defense lawyer. She had walked away more than once with a slap on her wrist and a firm lecture rather than the jail time she should have received.

He couldn't blame the judges or the prosecutors too much, though, because right now, he wanted to believe every excuse out of her mouth. And the thought of that didn't sit well with him at all.

Mason meowed plaintively from within what appeared to be a pillowcase converted into some type of sling.

"Be quiet, Mason," she mumbled. "If I let you go you'll become dog food. Is that what you really want?"

She was quiet now. As though she knew it wasn't going to do her any good to fight any longer. Conserving her strength, he thought in amusement. As aroused as he was right now, it might be the sensible course for her. He was so damned hard that if he did manage to get her into a bed, it would be a long time before she got out of it.

Shaking his head, Luc walked toward her, staring down at the mass of red-gold curls that had been tied back behind her neck, revealing the perfection of her pale profile. He hesitated in touching her. Rather, he stopped inches from her feet and stared down at her with what he hoped was a forbidding expression. It wouldn't do for her to see how easily he was softening toward her. Or how much he desired her. She was becoming a hunger. A need. In little more than a few days she had set his senses on fire, and despite the confusion, he found he had little resistance against it.

"Are you ready to go back yet?" he asked her sternly, pressing his lips together tightly to still the grin that would have edged them.

"Not really." Anger laced her tone as she kept her face buried at her knees.

She had to be exhausted. Despite her best attempts to appear as though she wasn't cleaning the house, several of the rooms damned near sparkled. He couldn't understand it. When he first set out the wealth of cleaning supplies he had bought her she had lifted her lip in contempt. But with each room he dragged her to, the improvement had been almost immediate.

Luc bent his knees, lowering himself until he could stare into her eyes whenever she deigned to look up. She kept herself still, refusing to raise her head.

"You proclaimed your innocence almost convincingly the other day," he said softly. "Then you do exactly what I would have expected of Maria. Only a guilty child runs from her punishment, Maria. Not an innocent woman."

"Oh God, the world has gone insane!" Her laughter was edged with disbelief as she shifted the cat to her side and sprawled out on her back, staring up at the black velvet, star-studded sky. "Did he even hear what he said?" she seemed to demand of the heavens. "A crazy man has kidnapped me. Have mercy, please," she prayed with exaggerated patience before staring back at him with glittering eyes. "What about innocent people who have no desire to clean your filthy messes?"

Luc watched her curiously, as did Lobo. The animal was a bit more forward about it, though. He scooted close to her, nudging her neck with his nose before yipping demandingly in her ear. Mason cried out plaintively within the crude sack that had fallen to her side.

She closed her eyes tightly before moving slowly to pull herself to her feet.

"Next time, I steal the fucking truck," she muttered.

Luc grinned as he rose as well, staring down at her.

"You have to steal the keys first. Want to know where they are?" He stuck his hand in his jeans pocket and rattled the keys teasingly.

"Figures. Likely where your damned brains are too," she snarled, heading back to the house. "Just my luck. All looks, nothing upstairs. Let's hope for the sake of your past and future lovers that at least you know what to do with the equipment a little lower, because my personal opinion is, that's all you have going for you."

Luc stilled his laughter. She was amusing. Had there been anything rather than irritation behind her tone, then he would have likely been just a little offended. But her tone was teasing, a bit abstract. She was plotting another way to escape while she hoped to piss him off enough that he wouldn't realize it.

"I've had no complaints," he assured her as he walked carefully behind her. "Perhaps you should test it for yourself."

A less than ladylike snort left her lips. "No thanks. As difficult as I'm sure you think the decision is, I'll have to decline your lovely offer."

"For now," he grinned. But not for long, he promised himself.

She came to a stop, turning to him, and he was surprised by the icy look she gave him, the pride and haughty disdain that filled her expression.

"Save your lust for someone who cares, Mr. Jardin. I don't. And I sure as hell don't want my sister's used seconds. Please be so kind as to keep that in mind."

Her sister's used seconds? She was good, he had to give her that. Damned good. Hell, he *wanted* to believe her and he knew better.

Nearly an hour later Luc was still fuming at the accusation as he dragged her into the house and up to his bedroom. She had fought him damned near every step until he had threatened to throw her over his shoulder instead. Her furious silence the rest of the way only edged his anger higher.

Fine. Maybe she hadn't really known what her friends were up to the day they had nearly killed him and Jack. She looked innocent enough. There were none of the signs of drug use on her and she was a hell of a lot more spirited than he had ever expected. She could make him feel like slime with one look out of those wounded, shadow-filled green eyes, and he wanted to cringe each time she turned them on him in accusation. And she was always so ladylike. She even moved like a lady. Smooth and supple, teasing and tempting him in ways he wouldn't have imagined she could.

She was fucking classy, was what she was. Moving with grace and a regal bearing that had him watching her even when he didn't want to. But she didn't have to lie about who she was. All she had to try was the truth. Stupidity was forgivable, lying wasn't. He hated liars. And she didn't have to call him used seconds when he hadn't even had a chance to fuck her. Yet.

That could change quickly, though, he thought as he headed for his bedroom. He was on fire for her. Less than a week in her presence and his cock was like hot iron in his pants, so ready to fuck he could feel the seeping of the pre-come from its slitted eye.

"This isn't my room," she finally yelled furiously as he pushed her into his room and slammed the door closed behind him.

Tension, thick and hot, filled the air. His body was hard and primed and she was soft, and he knew she would be so damned sweet to taste that it would send him over the edge of his control.

She looked more like a scared woman-child than a seductress, though, as she rounded on him, her eyes wide, her face pale as her fists clenched at her side. So innocent. Damn her. She had sucked his dick like a pro and now acted like a virgin wronged.

"No. It's not," he agreed coldly as he wrestled the sacked cat from her and released the tormented little feline.

For his efforts, the little black demon took a swipe at him a second before disappearing under his bed. He would have chased it out if Maria hadn't decided then to make a run for the door. The woman deserved a medal for sheer stubbornness.

He grabbed her arm, pulling her quickly to a stop before shoving her to the bed. If he had his hands on her for more than a second he feared he would lose any semblance of control. He was dying to take those lush sweet pink lips in a kiss and see if her mouth tasted as hot and arousing as he knew it would.

"Since I can't trust you to stay put, you'll stay where I can keep an eye on you," he snapped as he jerked the blankets off the four-poster bed, fighting the hunger. "Now strip."

He turned back to her as her eyes widened in shocked outrage. "I will not."

She should be on stage, he thought furiously. She pulled off the innocent virgin too damned good. That was no virgin sucking his cock two years before. That was a well-trained, experienced woman who had swallowed every drop of semen spewing into her mouth.

"Stop with the damned act," he snarled back at her. "I'm tired and not in the mood for your snipey little protests of innocence. Strip your damned clothes off and get into the bed before I tear them off you."

His fingers clenched with the need to do just that, then to tear his own off and plunge his cock as hard and deep inside her pussy as he could. He could feel the blood surging through his veins at the thought of it. Of holding her beneath him, hearing her scream his name, her hips pumping beneath him as he fucked her past defiance.

"Adding rape to your crimes now?" she sneered, surprising him. "Luc, surely there's enough dumb women around here to take care of the stupid cowboys in rut. Or do you have to wait for a season, like the other animals do?"

Luc held onto his control carefully. He couldn't blame her for being angry, for striking out at him with fury. But he'd be damned if he would allow her to push him much further. Further than he felt his own temper would allow. And that surprised him. No woman had ever touched that dark core inside him. The restless, hungry desire he had always been careful to keep hidden. She was doing more than tempting that pulsing, aching core, though. She was making it hunger, seethe. She was rousing a side of him that even he was wary of.

"You have one minute to strip and crawl into that bed," he growled softly. Even Lobo, who had followed them into the room, looked at him worriedly when he used that tone of voice. "Starting now."

* * * * *

Melina felt trepidation suddenly wrap around her senses. His tone of voice was dark, dangerous, but the sudden shifting of the color of his eyes was even more so. They darkened, became almost feral in intensity, and caused her to suddenly second-guess the belief she had formed that Luc Jardin was in any way safe.

He hadn't hurt her yet, she reminded herself. He wouldn't hurt her now. But, damn if it wasn't hard to fight back the fear.

She felt perspiration dot her forehead as he stared at her, felt the aroused hunger leaping from him to wrap around her. Twisted, nightmare images of pain and cruel hands touching her body attacked her mind then. She fought the instinctive need to trust him. To believe in the fantasy visions she had of him since their first meeting.

"Please..." She backed away from him. "I won't do it again. I'll be good." She almost winced at the hasty words that suddenly flew from her lips. Dammit, she wasn't a child anymore. She swallowed tightly, steadied her voice and whispered, "Luc, don't do this."

There was no mercy in his expression. If anything, he appeared harder, more determined than ever.

Tension thickened in the room. It became heavy with his sexual tension, with her fear.

"Undress." She flinched as his voice hardened. The wolf that lay in the corner of the room whined in confusion.

She wouldn't do it. Melina straightened her shoulders, knowing she would lose the fight to come, but she wouldn't stop fighting. She shuddered at the thought of how he could still her defiance, though, how it had been stilled once before, and she wanted to scream out in fury.

Melina held back her screams. She would need the energy for those later, she feared. She backed farther away from him, watching him carefully as she fought to breathe. She could feel the hard throb of her heart in her chest, the blood pounding through her veins and the cold sweat that covered her body. She hated fear. Hated the weakness it brought and the sense of vulnerability that seemed to only intensify.

"No." She gripped the front of her shirt in defense as she defied him. He wasn't a man who would take that defiance easily.

They had gone for her shirt first, during that night of horror and pain in the cells. They had torn it from her body and then ripped the loose jail issue pants from her hips as she fought to cover herself. Every time she said no, the blows had only grown worse. But she hadn't stopped, not until she lost consciousness, not until the pain had become so great that she knew death itself had come to rescue her. But it hadn't. She had lived. And now she lived with the memories as well.

She was going to be sick. She could feel her stomach roiling, feel the fear washing over her as she stared back at his stony expression. It was a nightmare that she wasn't certain she could survive.

He took a step toward her and Melina jumped back, barely aware of the whimper that escaped her throat, or of Lobo's sudden, soft growl. But Luc stopped then. His piercing eyes went to the animal at the side of the room before moving slowly back to her.

Melina swallowed tightly, forcing back the bile rising to her throat. Luc was tall, strong. Stronger than any man she knew. If he tried to force her...

"Maria, I won't hurt you," he suddenly breathed tiredly, though his look was too intense, too knowing now for her to find any comfort.

He moved instead to his dresser and pulled out a dark T-shirt. "Take this to the bathroom and change. You will be sleeping in this bed. With me. Don't even doubt that. But I would never take anything from you that you don't willingly give me."

She was shaking. Melina hadn't realized how hard she was shaking until she heard her teeth chatter as he came closer. She bit her lip, fighting the need to run, to flee as he advanced. She couldn't scream, she couldn't trust herself to utter a sound, afraid that if she did, the memories she had fought so hard to keep contained would pour out of her like bitter acid, scarring them both.

"Here." He pressed the shirt to her then caressed her cheek as she flinched away from him. "Get ready for bed, Cat. Now."

She snatched the shirt. "My pajamas," she whispered as she fought to speak without stuttering. "Will you get me a pair? In my room."

The fleece bottoms would provide much more protection, more warning if he decided to change his mind. She needed that confidence more than she needed anything right now.

"No, Maria." He shook his head, causing her chest to tighten in dread. "You have to learn to understand I won't hurt you. We'll begin tonight. No pants. Now go change. You have five minutes, and not a second more."

She stared up at him, sensing the crisis had passed, though her mind refused to accept it. He seemed to surround her, to take up all the air in the room, all the freedom of movement.

Skirting around him, watching him carefully, she moved for the tenuous sanctuary of the bathroom and hopefully a locked door. She needed time to still the dark shadows that chased through her mind, time to repair the fragile control he had destroyed so easily.

Chapter Six

∞

He was shaking. Luc stared down at his hands as though they belonged to someone else, wondering at the trembling extensions. Suspicion coursed through him like a tidal wave, and he didn't like the conclusions he was drawing.

Maria was like a light, fluid and bright whether she was angry or teasing, and hot as a damned firecracker. Until he had let the anger simmer to the surface. Until she had realized she would be in his bed—naked, at his mercy. And terror had swamped her. And there was but one reason for such overriding fear.

Had she been raped? Of course she had. He shook his head, fighting the rage that began to burn in his chest. There was no other reason for it. No other way to explain her reaction to him.

If it hadn't been for Lobo, he feared he would have missed the sheer terror in her eyes as he fought her defiance of him. He had seen her beauty, felt his sudden arousal for her, but only at Lobo's warning growl had he understood the true cause of the desperation. The animal had sensed what he had been too stupid to notice.

"Fuck," he whispered as he pushed his fingers restlessly through his hair.

His arousal had slammed to a stop the minute he realized how truly frightened she was. He knew the fear didn't come from his confrontation with her two years before. There had been no fear in her then, only remorse. And something that didn't make sense. Confusion. He remembered that now. She had been confused, wary, but resigned.

What the hell was going on? Joe wouldn't lie to him. He had spent enough time with the man to know he wouldn't willingly place his sister in danger. And he sure as hell wouldn't place an innocent sister in the line of fire.

He moved quickly to his feet as the doorknob turned slowly long minutes later and then opened. She left the bathroom, her shoulders straight, her head held high as she faced him, dressed in his T-shirt. Damn. He envied that shirt in ways he couldn't name. It fell over full, luscious breasts and ended mid-thigh. Her legs were shapely, well toned, and so tempting he could have spent hours touching them. Her eyes blazed, though. Green fire sparking with anger and the remnants of her fear.

"Lobo, keep her in here," he ordered the wolf as he watched Maria carefully. "Get in the bed. I'm worn to the bone and don't feel like fighting with you anymore, Maria. We'll talk in the morning."

"I'm going home in the morning," she stated quietly. "And my name is Melina, not Maria. I am Melina."

Luc sighed roughly. "You're acting more like that damned spoiled cat than you are anything. And you're not going anywhere tomorrow. Now get in the bed before I have to tie you in it. I'm not in the mood for theatrics or temperaments. I've had enough for the day."

He stalked to the bathroom before he did something stupid. Something like pulling her into his arms, holding her to his chest and swearing he'd never hurt her, never let anyone else hurt her. Making promises he knew she would never believe.

As he slammed the bathroom door he came to a startling, horrifying realization. He was starting to care for her, and that just would not do. He couldn't afford to care for this little wild cat. Not and survive with his heart intact. But damn, if it hadn't already happened.

Shaking his head at his own foolishness, Luc prepared for bed. He stripped to his briefs, washed the dust from his face, hands and arms and quickly brushed his teeth. Weariness dragged at him, as well as arousal, and he wondered at the sanity of having her sleep in his bed.

He could have set Lobo to guard her. Had actually considered doing it until he watched how the wolf merely played with her rather than displaying the aggression he should have in turning her back earlier. She had charmed the animal Jack called a demon beast and Luc wondered if he could trust him to do anything other than pant at her heels now. He snorted at that thought as he flipped the light out and left the bathroom. Lobo wasn't the only one willing to pant at her heels right now.

She was in the bed, hugging the edge as though her life depended on it, the sheet and comforter pulled up to her shoulders as she lay on her side, her back to him. When he got into the bed he was careful to keep the upper sheet beneath his body and used the comforter alone for warmth. He flipped out the light and settled in the bed, resigned to a miserable night.

For long minutes silence filled the darkened room as Luc fought every instinct in his body to turn to her. He needed her as desperately as he needed air now. His cock was throbbing, making him insane with the desire to fuck her, to fill her with every hard inch of it.

Finally, he sighed wearily. He could feel her wariness stretching between them, the nerves that held her body rigid and kept her from easing into sleep.

"I won't hurt you, you know," he finally told her softly. "I might paddle that tempting little ass of yours if you don't obey me, but I won't damage you, little Cat."

She had claws, just like that bag of fur she claimed as a pet. But there was something warm and soft about her despite the bite. He hadn't expected to see that in her, and he found it drew him more than he liked.

"You have no right to hold me here, Luc," she finally answered him.

"Is prison preferable, Cat?" he finally asked her.

He couldn't imagine her in prison, her passion and energy restrained, the traces of vulnerability he had seen in her forever destroyed. She was too soft, too gentle for such an atmosphere.

187

Silence greeted his question and though she didn't make a sound, he could feel the sadness that seemed to wrap around her as snugly as the blanket on the bed. He turned over on his side, staring at the fall of fiery curls that lay over her pillow and down her back.

"No," she whispered, and the sound of her voice had him frowning in confusion. It was rife with pain, with throttled rage, as she breathed in shakily. "Prison is not preferable."

"Well now, aren't you a pretty little thing…" At the sound of a woman's coarse, spiteful voice, Melina opened her eyes and stared around in horror.

Where had the guards gone? There were supposed to be guards outside the cells. Her door was supposed to be locked at all times. She wasn't supposed to be harassed again. Not after the last time. The warden had promised.

"Why are you here?" She tried to sit up in the bed, to somehow put herself into a defensive position, but there was no place to go. Above her was another cot. There was no way out, no way to protect herself.

Dear God, where was Joe? His secretary had said he would come for her, that he would get her out of here. Why wasn't he here yet?

Panic welled in her chest, made her stomach roil in waves of fear as a cold sweat began to cover her body. For a moment, just a moment, the image of Luc Jardin flashed in her head. He had made certain her sister Maria was given the sentence in the detention center. Luc Jardin who had come to her parents' home, fury throbbing through every inch of his body as he stared into her eyes thinking she was Maria, and swore she would pay. Swore she would spend as much time incarcerated as he could manage.

But it was her sister, her cold, deceptive sister, who had made certain Melina was locked up in her place. Not Luc. Handsome, strong Luc. Oh God. She was going to die, Melina thought. She would die by the hands of the female rapist now staring back at her.

"Thought you'd get away from us, didn't you, pretty thing?" Bertha Saks was a towering woman, built like a man with long black

hair and faintly almond-shaped eyes. Her lips were twisted in a sneer as three other inmates crowded into the room.

"Let's see if we can't teach you better than to run tattling to the nice warden next time I decide I want a little kiss from those sweet lips," Bertha chuckled. "Don't worry, sweet thing, it only hurts if you fight it."

Melina shuddered in distaste. The thought of giving the woman what she wanted nearly caused her to throw up.

'Bertha, leave me alone." She tried to keep her voice firm, reasonable. "You don't want to do this. My family can help you…"

A short, vicious laugh sounded from Bertha's lips. "Your family?" she sneered. "Darlin', haven't you figured it out yet? You don't have no family. They left you here all alone to my tender mercies. And I can be tender, sweet thing. You just lay back and spread those pretty legs and I'll show you how tender I can be."

Melina pushed herself deeper into the corner of the bunk, pulling her legs up in front of her, shaking, knowing there was no way to escape the other woman now. There were no guards, no sounds of movement outside the cells, only the echo of her own heart in her ears.

"I won't do it." She swallowed tightly.

"Oh, you will, bitch," Bertha assured her. "Before this night is over, you'll do that and more."

"Oh God. No." Melina tried to escape the suddenly grasping hands. Hands that tore at her clothing, ripping the cheap tunic and cotton pants off her body as others held her down.

"Now just settle down, sweet thing." Bertha's laughter echoed around her. "Oh, what pretty little tits. I bet they taste just as pretty as they look."

Cruel hands stretched her arms above her head as Bertha moved, her hands outstretched, fingers curling into claws as they lowered to Melina's breasts.

Enraged, terrified beyond anything she had known in her life, Melina began to fight. Her hands were restrained, but her legs weren't. She kicked out forcefully, catching the larger woman in the midsection and sending her flying back as Melina twisted against the others who held her to the small cot.

Bertha's curses echoed around the room a second before pain shattered Melina's body. A heavy fist had landed into her tender, undefended waist. Her body bowed as an agonized scream tore from her throat and her stomach began to revolt against the pain.

"Let the bitch go," Bertha ordered furiously. "I'll take her to my hand or I'll kill her."

Before she could find the strength to stumble away, the other woman was stretched on the cot beside her, staring down at her with an evil smile, her dark eyes malicious and determined.

"No, babycakes, you'll let me take you and you'll like it, or I'll make sure that sweet little body hurts real bad before you take your last breath."

Fighting to breathe, Melina stared back at her, seeing her own death in her eyes. Weakly, she sneered into the other woman's face. "I'd rather die..."

The next driving blow went into her stomach. As Melina's eyes widened at the pain, her mouth opening as she fought to gasp for air, cruel hands grabbed at her breasts, hard fingers pinching at her tender nipples as the order was given again.

Wheezing for breath, tears of agony streaking her face, Melina stared into the eyes of hell and repeated her preference. "I'd rather die..."

"Then die, " Bertha sneered. "I'll fuck your cold body and make you like it..."

* * * * *

Melina's scream brought Luc instantly awake, his hand reaching automatically for the gun he kept beside his bed before he realized the agonized cry was one of sleep-induced terror rather than reality.

Turning to her, he caught her automatically in his arms as her body jackknifed, her eyes flying open, glazed with terror and pain as she stared back at him. A second later, she began to fight. Tears poured from her eyes as she screamed his name, yet her nails clawed at his arms, her body shuddering, sweat pouring from her as she fought against him.

"Cat!" He yelled her name, his hands gripping her arms as she struck out at him, shaking her furiously before jerking her against his chest, holding her tight. "God damn, wake up, baby, please wake up."

Her sobs were horrible to hear. Deep, gut-wrenching cries that tore at his soul.

"Oh God. A dream." she gasped into his chest as the cat suddenly jumped to the bed, wailing, his feline howls grating on Luc's nerves. "Let me go." She pushed against him, barely able to speak for her cries, barely able to function for the hard shudders ripping through her body. "Let me go. Let me go…"

He released her slowly, staring at her in shock as she grabbed at the fat little cat and hauled him into her arms. Her face buried into the fur of his neck as the cat's cries eased and glowing feline eyes stared back at him with a somber weariness that had him shaking his head in shock.

The fucking cat was meowing now, a low, soothing sound, a shushing sound, as she trembled, her arms holding the animal close, his fur absorbing the terrorized sobs that were finally growing weaker.

"Cat." He wanted to touch her, needed to touch her. God help him, but the sound of her cries was breaking what was left of his heart. "Sweetheart, you're going to make yourself sick crying like this."

He tried to keep his voice soft, as soothing as the cat's meows had become.

"Go away." She was almost gagging as she fought for breath. "Leave me alone, Luc. Just leave me alone."

Like hell. He moved closer, his arms going around her despite the stiffness that suddenly seized her body.

"Do you think squeezing the life out of that cat is going to make it better, Cat?" he asked her harshly. "That's not what you need and we both know it."

She quivered against him.

"Let me help you, baby," he whispered into her hair. "Come on, let poor little Mason go." He smoothed his hand down her arm, his hand covering one of hers as he tugged at it gently. "Come on, baby. Let's chase the demons back the right way."

He tipped her tear-drenched face up, surprised that she wasn't fighting with him. Bleak, overwhelming pain filled her gaze, tearing at his heart.

"It's okay, baby." He lowered his head, sipping at the salty tears that fell from her eyes. "Come on, let me hold you. That's all. Just hold you."

She eased her grip on the cat slowly, allowing the animal to leave or stay as he pleased. Luc pushed at the fat little body, reminding himself to buy the animal his own stash of tuna for the comfort he so obviously had brought her in the past. She had turned too quickly to the cat for it to be anything other than habit. He comforted her. The cat was aloof and cold at any other time, superior in his place in the world, until her screams had brought them awake.

"Come on." Luc pulled her against him more fully, hating the tremors that ripped through her. "It's okay."

His lips touched hers. Gently. Soothingly.

"Luc," she finally whispered. She drew in a deep breath and stared back at him with slowly dawning awareness. "I'm sorry. I'm so sorry."

She tried to draw away then. Tried, but he wasn't about to allow it. Luc didn't give her time to protest. His lips covered hers gently, his tongue licking its way past them into the velvet heat of her mouth.

He felt her still. Felt the shudders ease into a reluctant tremor as he moved his lips over hers gently. Cajoling, nipping playfully, watching her carefully through the fringe of his lashes as she stared up at him in the darkness.

"Nightmares are nasty little creatures," he murmured against her lips as his hands smoothed up her back, one moving to bury in the mass of silken curls that fell from her head. "You have to chase them back, show them that when they come callin', you'll fight dirty."

He smiled at the flicker of confusion in her gaze. He nipped gently at her lips, teasing her now with the threat of his kiss, keeping her waiting, watching.

"They don't come creeping out if they know something good is going to follow their harassment. So we just have to show them you'll fight dirty, huh? Do you like this, baby?"

His hands cupped her head as he lowered her back to the bed, coming down beside her, keeping his movements slow and easy, not threatening, not intense, just a silken slide of desire and pleasure to soothe and tempt her.

"I'm not Maria," she whimpered suddenly, causing him to still. "Don't hold me like this and think I'm Maria, Luc."

He frowned down at her as he moved one hand to allow his fingers to caress her cheek.

"Cat," he whispered then. "All graceful and smooth like a little cat. Curious and tempting as sin. Come here, little Cat, let me show you how to chase away the nightmares."

He would figure out the thread of fear and longing in her declaration later. Right now, pouty, tear-swollen lips awaited him. He wanted them reddened with his passion, moving beneath his with hungry abandon. And they were.

A soft moan of surrender escaped her as he slanted his lips over hers and once again used his tongue to tempt her higher. Within seconds her arms were wrapped around his shoulders tentatively as she relaxed into the fiery embrace.

Control, Luc reminded himself. He couldn't take her now. Not while she was weak, frightened. He wanted to soothe her, wanted her to know he would hold her through whatever fears besieged her. He wanted — God help him, he *needed* — her trust.

"There, now." He drew back long seconds later and pulled her closer into his embrace. "See? It's all gone, baby."

A small grin suddenly edged her lips. He knew she could sense the sexual tension wrapping around them.

"I'm supposed to go back to sleep now?" she finally asked him, her voice hoarse, but thankfully without fear.

"Well," he finally said with no small amount of amusement, "unless you want to take care of this hard-on killing me. Otherwise, I'd advise you to go to sleep fast or I might be tempted to convince you to help me out with that matter."

She was definitely considering it. For a second his heart stilled in anticipation before going into overdrive and beating a fierce drumbeat of lust inside his chest. Then her eyes snapped closed, though the corners of her lips were still edging into a grin.

"I'm asleep," she murmured drowsily.

Luc snorted and settled deeper in his pillow, holding her to his chest and trying to fight back his own fears. Her screams would haunt him forever, he thought. What the hell had happened to her?

"You convince yourself of that, baby." He kissed the top of her head and sighed wearily. "Now, go to sleep before my lust overrules my head and convinces me you're well able to handle a good old-fashioned tumble."

Her laughter was more relaxed now as her body softened against him.

"Thanks, Luc," she finally whispered.

"For what? Baby, I didn't do anything but make myself hard as stone with no relief in sight. You should feel sorry for me. Real sorry." He exaggerated his slow drawl, relishing her low laughter in the dark.

"Thanks anyway." She snuggled closer, sighed deeply, and within minutes was drifting back to sleep.

She left Luc staring into the darkness, a frown on his face and suspicion building in his head. If he weren't so certain of Joe, he would have sworn this couldn't be Maria after all. But one thing was clear. Whatever the hell was going on, she wasn't the type of woman he had been led to believe, nor was she the drug-dazed whore his information had hinted at. She was almost...innocent. He wanted to shake his head to dispel that image. The woman who sucked his dick two years before wasn't innocent, not in any way. But strangely enough, the woman clearing his house, and now sleeping in his bed, was just that.

Chapter Seven

෨

Melina did her best to ignore Luc the next day. It wasn't that the nightmare had left her frightened. Strangely enough, it had left her more comforted than she had ever been after such an episode. No, she was avoiding Luc because that single act of comfort had suddenly shifted the balance of her emotions. What had been simple lust, a desire for that tough-as-hell body, was turning into something she didn't understand, something deeper, something more intense. Something that was almost frightening.

He had held her through the night. His arms, so muscular, strong and warm. God, he was so warm.

She paused as she loaded the washer with dusty jeans and closed her eyes at the thought of it, remembering the feel of him holding her. A shudder raced down her spine. Like live bands of flexible steel, his arms had surrounded her, wrapping around her and holding her close to his chest.

And his chest... She sighed. She was a lost cause. One of those silly, insipid females who caved for lust. She stuffed his jeans into the washer as she grimaced at the very idea of it. It was bad enough she had been a doormat for her family her entire life, but this was ridiculous. She despised women who caved so damned easily.

"But it's just for a little while," she muttered to herself as she stared into the depths of the washer as though it could actually hold answers.

He would realize his mistake soon. Luc wasn't a stupid man, just a determined man. And when he did realize what he had done he would pack her up and take her back to her empty apartment and her empty life.

It wasn't that she couldn't find a lover, if she wanted one. It was, unfortunately, a matter of having only wanted one man. Luc. *Silly wimp*, she berated herself. *Take one look at six feet plus of hot cowboy and what do you do? Goodbye, common sense, hello, hormones.*

She slammed the washer lid closed.

"I am not this insane," she mumbled to herself. "God, I have to have more self-control than this."

"I don't know, Cat. If you start answering yourself, though, I'd worry if I were you."

Melina swung around, her eyes widening in mortification, her body flushing in embarrassment as she stared back at the object of her insanity.

Luc leaned casually against the doorframe to the washroom, his gray eyes glinting with amusement, a smile quirking those eat-'em-up lips. That full lower lip was as tempting as chocolate and she knew his kiss was anything but sweet. It was hot and wild and mind-destroying and she wanted to feast on it.

"I thought you were outside," she snapped, turning quickly away from him to check the clothes in the dryer before turning it on with a quick flip of the switch.

"I was." She could hear the shrug in his voice.

A second later she heard him move closer. She tensed, though her pussy began to weep in serious distress. That particular part of her body was not pleased with her reticence in jumping his bones. It really wasn't fair, she thought. Men like Luc Jardin should seriously be outlawed for the good of all females.

He was too close. She could smell him. She straightened the containers of fabric softener, laundry detergent and various stain removers as she fought the racing of her heart, the tightening of her nipples. Why did he have to be so darned gentle last night? If he had been a bastard, she could have resisted him, could have reminded herself how mean and rude and totally irrational he was.

"Cat." His chest brushed her back as she drew in a long, hard breath. "You feel it too, baby. It won't just go away."

She shook her head, denying him, denying herself.

"Do you have any idea how hard it was to just hold you last night?" he asked her. "Your hard little nipples burned holes in my chest, even through that shirt. I bet I have the singe marks to prove it."

She couldn't stop the smile that begged to curve her lips, but she kept her back to him, trembling, jerking in response when he kissed her bare shoulder. The sleeveless tank top was no defense against him. The gauzy slip-skirt she wore with it suddenly seemed too heavy, too restricting. She wanted to get naked with him. Wanted to roll across beds and floors and tables and scream in pleasure as he fucked her sillier than she must already be.

"I have half an hour before a buyer shows up," he murmured, his lips brushing over her bare skin once again. "Plenty of time, baby, to show you how good it could be."

Oh hell. Like he had to tell her anything. Even her womb was rippling with pleading little tremors. Her panties would have to be changed. And she didn't dare turn around because her nipples were about to pop through the cloth of her shirt, they were so damned hard. Yep, she was in trouble here.

"I have to clean…something." She rolled her eyes at the betraying squeak in her voice. *Silly twit,* she accused herself.

"Hmm." The soft hum against her neck had her shuddering in response.

"Luc, please…" She licked her suddenly dry lips as she fought to hold on to her control. "This isn't the wisest course of action here."

"Do you know how sexy that little skirt looks?" He ignored her statement as his hands gripped her, one smoothing down her thigh. "I've denied myself all day, Cat. Turn around, baby, and tell me why I shouldn't raise that flimsy excuse for a covering and push my cock as deep inside your sweet pussy as I can get it."

Why he shouldn't? There was a reason why he shouldn't?

Twit.

She flipped around, opened her mouth to say…something, she was certain, though she quickly forgot what as his lips covered hers. He lifted her against his chest, his arms coming around her, causing her to whimper at the warmth, the security of being enfolded so snugly against him.

Her lips opened to him, her tongue meeting his with a speed and hunger that she knew should have shocked her. Her hands went to his hair. All that long, thick black silk hiding beneath his Stetson. The Stetson was pushed quickly out of the way — who the hell cared where it landed?

Could fingertips have orgasms? Her fingers flexed, the flesh covering them rioted with pleasure at the feel of the cool, incredibly soft strands they suddenly gripped.

His lips ate at hers, but she dined in return. Hard, deep kisses that drew the breath from her body and left her dependent on him alone for survival. His head tilted, his lips slanting over hers as he growled into the kiss and lifted her further.

"Luc…" She tore her lips from his. crying out his name in dazed pleasure as she felt the cool metal of the washer beneath her bare butt. Panties were no protection.

Her head fell back as his lips moved down her neck. His tongue was a demon. It licked as his lips created a delicate suction along the sensitive points of the column of flesh. One hand smoothed beneath her skirt, spreading her thighs, drawing ever closer to the hot center of need that tormented her.

"God, you're like a flame," he groaned as his other hand — sneaky, diabolical — gripped the hem of her shirt and jerked it over her swollen breasts. "Sweet heaven," he muttered harshly. "Cat, baby…"

Melina opened her eyes, staring into his flushed, lustful face and she swore she nearly came in that second. Had any man ever looked at her with such hunger and need? Never, she quickly answered herself. Not at any time.

"Bad idea..." She trembled as his hand cupped the full curve, his thumb rasping over the sensitized tip. She wasn't about to make him stop.

"Good idea," he denied. "Best damned idea I ever had."

His lips covered the engorged peak and Melina lost the last bit of common sense she might have originally possessed as the heat of his mouth surrounded her needy nipple.

Could she bear the pleasure? She arched to him, a thin wail escaping her lips as her fingers sank deeper into his hair, holding his head to her as he suckled at the tight flesh deeply. Her legs tightened on his hips as he jerked her closer, grinding the hard ridge of his cock against the swollen mound of her pussy.

Ah God, it was too good. His teeth nibbled at the hard peak his mouth surrounded, his tongue lashing at it with fiery demand before he sucked at it firmly once again. She couldn't stay still. Couldn't stop her hands from holding him closer, her hips from moving, rubbing her cunt against the hot wedge of flesh behind the tight fit of denim. Her clit was swollen, throbbing, so agonizingly sensitive she knew it would take very little to send her exploding into orgasm.

"God. I'm going to end up fucking you blind on this damned washer," he muttered as he drew back, despite her attempts to hold him to her.

She was supposed to protest that? She shuddered as he pushed her skirt higher, his thumbs edging around the elastic at the side of her lacy panties. She was dying with anticipation, her pussy saturated with it as she stared back at him in dazed awareness of exactly where this was heading.

"I want to taste you," he whispered as his fingers delved beneath the lace slowly, pulling it to the side as his other hand rose to press her back until her shoulders touched the wall behind the washer. "Just like this, baby. Just a taste…"

His tongue swiped through the hot slit of her cunt, curled around her clit then traveled back down to suddenly plunge into the entrance of her vagina as he lifted her legs over his shoulders.

"Oh God! Luc!" He would kill her. She didn't have the experience to combat this, didn't have the self-control to deny it.

"Mmm." The sound of male pleasure, the feel of his tongue fucking inside her was nearly too much. She was reaching, desperate…oh God, she was so close. Her hands were in his hair again, holding him to her as he ate her with such sensual abandon that she felt lost in the headlong flight to wherever he was determined to push her. Insanity, she imagined. Complete, hedonistic mindlessness.

His tongue was a weapon of sensual torture. It flickered in and out of her vagina, licking up the shallow cleft to torment her swollen clit, his lips covering it, suckling it, his tongue rasping over it. She was seconds from an orgasm. She could feel it building in her womb, her nerve endings gathering themselves for the explosion to come.

"Hey Luc, where the hell are you?" She froze at the sound of the unfamiliar voice echoing through the house. "Dammit, boy, thought you wanted to sell those horses."

Luc jerked back. As he looked up at her in surprise, Melina felt her womb contract in vicious need at the sight of his lips glistening with the proof of her arousal.

"Fuck." His voice was brutally rough with lust, his eyes nearly black as he straightened quickly.

He pulled her shirt down swiftly then her skirt. Grabbing a clean cloth from the rack over the washer, he quickly dried his lower face, his expression rueful as he stared back at her.

"Sam August," he muttered. "Hell. Get presentable, baby. That's one ole boy you don't want to tempt."

"Well hell, no wonder you didn't answer." Amused and blatantly confident, the laughing male voice was like a splash of ice water to Melina's hormones.

The big cowboy suddenly framed in the doorway was breathtakingly handsome. Laughing blue eyes watched them in amusement as sensual lips curved upward in response to Luc's curse. "Should I come back later?"

"You should get your ass back in the kitchen until I get there," Luc snapped, frowning at Melina's surprised look.

Sam August laughed quietly. "That's okay, Luc. Heather would have my balls if I even considered it. Do what you have to do and get out here. I brought her with me and she gets a mite impatient if she has to wait too long."

Melina looked between the two men in astonishment as Luc helped her from the washer, shielding her body with his as though trying to hide her from the other man.

"Maria Angeles, right?" Sam craned his neck to see around Luc. "Hell, son, she don't look tough enough to be a criminal…"

The kick Melina delivered to Luc's shin was anything but weak as she pushed past him and moved for the doorway. Fury engulfed her. Damn him to hell and back.

"What the hell…" Luc stared down at her with a glimmer of his own anger. "What was that for?"

Rather than answering him, she turned back to his friend.

"Maria Angeles, my ass," she informed Sam heatedly. "Try Melina or I'll take your head off right after I get finished taking his off. Now, excuse me while I go try to find my sanity. I'm sure it's floating around here somewhere."

She stalked from the washroom past a surprised Sam August, her head held high as she mentally kicked herself for ever believing, for even a second, that there was a chance in hell that Luc Jardin could have even considered suspecting she wasn't Maria. Hell, he had even told his friends about her. And only God knew what he had told them.

Twit, she accused herself again. And it wasn't like she didn't deserve it. She had fallen into Luc's hands like the silly ninny he thought she was. And this time, she couldn't even blame it all on him. She had done everything but beg for the humiliation. *Twit*.

Melina had every intention of rushing straight upstairs as she cursed herself for her lapse in common sense. And she would have. if she hadn't nearly run over the slender redhead who had her head buried in the depths of the nearly empty refrigerator.

'Oh. Hello." The other woman straightened and flashed Melina a bright smile before glancing back at the cavernous interior of the appliance. "I'm convinced Jardin is a vampire. The man has to exist on some sort of nourishment, but you never see anything in his fridge." She gestured to the half empty gallon of milk, a few jars of pickles and a full package of lunchmeat.

'That's because his cooking abilities are zero." Melina reached up and jerked open the upper freezer to display the myriad TV dinners, and frozen entrees he kept stored there

'Oh." Her expression seemed to drop as she sighed in disappointment. "I knew I should have made Sam stop at the hamburger joint in town." She closed the door and stuck out her hand. "I'm Heather August You must be Luc's kidnap victim. You know, it's against the laws of the Geneva Convention to starve prisoners. You should mention this to Luc."

Melina shook her hand automatically as she stared back into the amused green eyes regarding her. Heather August wasn't much taller than Melina. She had a healthy, wholesome appearance, clear creamy skin with only a scattering of freckles across her nose. Long red hair, pulled back from her face and bound into an intricate braid that fell past her shoulder blades, hinted at a temper that was nowhere in sight at the moment. She was dressed in jeans and a loose, dark blue silk blouse.

Her hands were propped on her hips as she regarded Melina curiously.

"It amazes me how everyone knows and yet I'm still stuck here. Kidnapping is against the law," Melina grunted as she stood aside for Luc and Sam to enter the room.

"So is drug running," Luc retorted as he passed her. "Beats prison. Remember?"

Heather laughed softly before Melina could snap out a reply to Luc. "If I thought you were in any danger, I would kick his ass myself. But I have to admit, you're not what I expected. You're definitely not the drug runner type."

Melina felt like rolling her eyes. "Could be because I'm not a drug runner." She cast Luc a hateful glance as he followed her into the kitchen. "Exactly who have you told anyway? If I find out the law enforcement in this godforsaken...wherever I am...knows about this, I'm not going to be happy."

Luc arched his brow mockingly as his dark gray eyes filled with amusement.

"I haven't seen the sheriff in a few weeks, actually. I didn't get around to telling him about it."

"Why not just take out a damned newspaper ad?" Melina snapped temperamentally. "Then you wouldn't have to remember to tell anyone."

Luc chuckled, though Sam and Heather both seemed to watch her curiously.

"A newspaper ad isn't nearly as fast as some people's wagging tongues," Sam laughed. "Luckily for Luc, we're trustworthy." He turned to Luc then. "Let's go do some horse trading. Maybe your woman will have pity on mine and fix something edible. Those frozen dinners are gonna kill you, boy."

Melina crossed her arms over her chest and stared at the two men furiously. "I am not his woman. He didn't court me, he kidnapped me."

"The best marriages in the west started that way." Sam shrugged, then chuckled when his wife's fist landed on his thick shoulder. "That's my cue to go." He turned to Luc. "Let's go check out my horseflesh, Luc, before I get myself in trouble."

Melina watched Luc, her eyes narrowing as he struggled to hide his own grin and followed Sam from the house. She wanted to hate him, wanted to blame him, but the more time she spent with him the less she looked forward to him learning the truth of who she was. And that only made her madder. Though the anger was directed more at herself now than at Luc.

'He's a hard man, but he's a good man." Heather's voice suddenly interrupted her musings. "And I think he's a little bit fonder of you than perhaps he's letting on."

Melina sighed and looked over at the other woman. "You're hungry?" She ignored Heather's observation.

"Not really." She shrugged. "I just like to hassle him over it. He never eats properly."

Melina snorted. "The man can't boil water safely. Thankfully, he kidnapped someone who does know how to cook. How about some coffee and cinnamon rolls instead?"

"Sounds great. Can I do anything to help?" Heather asked as Melina moved to the coffee maker and began making a fresh pot.

"The rolls were baked this morning and coffee won't take but a few minutes." Melina shrugged. "Go ahead and sit down. I'll have it ready soon."

Silence filled the small room as Melina prepared the coffee, removed the cups from the cabinet and set out the fresh baked rolls she had fixed that morning. It took only minutes for the coffee to brew. During that time Melina laid out small saucers, sugar and cream and endured Heather's narrow-eyed perusal.

She wondered what Luc had told the couple about her. Of course, they would have known about Maria's part in the shooting two years before. Luc seemed rather close to the other man, so she had no doubt that Sam August knew about it. There had also been a glimmer of resentment in the other man's eyes when he watched her. He was polite, a bit mocking maybe, but she could tell he was concerned about Luc.

Heather seemed more direct, though she had yet to say anything. She merely watched as Melina prepared the coffee, poured it into oversized cups and then returned to the table.

"You're the sister," Heather finally said softly. "You're not Maria."

Surprised, Melina stared over at the other woman.

"Luc swears there isn't a sister," she said sarcastically. "So you must be wrong."

Heather laughed gently. "I would say Luc spent very little time researching his subject. The minute Sam told me what Luc had done I got on the computer. I have to admit, I'm glad he didn't kidnap Maria. She would have made certain he went to prison for it."

"And you think I won't?" Melina asked coolly as she stirred sugar into her coffee.

Heather tilted her head to the side and regarded her for long moments.

"I don't think you will. I think you're more likely to fuck him silly than you are to see him locked up behind bars."

Melina could feel the heat filling her face and knew she was flushing in both embarrassment and knowledge. The other woman was far too perceptive.

"I'm more likely to kill him myself." She sighed. "Do you intend to help me convince him he has the wrong woman?"

Heather leaned back in her chair and watched her silently. Melina found that those green eyes could be uncomfortably focused as she stared back at her.

"Why not just let him hang himself?" Heather finally shrugged. "I've rarely seen Luc smile as he did today. He's more relaxed — almost happy. And I don't sense a burning desire in you to be free."

She was much too close to the truth.

"I should be desperate to escape." Melina shook her head at that knowledge. "I think I'm a failure as a kidnap victim."

The episode on the washer earlier proved that. She would have begged him to take her then and there if Sam hadn't shown up. And she wouldn't have regretted it, she thought. She would have gloried in it.

"I think maybe you're just what he needs right now." Heather leaned forward again and picked up her coffee cup. "Teach him how to cook while you're here. Maybe he won't kill himself with frozen dinners after you leave...that is if he lets you leave."

Melina wondered at the smile that played about the other woman's lips as she lifted her coffee cup and sipped at the hot brew. Heather seemed much too convinced that leaving wouldn't be an option.

"He has to let me go soon." Melina glanced out the window to her side, watching as Luc led one of the huge horses from the barn for Sam to examine. "He won't keep me forever."

No matter how much she wished he would. For a moment, shock vibrated through her system. This wasn't what she wanted, was it? It wasn't a question she could answer right then.

"Stranger things have happened." Heather shrugged. "But what will be, will be. Now tell me about your sister and how the hell you ended up being kidnapped in her place. I'm dying of curiosity."

Chapter Eight

෨

Heather and Sam hadn't stayed long, but by the time the two men had concluded their visit, Melina knew she had made a friend. Not that Luc seemed comfortable with the idea, nor did Sam. But both men seemed smart enough not to comment on it. Besides, as the evening wore on, Melina could tell that Luc had something much more serious on his mind.

He kept watching her silently. His dark gray eyes were reflective, his expression too serious to suit her. She had a feeling she knew what was coming, but when the question was voiced, she found that she still didn't have the answers that would have placated him.

"What happened to frighten you last night?" Luc's softly voiced question finally came after dinner.

Melina stood in front of the sink finishing the last of the dinner dishes and staring through the window at the steadily darkening backyard. She lowered her head, focusing on the thick mass of suds that covered her hands and wondered what to tell him.

The truth can often hurt, and Melina had no desire to hurt Luc. The fact that he had been the catalyst that ended with her in that jail cell that week had been forgiven long ago. Her own foolishness, she realized, was the reason she had landed there. She had trusted her parents, had trusted Maria, when she knew better.

She flinched as she heard the chair he was sitting in scuff across the floor. Her gaze rose to the window, her heart speeding up in her chest as he approached her. His expression was somber, his black hair falling over his brow, his lips compressed into a controlled line as his eyes met hers in the reflection.

'Wouldn't any woman be frightened at the thought of being tied naked in a stranger's bed?" she finally snapped in defense.

He was getting too close. She could feel the heat of his body along her back now, the intensity that was so much a part of him wrapping around her with gossamer threads of emotion.

He stared at her in the glass until she finally dropped her eyes, covering her retreat by letting out the water and rinsing her shaking hands with a quick motion.

"Cat?" He touched her.

Melina stilled, wanting nothing more than to close her eyes and escape the merciless perception in his gaze. She felt trapped by his look, drawn into it, captivated by the dark clouds of concern that shifted within them as his hand settled on her hip.

She swallowed tightly.

"I have to finish the kitchen…"

She was not giving in to him. Not again. She couldn't let herself forget who he thought she was. She couldn't let herself forget *who* she was. Despite her desire for him, despite the hunger that sped through every cell in her body, she couldn't forget what they had both suffered at her sister's hands.

"Fuck the kitchen, Cat." A frown snapped between his brows as he turned her to face him, both hands gripping her hips now, holding her so close that a breath of air would have had trouble passing between his body and hers. "I want answers. Do you think I didn't see your terror? That I wouldn't wonder what's behind it? What happened?"

Melina breathed out with a short angry burst of air.

"I don't owe you answers, Luc. You've kidnapped me. Refused to listen to reason once you were informed of the mistake you made. And you push and prod at me every chance you get to force admissions that are no more than lies to appease you. You have no right to be concerned about anything."

Melina pushed away from him, stalking across the kitchen to replace his chair beneath the table and straighten the small, cloth placemats. The old oak table gleamed with its fresh coat of wax, a testament to her hard work that day.

"Cat, freedom comes with a price." His voice was gentle but the meaning was clear. "You can't change if you don't learn from your mistakes."

Amazement filled her. How gentle and concerned he sounded. It was almost enough to make her sick.

"God, can you get any more pompous?" She rounded on him furiously. "Listen to yourself, Luc. I've told you at every opportunity what a fool you're making of yourself here and still, you aren't listening. You know what?" She propped her hands on her hips, tired of the arguments, sick of dealing with his determination to believe she was Maria. "You just believe what you want to. Everyone else has. You want to believe I'm Maria? Knock yourself out, asshole, but don't expect me to cooperate. I grew sick of wearing my sister's shoes quite a while ago. I won't let you force me back into them."

The situation would have been laughable if it weren't for the fact that she was aware she was losing her heart to the knucklehead.

"This isn't about your refusal to admit who you are," he retorted, his voice harsh, dark. "I don't give a damn who you want to pretend to be. Dammit, Cat, have you considered the fact that the drugs could just be an escape from whatever happened? If you admit you're frightened, wouldn't it be easier to accept you have a problem? Now, I want to know why the hell you looked at me like I was within an inch of raping you last night, when you should have known damned good and well that's not a danger you face. If I don't know the problem, then I can't help you fix it."

Some men were just too damned stubborn for their own good.

"Oh, you know the problem," she snapped. "You just won't admit it. Dammit, Luc, when are you going to admit that maybe, just maybe, I'm not Maria?"

"Cat, do you think I didn't make certain before taking you?" he growled in frustration.

"Evidently you didn't" She shrugged, lifting her brow mockingly. "Listen to you, you don't even call me by my name. You call me Cat. Why, Luc? If you're so insistent you know you're right, why not call me by Maria?"

He grimaced, male irritation filling his gaze as he stared back at her with a determined glint in his eyes.

"You're deliberately trying to change the subject," he said darkly. "You're good at that, Cat, I have to commend you. But I won't let it continue. Why were you so frightened of me last night? You knew I wouldn't hurt you."

"Oh, did I?" She arched her brow with mocking inquiry. "And how am I supposed to know this, Luc? You threaten things when you don't get your way. You threatened Mason's safety before I admitted to who you thought I was. You made me lie to you." It still infuriated her. "But I let it go." She threw her arms wide to indicate her former surrender. "I wasn't about to strip naked for you so you could tie me down and do whatever the hell you wanted with me."

He stared at her. He didn't argue with her, didn't answer her accusations. He merely tucked his thumbs in the waistband of his jeans and watched her for long, nerve-racking minutes. She could see a storm brewing in his eyes. Melina stilled. He looked dominant, forceful. He looked like a man unwilling to accept the answer she had given him.

She wasn't afraid of him. She was wary of the threat he represented to her heart, but last night, as darkness closed around them, she had admitted, to herself at least, that Luc would never harm her. He might infuriate her. He might drive her insane with his complete confidence in what he thought he was doing, especially when he was wrong. But he would never force himself on her.

"Who raped you?" He finally asked the question she had been dreading.

God, why did this man, of all men, have to be the one her heart had set itself on? If it had just been lust, maybe it would have been easier to handle. But the moment she met him, despite his fury, she had been drawn to him. In the months after that, all she learned about him had only increased her fascination with him. Now, spending the days with him, seeing his quiet humor and dealing with his stubbornness was turning her into a fool. A fool because she could feel her emotions peaking, edging toward him, yearning for him.

"Because I'm not ready to spread my thighs and invite you in, then I've been raped?" She crossed her arms over her chest, praying now for an interruption. Any kind of interruption would be nice.

He advanced on her. There was no way to retreat. The table behind her came against her rear as Luc pressed against her front. This time, when his hands gripped her hips she knew there would be no escape from him.

"Cat." His head lowered, his gaze dark, deliberate, as his lips stopped within a breath of hers. "Tell me why I care," he whispered, staring at her somberly, his voice filled with his own confusion, his own need for answers. "Tell me why the thought of your terror last night has driven me insane to find an explanation for it. And tell me why in the hell all I can think about is how to ease those fears long enough to get you beneath me and show you I would never hurt you."

Lust slammed into her womb. Melina's eyes widened at the hard, convulsive shudder of hunger that rippled through it. She swallowed tightly, fighting for breath. Fear was the last thing on her mind. All she could think about now was the sheer, unbridled hunger glittering in his eyes and the liquid heat pooling in her vagina.

And he knew it. He knew what he did to her. Knew how damned hot he could make her.

"You're imagining things." She cleared her throat nervously, trying to push away from him, desperate to escape the building desire.

"I watched you wax this damned table," he whispered, his lips glancing hers, freezing her in place. "Bent over, that tight little ass bouncing around, and all I could think about was stretching you across it..."

He lifted her. Melina gasped, gripping his hands as he set her on the table and quickly moved between her thighs.

"Luc." She meant for the words to come out as a protest, not the plea that it seemed to be.

"I wanted to make a meal out of you on this damned table," he growled, baring his teeth in a tight grimace. "And all I could think of was the fear in your eyes last night and how much I hated knowing you were frightened of me. That, and cursing myself for letting my own lust interfere in what should be a punishment rather than a vacation for you." His voice deepened in self-disgust and bemusement.

"Yeah, us naughty girls definitely shouldn't have any fun." She meant it to come out with a wealth of sarcasm, not the sultry tone it was wrapped in.

She couldn't forget the episode in the washroom. Couldn't get it out of her mind and couldn't make her body accept that this man was the wrong man for her heart. Her hormones just didn't give a damn. This was the one they wanted.

His eyelids lowered, giving him a drowsy, sensually dangerous appearance as his hands tightened on her hips.

'Don't tempt me," he whispered.

Tempt him? What the hell did he think he was doing to her? He was killing her. There was no fear of him, which left only the need. She wondered if she would be safer being frightened of him. Because she was just confident enough of her safety, and his desire for her, that her own need to tempt him in return surged ahead of any caution she may have displayed.

"Hmm. Admit who I am, Luc, and I might help you with that," she murmured, almost shocked at the impish impulse to torment him now. "Come on, big boy, tell me what I want to hear."

His eyes flared, his cheeks flushing as his breathing began to match hers.

"You're playing a very dangerous game, sweetheart." The rough warning only made her braver.

For a moment, she wondered at her own daring. Never would she have attempted to spar with another man in this manner, especially not in the past two years. But this was Luc. She had dreamed about him for years, lusted for him, ached for him.

She licked her lips slowly, staring back at him sensually.

"Who am I, Luc?" she asked him, her thighs softening against his hips as she fought a whimper of longing. His jeans-covered cock settled tighter against her pussy, a hard, thick wedge of heat that made her clit swell in need and her vagina ache in emptiness.

His eyes narrowed. The cloudy gray was nearly black now, his expression slack and filled with hunger as he stared at her moist lips.

"A minx," he growled, though a smile edged his lips. "One who's going to end up spanked if she isn't careful."

"Hmm. Hurt me so good." She licked her lips, pushing her luck and knowing it. But damned if he didn't look hot as hell. He was staring at her as though he could consume her at any minute. Lust and perhaps even a shade of confusion filled his expression.

"You like pushing your luck, don't you?" he asked her softly as he moved away from her.

Nothing could dispel the heat that wrapped around her, though, as he watched her. She could feel it licking over her flesh, stoking the fires in her pussy and leaving her almost weak with arousal. She wanted to touch him more than he could ever know. But she would be damned if she would let him kidnap her *and* break her heart.

"Actually," she stated a bit regretfully, "pushing my luck has been my choice, Luc. At least, until now."

Flashing him a saucy smile she moved quickly away from him, aware she was only delaying the inevitable. She knew she couldn't hold out much longer against the sensual promise he represented. She only hoped that when the time came, he didn't whisper Maria's name. That would be one insult she didn't think she could bear.

≈ * * * *

Luc couldn't push aside his certainty that Catarina's fear had somehow been rooted in sexual violence. Though her good humor restored itself quickly, he could glimpse the shadows in her eyes, the lie spilling from her lips. He knew she was evading him.

Going to bed with her was hell, though. Dressed in another of his shirts that night, she pulled the blankets to her chin and went quickly to sleep. Luc was left to stare into the darkness, aroused and confused by the woman he was sharing his bed with. There was no doubt by now that she wasn't taking drugs. Withdrawal was a son of a bitch and impossible to hide. Catarina wasn't in withdrawal. And she sure as hell wasn't taking anything.

He didn't like being confused. And he sure as hell didn't understand the strange emotions that were beginning to fill him. He wanted to believe she wasn't Maria. He found himself daily attempting to come up with reasons why Joe might have lied to him. He was attempting to fool himself, and it wasn't sitting well with him.

Confirming his suspicions would have to wait until he could talk to the other man, though. Each time Luc had called him in the past few days he had been unavailable, which only roused Luc's suspicions that much more.

He sighed tiredly, thumped his pillow and closed his eyes. Sleep would have to come soon. If not, he would make himself insane trying to make sense of it all. But one thing was for certain, this was not the Maria he had expected. If she was Maria.

* * * * *

Melina awoke in the least likely position. She had grown used to waking up draped across Luc's chest, but never like this.

One of her legs had crossed over his, her knee bent, resting uncomfortably close to the center of his thighs. His leg was pressed firmly to the mound of her pussy and as she awoke, she realized in mortification that she had been slowly rubbing herself against him.

Now how did she get herself out of this one? Better yet, how had she managed to get herself into it?

She tried to keep her breathing slow and steady, to ignore the heat building in the depths of her cunt. She had never felt so moist, so on fire there. Her clit was sensitized, swollen, and when Luc shifted against her she caught her breath at the sudden pleasure that whipped through it.

His hand tightened in her hair, the fingers of the other smoothing against the bare flesh of her side where it had burrowed beneath her shirt. The pads of his fingers were calloused, warm, and the feel of them pressing lightly against her skin had her fighting to control the shiver that raced up her spine.

She could feel excitement sizzling over her flesh, pleasure and need mixing in her bloodstream until she could barely breathe for it. One of her hands lay flat against his hard abdomen only inches from where the bulbous head of his cock had risen past the soft elastic of his briefs. A small, pearly drop of pre-come glistened on the tip of it as it throbbed erotically.

Melina knew the minute he became aware of their positions. His stomach tensed, his heart began to race furiously beneath her ear. She could feel the sexual tension heating his big body now and the careful control he used as his hand flattened against her hip.

"Better move," he whispered with drowsy amusement. "I'm about two seconds from doing something stupid."

Melina lay still. How long had she fantasized about him like this? His arms wrapped around her. his hunger heating the air. It hadn't made sense. even before she met him, and it made less sense now. But she couldn't deny the incredible pleasure or the desire that sang through her blood at his touch.

His fingers moved, playing lightly with the band of her lacy, French-cut panties as she stared at the dark head of his cock in fascination. The feel of it against her lips that first day had been a temptation that only her fury had allowed her to deny. He had no idea how much she wanted to open her lips and take him inside her mouth. Taste the thick moisture that had gleamed on the tip, and lick the rounded head slowly.

She moistened her lips in hunger.

"Cat," he warned her tightly as her fingers flexed against his hard abdomen. "This is a dangerous game, baby."

His voice was tense, his big body almost vibrating beneath her.

Melina turned her head a fraction, her lips pressing beneath his breastbone as her tongue peeked out to taste.

"Fuck." He tightened as though he had taken a lash rather than a small warm lick.

Fascinated at his response, she let her fingers caress the flesh of his lower stomach as her lips and tongue caressed him again. All the while she kept her gaze on the thick erection below.

The mushroomed head had darkened, rising toward her as his hips jerked, and she imagined it was pleading for attention.

The little slitted eye spilled another lush drop of creamy moisture, tempting her to taste.

There was no fear as she felt the leashed arousal in his body. He was careful, controlled. And she was hungry for him. There was none of the previous anger or male dominance, there was only hot, thick need filling the air now. The same need she had dreamed of — ached for — for the past two years.

"Cat," Luc groaned, the sound vibrating against her body as his breathing accelerated. "You have two choices, baby. You can move or accept the consequences."

The consequences being his touch, his passion.

Her hand slid lower, her finger reaching out hesitantly to slide over the moist, turgid head of his cock.

His indrawn breath was a sound of excruciating sensation as a throttled groan slipped past his throat. His hips lifted, pressing his erection closer as her tongue flickered out to once again taste the flesh below his breastbone. She watched as her finger smoothed over the hot male erection, feeling the heat and hardness that awaited her there.

Her clit throbbed in demand, a piercing sensation of unbearable need streaking into her womb. Melina pressed against the hard leg, her eyes nearly closing at the rasp of pleasure.

"Cat," he growled. "Sugar, if you don't want to be fucked, you'll stop now."

She smiled slowly. She did want to be fucked, though. Maria had only taken his cock into her mouth, she knew that from her sister's snide comments. But Melina wanted so much more. She wanted all of him, every inch of his hard body covering her, taking her, making her scream with pleasures she had only heard about.

Shudders of sensation worked over her body as she let her finger slide idly around the crest of his erection. It throbbed, darkening further as she pressed her pussy tighter against his knee.

"Cat, what do you want, baby?" His voice deepened as one hand tangled in her hair, the gentle pressure against her head encouraging her to go lower, to draw closer.

"Luc," she whispered beseechingly.

"Whatever you want, baby," he whispered as the bulging head came closer, his hand urging her down the hard muscles of his stomach as she whimpered in a hungry desperate need she hadn't known she was capable of.

She wanted to taste him. She wanted to know how hard and hot his cock would be within her mouth, feel the hard pulse of life beneath the tight flesh and know it was for her.

Melina was but a breath away, fighting to control the hard tremors of response quaking through her flesh as her tongue reached out and licked slowly over the small eye that pierced the head of his cock.

Oh yes. Hot. Hard. He was all male, huge and ready for her.

"Cat..." The hand at her head grew heavier. "Take it, baby. Put that hot little mouth over my cock before I die for it."

She could have possibly denied herself. But Luc? She had dreamed of him for too long, lusted after him through too many of her own darkest fantasies. There was nothing he could do to her that she would object to. Nothing that he would want that she could deny him. Not here. Not now.

Her mouth opened, drawing the bulging head of his erection between her lips as her tongue began to stroke and caress, tasting the small drops of semen that escaped it.

"Oh hell..." His hips lifted as a sound of sharp surprise left his lips. "There you go, baby. Ah yes, Catarina, suck my cock, baby. Take everything you want."

* * * * *

She was going to kill him. What the hell had happened? This was not the experienced little cocksucker who had swallowed his dick like nobody's business two years before. This was sensual, sexual—a hungry little vixen consuming his erection. And she was destroying him. No experience here, but none was required. Only hot, wet suckling strokes that drove him to the very edge of his control.

Her cool, silken hand cupped his testicles, tested their weight gently a second before her mouth slid lower, the flared head of his cock nearly touching her throat as she began to suck him with hungry abandon. Small, lusty mewls escaped her and vibrated on his erection, nearly sending him over the edge.

"Cat. Baby." He clenched his teeth as he fought to hold onto his control.

His hands tangled in her soft hair, holding her to him as he pushed his cock deeper into her mouth, glorying in the sounds of the pleasure she was taking from an act that drove him steadily closer to ecstasy.

She moved, though her mouth never left the shaft throbbing heatedly beneath her touch. She came to her knees, moving between his thighs as he lifted the curtain of hair to see his cock disappearing between her tightly stretched lips. Her eyes glittered up at him with drowsy sexuality, her cheeks flushing and any control he may have had was shot in that second.

"I'm going to come," he growled as she worked his flesh with moist hunger. "Cat." He could feel the fire arcing up his spine. "Baby. I'm going to lose it."

His cock flexed and her eyes darkened further. His hands tightened in her hair as his balls drew up against the base of his shaft and he felt his semen surging from the very depths of his soul.

"Fuck." His lips drew back, his eyes threatening to close, but he didn't want to miss so much as a moment of this.

He felt his seed erupt from the tip in hard, jetting pulses of release. Her eyes widened, her lips paused for a bare second before she shuddered, moaning wildly, swallowed and began to draw on him again as each pulse thereafter was greedily consumed.

"Luc." She licked her lips as she drew back from him long seconds later.

She was wild—her eyes glittered feverishly, the flush of arousal on her face now spread to her hard-tipped breasts, making him insane to fuck her. If he didn't get his cock inside her, he would go mad from the desire.

Chapter Nine

ॐ

Had anything ever been so wild? So impossible to deny? Melina gasped as Luc bore her back upon the mattress. Each inch of his broad, calloused palms smoothed over her flesh before he stretched her arms above her head and came over her slowly.

"I keep telling myself to wait." His voice rasped over her nerve endings, sending a shudder of pleasure down her spine as her womb convulsed in need.

His body was taut, glistening with perspiration as he braced himself above her, his thighs on either side of hers, his hands moving slowly back down her upraised arms. Melina couldn't control her breathing or the response surging through her. She was trembling with the need to have him fill her tormented cunt. Her clit was a pulsing knot of painful desire now, the slick heat coating the curves of her mons, intensifying its sensitivity.

"Why wait?" She was panting, staring up at him, shuddering as his hands slowly framed her swollen breasts.

His expression was drowsy, his black hair falling over his forehead as his gray eyes darkened to almost black.

"Because I want to make you as hot and as crazy as I am right now," he whispered, his voice so sexy, so sensually dark and deep that she whimpered at the sound.

She could almost climax from the sound of his rough voice alone. It was powerful, hinting at forbidden secrets and ecstatic pleasures only guessed at.

"You mean I'm not yet?" she moaned weakly, her fingers clenching in the sheet above her head as he continued to stare intently at her firm, peaked breasts. "Luc, if I get any hotter, we're both going to go up in flames."

He raised his eyes. Pure carnal hunger reflected in his gaze.

"Yeah." He bared his teeth in a tight grimace. "We just might at that."

Her breath caught in her chest, pushing her breasts closer to him as his thumbs raked over the sensitive tips. Pleasure shuddered through her. It was exquisite, the sharp, racing spears of sensation that pierced her nipples and sped to her womb. She caught her lower lip between her teeth, fighting to hold back the cries that threatened to erupt from her throat.

She could feel the pleasure from that simple touch swirling through her body, building the growing band of tension in her womb tighter. He watched her as his thumbs rasped the tender peaks again. His eyes gleamed in satisfaction as she flinched from the extreme sensations.

"So responsive," he muttered as his head began to lower, his tongue moistening his lips a second before it curled around one taut peak.

"Luc," she almost screamed as her hands loosened the sheets and flew up to grip his damp shoulders.

Melina arched involuntarily, sizzling excitement bowed her body as he drew the tip into his mouth, applying a firm, strong suction that had her writhing beneath it. It was too intense, too much pleasure. Her eyes closed, her hips straining toward the length of his cock lying against her lower thigh.

A second later, he freed her from the exquisite torture, his gaze rising as her eyes opened drowsily.

"God, you're beautiful," he whispered as his lips moved to hers. "So beautiful you take my breath away. But you know that, don't you, Cat?"

Guttural and intense, the words didn't matter as much as his lips smoothing sensually over hers, creating a rasping pleasure that had her begging for more.

"Please, Luc," she whispered as he kissed the corner of her lips while his hands cupped her breasts, his fingers plumping and stroking her nipples, sending arcs of diabolical pleasure straight to her aching cunt.

He licked her lips as she opened for him, her breathing hard and erratic, need slicing along her nerve endings as she fought against his strength. He held her still, arched over her, his bigger body controlling her smaller one easily.

"Let me pleasure you, Cat." His lips caressed hers as he spoke. "Let me show you how much I love hearing your cries and your pleas. Let me show you how good it can be, baby."

He was going to kill her. The kiss, when it finally came, was greedy, hot and hungry as his lips and tongue tore through any resistance she may have thought she had. His hands roamed over her body, one smoothing along her tummy as he shifted her legs and spread them slowly.

Melina gasped for breath as her hips rose. His eyes, shielded by thick lashes, watched her with heated lust as his fingers slid between her thighs. Melina's eyes widened as his fingers circled her swollen clit. The touch sent her system into a riot of sensations as she fought to breathe through the pleasure exploding along her senses.

"God you taste good here, Cat."

A sharp detonation of pleasure exploded in her womb at his words. She jerked, whimpering against the intensity of it. Her hands clenched on his shoulders as he spread her thighs further, moving lower along her body.

His tongue swiped through the bare, plump curves then curled around her clit an instant before he drew the little nubbin into his mouth. He hummed against it, a sound of lust and satisfaction as her hips surged closer to his hot mouth.

Tightening his hands on her hips, Luc held her in place as he began his campaign to drive her crazy with the slow, hungry licks and carnal sips he took from her weeping pussy.

"So good..." he muttered as he traveled lower, his tongue rimming the entrance to her vagina. "So sweet and hot..." He invaded her slowly as Melina's tumultuous wail echoed around them.

She scrambled to hold on to the last shred of control. Fought to hold back, to enjoy without losing herself in his touch, but from the first caress she had been a goner and she knew it. When he lifted her thighs, opening her further, and plunged his tongue into the snug cavern of her cunt she gave up the last measure of sanity.

His tongue fucked deep inside her burning pussy, pumping into her with fierce strokes as he threw her higher, deeper into the maelstrom awaiting her. Whipping arcs of heat flickered through her, heating her flesh, sensitizing each nerve ending as she strained closer to the inferno building in her womb. She hadn't imagined it could be like this. That a touch could consume her, that a man's mouth alone could destroy her.

"Luc. Oh God. I can't stand it..." Melina thrashed beneath him, her voice rising in reaction to the extreme pleasure rushing through her. "Luc..."

She was terrified, exhilarated, yearning and yet desperate to draw back. The conflicting impulses were shattering her sense of reality.

"No." She nearly screamed the word as he jerked back from her, moving quickly between her thighs as he bent across her and opened the small drawer in the table beside the bed.

"Condom," he gasped.

At the same time, the thick head of his cock nudged into the snug entrance of her pussy. They froze, breaths rasping, lust sizzling around them.

"Fuck," he seemed to wheeze as his hips jerked, only to bury him marginally deeper.

Melina felt the convulsive clenching of her vagina, the hungry milking motion of her muscles as Luc's flesh stretched them tight. Bare, hot flesh buried inside her. A danger. She panted, fighting not to tempt the control he was trying to impose over his big body. But it was so good.

"Luc…" She jerked as she felt the head throb within her, driving him deeper.

"Condom," he rasped again, jerking one free of the drawer a second before he drove deep inside her gripping flesh, tearing through the thin veil of innocence and piercing her soul with a pleasure she knew would change her forever.

Reality no longer existed in any way, shape or form. There was only this. Luc buried within her, hot and steel-hard, fucking her with deep driving strokes as she screamed out beneath him. Melina's legs wrapped around his pounding hips, her hands gripping his shoulders as he held her close, lunging forcefully into her wet sheath.

Each stroke sank to the very depths of her cunt, caressing sensitive tissue, rasping delicate nerves until with a final, weak cry Melina fought the final battle with the orgasm overtaking her and lost. She exploded beneath him, the white-hot streaks of ecstasy surging through her body as her pussy tightened spasmodically around his plunging cock.

A second later she felt Luc's release, hot, hard jets of semen spilling into her as he groaned her name roughly, his voice tortured, dark and hungry. The heated warmth shattered her again, sending her plunging headlong into a smaller but no less destructive orgasm that left her weak and terribly frightened that she had just given this man more than her body. She had given him her heart.

* * * * *

She wasn't Maria Catarina Angeles. Luc held her close in his arms, feeling her soft breathing against his chest, her body relaxed in exhaustion, and admitted the truth she had been trying desperately to convince him of desperately. She wasn't Maria. She was Melina.

Which meant Joe had lied to him. But why?

He smoothed back the fall of red-gold curls and stared down at her sleeping face somberly. What the hell had he done? He had somehow managed to fall in love with a woman and not even know who she was. It was terrifying. It was— Hell, he was in deep.

He drew in a deep breath and ignored the erection pleading for another dose of rapture. Nothing had ever come close to the pleasure he had experienced as he plunged his cock inside her snug pussy unprotected. He had been a goner the minute he had unintentionally buried the head of his erection inside her. He had tried, though, he assured himself. Hell, he had been clutching the condom in his hand even as he spurted his seed deep inside the hot depths of her vagina.

And she was a virgin. A fucking virgin. What the hell had he done?

What now?

God, she was pretty. Now he understood the innocence in her eyes, the unlined, unblemished skin of her face. Her laughter, unaffected and so often freely given. Her joy in that black mouse catcher she gave so much affection to.

He doubted she had ever taken a drug in her life. There were no tracks on her arms, no furtive behavior, no withdrawal. There was none of it, because she wasn't Maria.

What the fuck was Joe trying to pull on him? Luc frowned heavily as he gently disengaged himself from his sleeping lover and pulled on a pair of loose pajama bottoms before leaving the bedroom quietly. Joe had called several times the first two days to check up on *Maria*. Luc snorted. The other man knew what the hell he had done, now Luc wanted to know why. And the reason had better be a damned good one.

He slipped downstairs and into his study, his anger building with every step. There had been times that he had been unjust in his treatment of her. He hadn't gone easy on her. The house was spotless, dust was now afraid to enter, and the place smelled like her. The tempting subtle scent of woman seemed steeped into every nook and cranny of the house.

Sighing wearily, he picked up the phone and quickly dialed Joe's number. Several rings later, the other man answered.

"You have two minutes to tell me why you fucking lied to me. If the explanation isn't satisfactory, then your voice will rival Melina's for soft feminine sweetness."

There was a long silence on the line. Shock and sudden comprehension filled the line.

"Fuck," Joe finally said. "No matter what you do to me later, Luc, don't let her out of your sight right now. She's in more danger than you know…"

* * * * *

Every time she said no, they hit her again…

She was beaten so badly we didn't think she would make it…

The doctors doubt she'll ever conceive due to the internal injuries…

She was tricked, Luc. Maria didn't spend that week in jail that you demanded, Melina did…

Luc pushed shaking fingers through his hair as the words replayed through his mind. His fault. It had been his fault that an innocent woman had nearly died. The same woman who had called him, apologizing for what had been done to him, her voice whispering in regret and sadness.

The woman he had confronted in her parents' living room hadn't been Maria. He remembered his fury when he had faced her, seeing the confusion and fear in her eyes when her parents introduced her as Maria. The memory of the awareness that had sizzled between them that day had haunted him over the years. For some reason, his cock had strained in urgent demand when her soft lips had trembled into a self-conscious smile that day.

He had allowed his rage free. His voice hard, harsh, his words damning as he watched her face drain of color.

You'll pay for it, Ms. Angeles, he had warned her furiously. *By God, I'll make sure you spend time in jail if it's the last thing I do in my life.*

At the time, he had ignored the bleak pain that filled her expression. Her gaze had dropped, her soft lips pressing together a second after a betraying quiver had shaken them. He had wanted to haul her into his arms and apologize, which only made him madder at the time.

Now he knew why. Some instinct, some primitive part of his mind, had recognized the fact that he was punishing the wrong woman. That he was punishing *his* woman.

Damn. Where had that thought come from?

Shaking his head, Luc rose to his feet and paced from his office through the darkened house and back upstairs to his bedroom. She was still sleeping in his bed, curled in the middle, her hair tumbling around her head and shoulders like a fall of silk.

She hadn't been raped. Thank God. Out of all the horror she had faced at least she had been saved the destructive pain of having been raped by her own sex. His fingers clenched as pain threatened to swamp him. He had put her there. Unintentionally perhaps, but he had been to blame all the same.

He sat down in the wingback chair beside his bed and stared at her. He simply watched her sleep, realizing he had never done that before. He had never watched a woman sleep nor would he have thought he would have gained any pleasure from it. But he did. Seeing the steady rise and fall of her full breasts, the way her lips parted just the tiniest bit, the small shadows her light colored, surprisingly lush lashes cast on her cheeks.

She was exquisite. In admitting that she wasn't the shell of a woman he had thought she was, he was able to look beyond what he thought was there to the woman beneath. There was no longer the conflict that had warred between his head and his heart where she was concerned. Now, if only he could find a way to keep her safe.

Maria was missing and, with her, two of the dangerous drug runners she associated with. According to Joe's information, she was looking for Melina. There was only one reason for Maria to be searching so hard for her sister. To find a way to ensure that Melina endured the coming prison sentence rather than her.

God, what kind of monsters raised a child to believe her sibling could always stand in front of trouble for her? What hold did Maria have over her parents' hearts to have allowed something like that to happen? How did a sister—a twin—turn so dark and black against the other? It made no sense to Luc.

He knew twins, the August twins, especially. Men whose battles had left them, for a while, scarred and almost broken. But they had always protected one another, and their older brother, Cade, had protected them all. They were brothers. There were no questions of loyalty or determination to help each other. It was a part of them. How had Maria managed to be born without that innate love for her sister?

And Melina. How had she endured it? To be betrayed, not just by her twin, but by her parents? They had left her in that fucking jail cell while they vacationed in the Bahamas, accepting Maria's word that her sister had been released. Accepting, without question, the word of a known liar, thief and drug addict.

Melina had nearly died. He stared at her, horror streaking through his system as he noted the almost fragile build of her slender body, the delicacy of her bones. She had been beaten so badly that she had received two broken ribs, suffered internal bleeding and contusions, scarring that might never heal. She had been only minutes from death when Joe had carried her into the emergency room of a local hospital. For days, it had been touch and go.

Hell, what had made her even fight to live? What did she have to hold on to at that time?

One of the inmates heard her scream your name... That had surprised Luc, when Joe told him that. Why would she scream for him? It had been his fault she was there to begin with. But she had screamed his name, cried out for him.

He wiped his hands over his face as fury consumed him. God help him, he prayed he never had a chance to wrap his hands around her father's neck, or her sister's. He feared he'd kill them himself for what they had done to Melina.

Rising to his feet, he shed his pajama bottoms and returned to the bed. He pulled her gently into his arms, surrounding her, holding her to him. She moved against him with a murmur of satisfaction, pillowing her head on his chest as he pressed his lips to her hair.

She was where she belonged. In his arms. His bed. His life. He'd be damned if he ever let her go. She might as well get used to being his captive, because she had stolen his heart and there wasn't a chance he was going to let her leave with it.

Chapter Ten

🔊

Melina slipped out of bed the next morning, aware of Luc's stormy eyes opening, his silence as she gathered up her clothes and headed for the shower. He didn't speak and she was thankful for that. She wasn't entirely certain she could handle a conversation with him right now.

Never in her life had she experienced a pleasure as astounding as what she had felt in his arms the night before. She shivered beneath the pounding force of the hot shower, her eyes closing as she fought the sensitivity of her own body. She ached in places that she didn't know could ache. Her breasts were tender, the snowy globes marked here and there with the reddened proof of his passion. Even her hips carried one of the rosy brands from his mouth.

Her thighs clenched as she felt her pussy ripple in remembered pleasure. His mouth had lingered there, kissing her so intimately she had thought she would die from the sensations. If she wasn't extremely careful, she could become addicted to his touch, his kiss.

She shook her head, attempting to dispel the memory of his touch, and quickly finished her shower. She had to figure out what to do now. She hadn't expected things to progress to this point. She had never imagined she would be so weak as to allow Luc to actually take her while he still believed she was Maria. Yet, she had.

Rinsing quickly, she turned off the shower and dried her body roughly, wondering if there was any way to erase the feel of him from her flesh. The heat and hardness, strong thighs parting hers, his cock — so hard and thick — working inside her.

Melina sighed before dressing in one of the soft cotton summer dresses Luc had packed, and dried her hair. She was so screwed, and she knew it. She was falling helplessly, hopelessly in love with a man who thought she was her sister. Who believed to the very core of his being that she was a thief, a drug addict, a woman who would stand by and allow murder to be committed.

Her fists clenched at the thought as she stared back at the image reflected in the mirror. She didn't even look that much like her sister anymore. The basic coloring was the same, but Maria's lifestyle had hardened her, had shaped her face, tightened her mouth until there was little left of the woman she could have been.

The little enforced stay on Luc's ranch had been nice. It had given Melina a chance to think, to find her bearings after her parents disowned her. It had given her precious days to find a balance between the child she had been and the woman she was. Time to figure out the chaos that had existed in her heart and in her mind.

She loved Luc Jardin. She had known, two years ago, that she could love him. When she had first stared into the dangerous depths of his stormy eyes, saw the flicker of pain and rage that chased across his expression, she had known she could love him. Had known he could become the most important person in her life. If she wasn't who she was. If Maria hadn't gotten to him first.

But she wouldn't let her love turn her into something or someone she wasn't.

Taking a deep breath she opened the door, stepping into the bedroom with every intention of confronting Luc. Instead, she drew stock-still. He was still in the bed, the sheet pulled to his hips, and on his chest sat Mason.

"This black mouse chaser of yours is holding me prisoner." She saw his banked smile, heard the amusement in his voice as his fingers ruffled the cat just under his wide chin.

Could any man look sexier than he did at that moment?

"Thought you didn't like cats, Mr. Hardass," she grunted as she walked over to the bed and lifted Mason into her arms.

The animal purred in contentment, settling into her hold as he stared back at Luc with a hint of feline arrogance.

"I don't." There was that controlled quirk to his lips again. "I hate the little beasts."

He stared up at her, his gaze becoming drowsy, suggestive. "Put him down and come here. You can make it up to me for being nice to him."

She couldn't help the flicker of her gaze to where the sheet began to tent at his thighs. Melina swallowed tightly at the knowledge that he was becoming aroused right before her eyes.

"Don't you have work to do?" she finally asked, backing away from the bed and the temptation he represented. "I thought you had horses to train or something."

He sighed heavily, though the amusement in his eyes only grew. "Or something," he agreed, though she had a feeling he wasn't talking about the horses.

"Then maybe you better get to it." She turned away from him, trembling, wanting to lie back in that big bed with him so badly she couldn't stand it.

She took a step away from the bed, desperate to escape him and the carnal hunger rising inside her. She wasn't expecting him to move so quickly. His arm wrapped around her waist and before she could do more than squeak and release a startled Mason she was flat on her back on the mattress staring up at him.

Just that fast the blood was racing through her body, excitement and exhilaration thundering through her system as he stared down at her with a lazy sexuality that had her toes practically curling.

"Maybe I should get to it then," he agreed, his husky voice washing over her nerve endings and sensitizing them further.

With her hands braced against his bare chest, she could do little about the bare expanse of her thighs that his hand revealed as he smoothed the soft material of her skirt further above her legs.

"That wasn't exactly what I meant, Luc." Her fingertips curled against the hard pad of muscle beneath them as she felt his other hand move beneath her head.

"Do you know how good you felt last night, Cat?" he asked her, stilling the objections rising to her lips. "I wasn't even able to protect you, you stole my control so quickly."

Melina stared up at him, seeing a softening in his eyes that hadn't been there before last night. As though he had eliminated some barrier that had been there previously. He watched her in a way she had thought he never would. There was no hint of accusation, no shadows of suspicion. There was amusement, arousal, and a heat that blazed between them like an inferno rushing quickly out of control.

"Luc, this isn't going to work." She was not going to arch closer to him. She fought the need to rub against him in a sensual imitation of Mason begging for attention. But it was so hard not to. His body was sleek and hard as he lay against her, holding her to the bed.

His hand rested on her lower thigh, fingertips smoothing an intricate design into the flesh above her knee and slowly upward. Her thighs parted, though she was certain she meant to keep them tightly clenched.

"Sure it's going to work baby." His head lowered, his teeth catching her lower lip gently as he stared back at her, the hunger in his gaze growing.

When he released her, his tongue smoothed over the curves. Melina parted her lips for him. She wanted his kiss, wanted his touch. What was the point in lying to herself or to him? She was weak and he was so damned tempting. Her time here would come to an end soon enough, surely there was no harm…

"No, Luc." She shook her head, pulling back. There was more harm awaiting her if she gave in to him. He already held her heart, soon he would hold her soul.

"Hmm. Captives aren't allowed to say no," he told her, his voice rumbling playfully in his throat as he moved closer to her.

His hard chest raked over her cloth-covered breasts. The cotton did nothing to stop her nipples from peaking, growing hard and tight as they pressed demandingly against the bodice of her dress.

"Aren't you taking this too far?" She tried to still the weakening desire that flooded her pussy. God, she needed him.

"Nope." His fingers clenched in her hair as his lips moved to her neck, smoothing over the sensitive flesh just beneath her ear. The shudder that rocked her body would have been embarrassing if Luc hadn't groaned so roughly. "Taking it too far is tying you to the bed and listening to you beg while I paddle that sweet ass until it's rosy." Her thighs clenched. That should *not* be turning her on. "Then, parting the pretty little red curves and watching as I work my cock inside your tight little ass."

She could feel her pussy creaming, her anus clenching. This was perverted, she told her traitorous body. Not that it cared. She was fighting to breathe now, panting beneath the fingers that had moved to unbutton the bodice of her dress.

"Maybe that wouldn't be going too far, though," he mused as he folded back the material and bared her swollen breasts. "Do you know how hot, how hard, the thought of that makes me, Cat?"

No one had ever talked to her so explicitly. Especially not while they watched her face, hands going over her body, gauging the depth of her arousal.

"Would you beg me?" he asked her as his fingers gripped a hard nipple, working it between them, tightening to the point that pleasure and pain blurred and sent her body rioting into a plane of sensation that she had never known existed.

"You're killing me." Melina was well aware she didn't have the experience to combat the sexuality he was turning on her. "You know you are, Luc."

His smile was sensual, tight, a grimace of extreme lust and hunger.

"Tell me what you want," he whispered, his fingers tightening on her nipple again as she gasped and arched to him. "You like it, baby. See how much you like it."

He repeated the move and Melina swore she was going to orgasm from that sensation alone.

"Yes," she moaned brokenly. "You know I like it."

"What else do you like?" His head lowered, his tongue curling around the reddened peak of her breast. "Tell me, baby. What else do you like?"

He didn't give her time to answer. His mouth covered the tip of her breast, drawing it deep inside his mouth and suckling at it with sensual abandon. His teeth rasped the delicate point, his tongue licked until Melina dug her fingers into his hair, holding him to her, arching closer as he insinuated himself between her legs.

Traitorous body. She whimpered as her thighs parted for him, her hips rising, a keening cry of need echoing around her as his cock pressed full length against her pussy.

"This isn't fair," she panted, but she arched her neck as his lips moved around to her throat, then her collarbone, moving inexorably closer to her swollen breasts. "You're supposed to hate me. You can't hate me and want to fuck me."

He stopped then. His entire body stilled for several long seconds before his head raised, his eyes blazing into hers.

"Oh baby, hatred is the last thing I feel for you," he said, the dark cadence of his voice throbbing with lust and something more. That something more, undefined and yet hidden, had her senses reeling.

How could he do this to her? Was it fair that love should weaken her even as it made her feel stronger, taller, able to face whatever she must to hold his heart? Even when she knew his heart would never be hers.

"You're dangerous," she whispered, her hand moving to touch the swollen pad of his lips as she stared back at him, knowing she couldn't turn him away, knowing she couldn't do anymore than love him while she could.

His tongue swiped along her fingers an instant before he gripped them with his teeth.

"Let's see how dangerous we can get together then."

His hand reached down, gripped the side of her panties and ripped them from her body. Melina's eyes widened but before she could snap out a derogatory comment about cowboys and manners he was sliding his cock inside her.

Melina stilled, her eyes closing as she fought to breathe and to concentrate on the slow, sensuous glide of his flesh. Inch by inch he pressed his cock inside her, stretching the sensitive tissue, searing her with a heat and hunger that stole her sanity. It was a pleasure unlike any she had ever known before. A pleasure she couldn't deny.

"You're killing me." She was fighting to breathe, to survive the white-hot lash of pleasure streaking through her.

"Then I'm killing us both," he growled. "Damn, baby, you're so hot, so fucking tight it's all I can do to hold on."

He was buried in her to the hilt. A hot throbbing presence that filled her pussy to overflowing and sent her senses spinning. Then he was moving. Thrusting hard and deep, his hard breaths echoing around her as she held on to him with desperate fingers. Her senses were spinning, her body blazing.

She wrapped her legs around his hips, crying out beneath him as the tension began to tighten, the conflagration threatening to destroy her.

"Luc!" She screamed his name as he nipped at her shoulder, almost growling against her flesh.

"I have you, baby," he groaned, his voice rough, hard hands holding her to him, his lean hips moving harder, faster, plunging his erection through the tight muscles and delicate gripping tissue that enclosed his cock. "Fuck. Fuck. I have you, baby. Always. Always."

She shattered. Every cell in her body exploded in a fury of ecstasy at his words. Her pussy convulsed around him, clamping down to hold him deep, tight, as he began to jerk with his own release.

"Sweet Cat." He lowered his head to her breast, his big body trembling with pleasure. "Sweet. So perfect. So fucking perfect."

And it was. Perfect.

The aftermath was a gentle easing, a soft glide from chaos to the peace of Luc's bed where he had rolled to his side and pulled her into his arms. One hand held her head against his chest, the other clasped her hip. His heart was still racing, but so was hers.

"It can't last forever," she said aloud, a somber sadness threatening to disturb the cloud of pleasure that enfolded them.

"It can." He sighed. "But only if you want it to, baby. Only if you want it to."

Chapter Eleven

🔊

Now that he knew the truth, Luc found it harder and harder to hold back from Melina. He could see her emotions clearly in her beautiful eyes, in her soft face. She was falling in love with him—he refused to accept any other alternative. But he also knew the time was swiftly approaching when he was going to let her know that he knew the truth. He would have already, but he had a feeling she would pack her bags and head out just as fast as he had kidnapped her to begin with. That, he couldn't allow.

Whatever the hell Maria was up to, it couldn't be anything good. Joe was worried sick, more concerned with Melina than with the threat Luc had made to rip his damned head for lying to him. Had Joe told him the truth, he would have been more than willing to help. But not like this. Not in a way that threatened every shred of happiness Luc had ever dreamed of.

He sat on the wide front porch, watching as Melina tried to stand between Lobo and Mason. The wolf hybrid was amazingly patient with the feline invader to his home. Not that he didn't harass the fat-assed cat. He did, on a daily basis. But only if Melina was around.

Mason was growling from Melina's arms, staring down at the huge canine with a smug feline expression. Luc almost believed the wolf just wanted Melina's attention rather than a chance to harass the cat. Not that he blamed him.

"Lobo, you're as aggravating as your owner," Melina laughed as she pushed the animal back when he made a mock lunge at the cat in her arms. "Mason is not lunch. How many times do I have to tell you that?"

Neither was a warm, willing woman, but Luc had taken her for lunch before he ever got around to the sandwiches and soup she had fixed. She was addictive, he thought, watching the bunch and sway of her sweetly curved ass beneath her jeans.

Her laughter echoed around the ranch yard as Lobo grabbed at her jeans leg, growling playfully as he stared up at her.

"Luc, call this monster off." She turned to him laughter sparkling in her gem-bright eyes as she tugged back on Lobo's hold. "He's going to snack on Mason."

Her laughter was like an echo of light and beauty. Luc couldn't help but grin at the sappy thought. He stood to his feet, intent on joining the play, when Lobo suddenly released her, his body going instantly alert as he stared down the road.

"Get in the house." Luc moved quickly for Melina ignoring the confusion on her face.

"What?" She stared down the curving ranch road before turning back to Luc.

"Get in the house *now.*" He gripped her arm lightly and drew her to the porch as anger began to glitter in her eyes.

"Don't want anyone to know you kidnapped your houseguest?" she snapped, jerking away from him and stomping to the door. "Don't worry, Luc, I have a better revenge planned for your arrogant ass." She slammed the door behind her as Luc breathed out roughly and moved quickly to where Lobo stood in a guarded stance at the road.

He breathed a sigh of relief when the vehicle came into sight. The unfamiliar Jeep was the reason Lobo had reacted so quickly, not the driver behind the wheel.

"Luc, dammit, I was within a day of a killer sale." Jack jumped from the new vehicle, his long blond hair tied at the nape with a strip of leather, his white silk shirt clinging to his shoulders. "What the hell could be so important that you called me back on an emergency?"

Irritation flashed in the other man's brilliant blue eyes, his tall, corded body tense with it.

"Good to have you home, Jack." Luc grinned. "Let's go to the barn and we'll talk."

"The barn?" Jack didn't move from where he stood. "Fuck the barn. It's over a hundred in the shade here and I need a cold drink. What the hell is wrong with the house?"

Luc adjusted his Stetson carefully. "This involves an explanation." He sighed. "If you want to get out of the sun, we'll go to the barn. But you're not stepping into that house until we talk. So are you coming or not?"

Jack's eyes narrowed. They had known each other for a lot of years. Hell, they had nearly died together. There was a trust, a bond that flowed between them when danger threatened the other. They weren't brothers but they might as well have been.

"Hell. Fine." Jack sighed wearily. "But this one better be good, Luc. Damned good."

* * * * *

"You did *what?*" Jack's question rose in volume until he was almost yelling the last word.

Luc leaned back against the frame of the barn's entrance and restrained his smile. For a man who had been in more scrapes than Luc could ever hope to dive into, Jack was amazingly incredulous at Luc's daring.

"Are you aware kidnapping is a federal crime?" Jack growled furiously. "Doesn't matter the reason…"

"Yeah, well, so is stealing cars, but I remember helping your ass when you decided to try your hand at it," Luc reminded him.

Jack's eyes narrowed. "It was my fucking car," he snapped. "They stole it from me."

Luc shrugged. "They had the papers. You didn't. That makes it grand theft."

Jack grunted in irritation. "I can't believe you got messed up with that damned family again," he finally snarled. "Son of a bitch, a fucking twin sister. Just what the hell we needed."

Luc frowned at his friend's tone of voice. Jack could rage over Maria for hours and Luc would be more than happy to listen, but Melina was another matter.

"She's my woman, Jack," Luc said softly, his voice deepening. "Watch what you say."

A frown snapped into place over Jack's eyes as he stared back at him. That was Jack. He could be a mean gutter fighter when he had to be, but he could also be a hell of a strategist. Right now, he would be carefully considering the information he had, as well as the fact that Maria was now searching for her twin.

"So we protect her." Jack sighed. "Have you managed to locate the bitch yet?" he asked, obviously meaning Maria.

"Joe's working on it." Luc shrugged. "My main concern is Melina and keeping her safe. She's spitting mad at me right now, but she seems to like the ranch well enough. Until her sister is apprehended, my main concern is keeping Melina undercover here."

Jack released the leather tie that held his hair back while sighing again, roughly.

"This one could be a mess." He shook his head tiredly. "Maria is a viper, Luc. We both know that. I've kept up with rumors over the years, too, and there are a lot of them. The woman doesn't have a conscience. All she has is a hunger for drugs. She won't be easy to catch. And if she suspects her sister is here, it might not be that damned easy to keep her away."

Luc smiled coldly. "As long as I catch her," he said softly. "That's all I care about, Jack. Keeping Melina safe and making certain her sister never has a chance to use her again. These are my top priorities. Now, are you in?"

Jack stared back at him in surprise. "Of course I'm in, dammit. I don't have to like it to go along with it. I just have to be able to bitch about it. And don't you think I won't be bitching later, ole son. Hard and long. You can take that one to the bank."

And likely draw interest on it, Luc thought in amusement. Jack wasn't a man who kept his thoughts to himself until the situation required it.

"Come on to the house then. I'll introduce you. Remember, you don't know she's not Maria," he reminded Jack.

Jack grunted. "Like I could have made that mistake. I think you just didn't want to know. You weren't yourself after that meeting with her and her parents after the shooting. I had a feeling something was wrong then. I think, my friend, you might have known all along."

Luc restrained his smile. He might have. He knew damned good and well that even before the plane landed that day he had no intention of taking Maria Angeles up on her sexual offer. The desire to do so just wasn't there. She was a mean little cocksucker, but that was about it.

Melina was pure sweetness, though, head to toe. Soft and delicate, passionate. His.

He stepped to the porch, heard pots and pans rattling loudly and chuckled before opening the door. She was pissed too, which suited him fine. If she stayed a little mad for a while, then she wouldn't catch on nearly as easily to the fact that he had fallen so completely beneath her spell that he knew he would never recover from it. Now, all he had to do was convince her that she shared the madness with him.

* * * * *

Jack's arrival was a surprise to Melina. She stood in the kitchen, fighting back a sense of guilt as she watched the amused friendliness in his eyes.

"You're a sight prettier than the last time I saw you," he said, his blue eyes crinkling at the corners as he smiled down at her. "Being sober is good for you, Maria."

She clenched her teeth and shot Luc a hateful look. "I guess you neglected to inform him of exactly who I was," she snapped.

Luc grinned back at her. "No, I didn't. I told him exactly who I thought you were."

Melina sniffed sarcastically before turning back to Jack. "I don't answer to that name. You can call me Catarina or Melina, your choice. But call me Maria and you'll be taking your life into your own hands."

Jack scratched his ear thoughtfully. "Hell, darlin', I think just being around you would be a danger. But you're damned sure worth looking at."

"Cool it, Jack." Melina glanced over at Luc, seeing the irritation that filled his expression.

"Sorry, Jack, Luc thinks he's the only one who has the right to be ill-mannered and rude," she said with wide-eyed innocence. "Personally, I've decided it's just a part of being a cowboy. I mean, neither of you are actually sporting any *manners*." She stressed the last word sarcastically before turning away from them and heading toward the living room.

"Cat, you're forgetting dinner," Luc growled.

She turned back to him, smiling sweetly. "No, Luc, I didn't forget, I just decided to quit. Fix it your own damned self."

He caught her before she left the kitchen, his lips quirking as he fought a smile, his gray eyes hooded, but the amusement in them wasn't hidden.

"You can't quit. I kidnapped you, remember?" he reminded her.

"Then you better reconsider not just the crime, but the punishment." She jerked her arm from his grip, furious with him now. "Because I'll be damned if I'll put up with this much longer."

His brows lowered to a frown as he blocked her way, his hands gripping her hips, jerking her to him, ignoring Jack's smothered laughter as he lowered his lips to her ear.

"Punishment, my love, definitely comes later," he growled. "And I promise, you won't forget it when it does."

He nipped her ear, smiling into her furious face before looking over at Jack.

"Come on into the living room and we'll discuss those sales you made. I think Cat might need a break from us irritating cowboys."

"Hmm," Jack murmured. "Maybe it's just you. You go pout in the living room and I'll keep her company."

"In your fucking dreams," Luc growled, frowning heavily at Jack. "Get your ass in here and tell me how cheap you sold my horses for. And keep your damned eyes off her. Not to mention your hands."

Jack sighed as though disappointed. "One of these days, I'm gonna bring my own woman. You're starting to get downright unfriendly, boy."

* * * * *

Men were just strange, that was all there was to it. Luc had to be a Gemini. The alternate personalities of the zodiac sign made perfect sense. It was the only explanation for...this. He had gone from surly jealousy that evening to one of the most amazing lovers she could have imagined later that night.

Melina clenched her teeth to hold back a scream of pleasure as she felt Luc's cock sink slowly back inside her well-lubricated behind. She hadn't truly thought it could be possible. That a cock as large as Luc's could possible invade that small, tight channel and actually bring pleasure. But there she was, on her knees, her butt in the air, her shoulders to the mattress as the big cowboy pumped his dick up her ass.

Her pussy was sizzling. She could feel her juices literally dripping from her vagina as he held her tight, fucking inside her with slow, careful strokes that stretched her impossibly, sending streaks of fire blazing up her anus as pleasure tore at her very core.

"You're so tight." His voice was rough, so deep and dark she shivered at the sound. "So hot and tight around my cock it's all I can do not to come inside you now."

Melina moaned in rising lust. Yes, that was what she wanted. She wanted him to come now, to feel him shuddering against her, pumping his seed inside her.

"You like this, baby?" he asked her, the eroticism of his voice had her pulse rate jumping. "God, I wish you could see the way your tight little ass stretches open for my cock, sucking me in..." he groaned roughly. "I'm going to come up your ass, baby. I'm going to fill it so deep with my come that you'll never forget the feel of me inside you."

She never would anyway.

She had to be in shock, she thought as she moved against him, taking him deeper inside the forbidden little hole, glorying in the pleasure-pain tearing through her. She had awakened to his fingers smoothing through the cleft of her ass, his hot voice whispering his intent to fuck her there.

She had shivered at the threat, believing he only meant a bit of hot foreplay. She'd had more than a bit of the foreplay. She'd had more than an hour of it. And each touch, each lick, each nip was designed to drive her higher, make her hotter as his fingers stretched the nether hole. Until finally, she was begging him to fuck her there. Pleading with him to drive his cock inside her, take her, anywhere, she didn't care. Now, she was within a second of begging again.

Her clit was a swollen mass of torturous lust, her pussy was sobbing in its need and she could feel...something. An edge of dark, coiling need gathering in the pit of her stomach with each stroke of his cock up her ass.

Melina's fingers tightened in the already bunched sheet beneath her, a mewling whimper escaping her throat as he ground his erection deeper inside her. She could feel every inch of his cock boring through her sensitive flesh. Every throb, every pulsing vein as it tunneled through the tender tissue.

"Luc, I can't stand it." She could barely speak, the need was so great. "Fuck me harder. Do something, please."

She was writhing beneath him, or trying to. His hands held her hips tightly, keeping her in place, refusing to allow her to increase the pace of his thrusts.

"Easy, baby." He was fighting for breath, his voice was deepening further. "Patience. Just a little more. You're so fucking tight I can't stand it much longer."

He felt as thick as a baseball bat, as hard as iron, but each long thrust inside the tender channel was making her crazy for more. She wanted him driving inside her, plunging as hard and fast inside her ass as possible. She was dying for it.

She clenched the muscles of her ass as he thrust inside her again, thrilling to the moan that tore from his throat. He was moving faster now, shuttling in and out of her anus as he gasped for breath and she whimpered in longing. She could feel the pleasure building inside her. It was unlike anything she had ever known before. The hot fist of sensation gathering in her womb was tightening, burning.

"Luc, please." She tried to scream out the demand, but it sounded more like a sob. "Fuck me. Fuck me harder. Please."

He came over her then, covering her smaller body with his own, as his hand moved beneath her body. Before she had any idea of his intention, two broad fingers plunged inside her cunt as he began to fuck her ass in earnest.

Deep, driving strokes, a dual pleasure that shocked her senses and turned her into a creature of sensation, of lust and need so powerful that she was helpless in its grip. Her hips bucked into each driving thrust as the knot of need built within her womb. Tighter, tighter…

"Luc. Oh God. Luc…" She was dripping with sweat but so was he. He groaned, a thick, harsh sound at her ear that caused her to shudder as his fingers plunged deeper inside her weeping pussy.

It took no more than that. Helplessly her mouth opened to scream, but the sound that emerged was a low, keening cry as she erupted. Her orgasm exploded through her system. Radiant, blistering with heat and a pleasure so intense it was nearly painful. Muscles tightened locked, holding him inside her as he growled her name and began to pump hot jetting bursts of semen deep inside her anus.

She was shaking in the aftermath. Never had she known anything could be this intense, this incredibly erotic. She moaned in regret as she felt him slide free of the grip she had on his flesh and fall into the bed beside her. The dark entrance he had so thoroughly fucked still tingled almost violently from the possession he had taken of it. Her body was sensitized, exhausted and she didn't think she could drag herself from the bed if her life depended on it.

She could jump in shock as a fist pounded on the door, though, her eyes rounding in surprise at Jack's querulous voice. "If you two are going to fuck like minks all morning the least you could do is throttle the fucking sound effects."

Her face flushed a bright crimson as she heard Luc chuckle tiredly.

"Oh my God." She buried her face in her pillow as she remembered her screams. "Oh my God. This is terrible." There was no way she could ever face that man again. Not that facing him had been easy the first time, of course. He was the most mocking, sarcastic creature she had ever laid her eyes on. And he was nearly killed because of Maria. One thing about her sister that she could count on, she knew how to make enemies.

Luc grunted. "Come on, get up. All this exertion makes me hungry. I need breakfast."

"Well, have fun," she muttered. "I'm not facing him this morn—dammit, Luc." He hauled her out of the bed, laughing at her shrieks as he flipped her over his shoulder and carried her to the bathroom.

"Barbarian," she accused him when he set her on her feet by the shower.

"Wench." He leaned down and kissed her quickly. "Now shower. I need breakfast. If you're not downstairs in half an hour, I'll come carry you down."

She frowned up at him mutinously. "Don't you think you're taking this captive thing just a little too far? I mean really, even the worst prisoner gets time off for good behavior."

The fact that she was naked and his eyes were darkening in lustful appreciation wasn't lost on her. Just as the knowledge that he was naked and his cock was slowly taking notice of her once again wasn't lost on him. He frowned darkly. "Damn, you're going to kill me. I'm too old for 'round-the-clock sex. Shower." He pressed her toward the cubicle. "I'll use the guest bath. And hurry. I'm hungry."

He was always hungry. Melina shook her head in amusement as her heart clenched in longing. Damn, he was sexy. Sexy and fun and so hot he made her toes curl with the heat. He made her heart break with emotion too.

She quickly shook away the somberness of that thought. She would enjoy this while she could, she promised herself. Reality would come all too soon, and when it did, it was going to bust her ass hard. For now, she wanted to revel in his touch, enjoy his laughter and just be a part of him. Even if he didn't know she wasn't Maria, he knew she wasn't the woman he thought Maria was. She would content herself with that for now. It was all she had left when it came right down to it. All she had to sustain her in the future when, she was certain, Luc would no longer be a part of her life. Then she would allow herself to hurt.

Chapter Twelve

∞

Melina's breakfast of fried eggs, hash browns, sausage and homemade biscuits was consumed quickly, and within an hour both Luc and Jack were out at the barn with the horses. Several had been sold, Jack had told Luc at breakfast. The two mares were exceptionally beautiful, graceful despite their size, and evenly tempered. Melina had watched from the porch for a while as the two men went into the corral and began to go over each of the animals.

Summer was in full swing, and the East Texas weather was damned hot. It was a dry heat, though, one that warmed the bones and made her think of the sultry night to come. There was no doubt in her mind that as long as she shared Luc's bed, there would be no lack of physical exertion. The man had enough testosterone for three men.

Turning back into the house, she entered the kitchen, determined to get the dishes done quickly so she could get the rest of the house cleaned. Luc had mentioned taking a few of the horses out later if she felt up to it. It had been years since she had ridden, and never an animal as large and graceful as the Clydesdales he so loved.

It was easy to convince herself that the situation could continue indefinitely. Easy to let her heart and mind push back the problems that would await her when she returned home.

Her parents had disowned her. She likely didn't have an apartment now and she definitely didn't have a job. All she had was a fat cat, a fairly nice car and a nursing certificate that she hadn't used in two years.

But when Luc's arms went around her, when his lips touched hers, none of those problems existed. There was only here and now, his touch, the heat and the hard wash of pleasure that surged through her body. It was becoming harder, daily, to imagine being without him. A sigh of longing escaped her at that thought. She didn't want to be without him, that was her problem.

"Why the sigh, little sis, missing home?" The voice from the doorway made Melina freeze in shock. She stood still before the sink, desperately trying to convince herself she hadn't heard the voice.

"Maybe missing me." The coarse roughness of the other female voice had Melina swinging around in fear.

Melina blinked warily, certain it wasn't possible that the two women she was staring at could actually be there.

"Oh look, Bertha, we surprised her. Doesn't she look so cute when she goes all pale like that?" Maria clapped her hands together like a child, an expression of malicious amusement twisting her face.

"Yeah, just makes the juices flow." Bertha smiled in anticipation, her dark eyes glittering with an unnatural lust. "Wonder if she'll be as hot as you are, Maria? I bet once she gets worked up, she'll be better."

Maria grimaced distastefully as the back door opened and two unfamiliar men entered. For a moment, just a moment, she had hoped it was Luc, until she saw the men. There was no doubt these were friends of Maria's. They had eyes like snakes, cold and devoid of emotion as they stared at her.

"These are friends of mine, Mellie," Maria told her cheerfully. "You don't need to know their names, but they've come to help me take you home. Poor baby. I'm sorry you were kidnapped in my stead, but I'm sure I can take care of your big old cowboy. Besides," she glanced at Bertha, "your good friend Bertha has really missed you. I think she's looking forward to greeting you properly."

Maria was high, her eyes were glazed, the unnatural smile on her face too wide.

"God, Maria." Melina shook her head as she faced the sad waste of the sister she had once loved. "What the hell are you doing here?"

Maria frowned back at her, a flicker of anger in her gaze. "You refused Papa's plan, Melina. You aren't supposed to do that. I came to bring you back so you could reconsider." She smiled like a child proposing some wonderful adventure. "Papa has it all worked out this time, honey. And Bertha here…" She motioned to the large-bored woman lazily. "She came along with us to remind you of what happens when you refuse to do what she wants. And she really wants you to help me." The beatific smile that filled Maria's face shouldn't have looked so twisted and sinister, but it did. It terrified Melina.

"I nearly died last time, Maria," she reminded her, fighting to remain calm as Bertha's eyes traveled over her body. "Do you really want to see me dead?"

There was no compassion, no hesitation in her sister. "Better you than me, sweetie. You know I'm the favorite. The best. Papa wouldn't want to lose me, Mellie, you know this. And it would break Momma's heart. They don't love you nearly as well as they do me, so you're really protecting all of us."

It was no more than the truth, but it sliced across her soul like the sharpest blade.

"I won't do it, Maria." Melina breathed in roughly. She wasn't alone, she reminded herself. Luc and Jack were at the barn. They would be back soon. Luc wouldn't let Maria take her. He couldn't.

"Now see, sweet thing, there's where you're wrong," Bertha spoke as Maria giggled gaily. "You will come back, and you will stand in her stead and pray to God you do it right. Otherwise, the rape you would have gotten at my hands will look like a Sunday picnic when I get finished with you."

Her arm went around Maria. Melina watched in sick fascination as Bertha's head bent, her lips covering Maria's as her sister responded with such unrestrained passion that Melina wondered if this wasn't another nightmare rather than reality.

"Cut it out, Maria," the bigger of the two men on the other side of room ordered her harshly. "We need to get the hell out of here before those two head back. We don't need any trouble here."

The two women disengaged slowly. Maria cuddled against Bertha's breasts as the other woman smiled over at Melina viciously. "Ready to go, sweet thing?"

Melina stared at her sister. In that moment she realized that there would be no saving her twin. She was horribly thin, her skin pasty, her mind so corrupted by the drugs that there was likely no hope of ever bringing her back.

"I love you, Maria," she said softly as she watched her pitifully. "I hope you always know that I love you."

Maria blinked, her gaze flickering before going dull and cold again. "Then you'll have no problems going to prison for me." She reached up and fondled one of Bertha's breasts, humming in approval as the other woman's nipple hardened.

Melina shuddered in revulsion.

"I'm not going anywhere." She stood still, her hands gripping the counter behind her as all eyes turned to her.

"Sorry, lady, but you are coming," the bigger man sighed roughly. "Sucks, huh? Having a sister like that? But she's pretty damned useful to me. You aren't, so you lose."

He wasn't a handsome man, he was cold and she knew he wouldn't hesitate to kill. The gun he pulled from beneath his jacket proved that.

"Let's go."

She gripped the counter harder. "Once I start screaming, Luc and his men will be here. They won't come unarmed."

A flicker of unease passed across his expression.

"Then we'll just have to make sure you don't scream." Bertha pushed Maria aside and jumped toward Melina.

She did scream. Luc's name reverberated through the house, but she knew he would never hear her at the barn. A second later a hard blow landed against her head as she attempted to shove past the larger woman.

Melina could hear her sister's laughter as she fell to the floor.

"Luc!" she screamed again as she scrambled beneath the table, kicking out at Bertha and the man who grabbed her legs.

A hard blow went into her kidneys a second before a savage howl sounded and the sound of breaking glass over the table was heard. Screams, curses and feminine laughter echoed around Melina as she fought the pain sweeping through her body. As always, Bertha knew exactly where to aim when she used those brutal fists.

Lobo's snarling growls were followed by the sound of Luc and Jack. Melina struggled to regain her breathing and to see more than the dim, blurry shapes struggling across the kitchen. But Maria was no longer laughing, and if she wasn't wrong, the still form lying across the room was Bertha.

"You killed her," Maria suddenly shrieked. "You killed her, you bastard."

Melina cleared her vision in time to see her sister dragging the gun from her purse and pulling it up. Luc was struggling across the room with one of the men, Jack had the other on the floor and Maria was pointing the gun at Luc's head.

"No..." Gathering the last bit of her strength Melina threw herself at her sister, her hand gripping Maria's wrists as she fought to take the weapon.

"Damn you, Mellie." Maria's knees went into her ribs, sending pain exploding through her body as she went to her back. "You can die first."

The gun turned on Melina. Her sister's eyes were cold, hard, as her finger tightened on the trigger. Then Maria jerked, shuddered, the gun dropping from her hand as red began to bloom across her chest. Melina watched the horrible stain in shock as silence seemed to fill the room.

"Joey?" Maria whispered bleakly. "Joey, you hurt me. You hurt me…"

She toppled across the fallen figure of her lover, a last gasp heaving from her chest as she stilled.

"Melina." Luc lowered himself beside her, his hands going over her ribs as she cried out weakly.

The pain was terrible, just breathing was agony.

"Fuck, they broke her rib, possibly two. Jack…"

"Calling the sheriff and ambulance now," Jack called back, though the words barely penetrated the shock in Melina's mind.

Maria was dead. Melina stared up past Luc, seeing her brother's tear-ravaged face as he gazed down at Maria. In his hand he carried a gun. The gun he had used to kill his sister.

"She wouldn't have stopped," he said wearily, his voice tear-choked as he knelt beside his dead sister. "She would have never stopped."

"Easy." Luc eased her against him as she fought to sit up, pain streaking through her. "Lay still, Cat. The ambulance will be here…"

"No. I'm not Maria." He called her Cat. Surely he didn't think she was Maria now.

"No, baby, you're not." He kissed her forehead gently. "You're my little Cat, though. That won't change."

"You hate cats." She stared up at him miserably. "I love you. I've always loved you. But you hate cats."

"I've learned to tolerate one in particular." He smiled then, a weary curve of his lips as he smoothed her hair back. "The other, I can't live without. I love you, Cat. Now rest easy. Everything's going to be okay. It's all going to be okay."

But would it? She gazed over at her brother, his lowered head, the stoop to his shoulders, then stared back up at Luc. His faced was creased with concern, his eyes black, his shirt torn.

"I love you," she whispered again.

Gently he smoothed the tears that fell from her eyes, from her cheek. His touch was gentle, tender, but his gaze was fierce.

"No more than I love you, little Cat. Never more than I love you."

* * * * *

Maria's funeral was a small, quiet affair. Melina had been forced to miss it. Two broken ribs and a bruised kidney canceled any flight plans she might have wanted to make. She knew Joe had gone, despite her parents' formal request that he not attend. The media circus had nearly destroyed the family.

Her father's brief visit to the hospital had resolved nothing. His grief and the clear indication that they blamed her for their favored daughter's death had been abundantly easy to see.

All she needed was your love, Melina. You never understood, Maria just needed more love and never received it. She only had her family to understand and lean on... It made no sense, but then, it never had.

Joe, as always, was enduring most of the anger, though. He had been formally disowned rather than verbally. Had he not suspected Maria had learned where Melina was then Maria wouldn't have been killed. She wouldn't have been lost to them forever. It hadn't seemed to sink into them yet that Maria would have gladly killed Melina. They refused to accept it.

Luc brought her home after a short stay in the hospital. Their home. And there he had kept her, pampering her, caring for her until her ribs had healed completely. She still had nightmares sometimes, visions of her sister taunting and laughing as she pointed the gun in her direction. But Luc was always there. His arms surrounded her, holding her close, whispering his love to her. And throughout the night he would pleasure her, driving all thoughts of nightmares, death or sadness from her mind.

Three months later, after just such a night, he surprised her by going to his dresser, pulling a small velvet box from a drawer and nearing the bed. There, he dropped to one knee, took her hand and pushed an outrageously expensive diamond on her finger. The engagement ring glistened with shards of color and heat as she stared down at it for long minutes.

Then she looked up at Luc in surprise as he rose to his feet. "No proposal?" she asked him archly.

He stared down at her arrogantly, though the effect was spoiled somewhat by the glint of amusement in his eyes.

"Captives are not given a choice. Remember, Cat? I decide, you follow."

She arched a brow as she allowed her hand to trail slowly up her silk-covered stomach before circling her swollen breasts. She sighed deeply.

"Is that how it works now?" she asked him huskily as her thighs shifted to allow him a glimpse of the plump, bare curves of her pussy. His cock responded immediately.

"Some captives get stubborn, you know? They do all sorts of things to get back at their captors. Things like finding another bedroom to sleep in."

And she wasn't joking. She'd be damned if she would wait that long for a proper proposal just to have him try to slide out of it.

He stared down at her for long seconds before sighing roughly. He went to one knee once again, took her hand and stared back at her.

"Marry me," he whispered. It sounded more like an order than a proposal, but if there was one thing she had learned about her cowboy, it was his fierce arrogance, his determination and his love for her. His love for her still amazed her.

"Of course I will." She shrugged. She wasn't finished with him yet. "Who's going to explain to our son, though, when he asks why we're sleeping in separate bedrooms?"

"Separate bedrooms? Dammit, Cat, I love you past hell, but if you think they'll be separate—" He stopped. His eyes widened. "Son?"

Her hand smoothed over her still flat abdomen. "It seems some of the scarring healed," she said softly. "We're pregnant, Luc."

He trembled. She hadn't seen him tremble since the day Maria had nearly shot her.

"Pregnant?" He licked his lips almost nervously, his hand moving to flatten on her stomach. "You're sure?"

"Positive," she said softly. "The doctor ran the tests twice just to be certain."

He swallowed tightly, staring back at her. his eyes darkening like a summer storm as he watched her with such emotion it clenched her heart.

"You steal my breath," he said simply. "You're my heart, Melina Catarina Angeles. My heart and soul. Please say you'll marry me."

Melina blinked back her tears then.

"You're my world. My life. Of course I'll marry you."

He moved quickly, coming over her, his lips covering hers as he moved between her thighs, opening her, his cock sinking slowly, gently, inside the sensitive depths of her pussy.

Melina's breath caught at the pleasure. It always did. He was hers. Her heart and soul and she breathed for his touch, his kiss.

There were few preliminaries. Emotions seemed to strip Luc's control as nothing else could. The depth of her love for him still seemed to amaze him, just as his amazed her

Her legs clasped his hips as her lips moved hungrily beneath his. His thrusts were gentle, tender, but no less fierce than they ever had been Within minutes her orgasm swept over her, shuddering through her body as she tore her lips from his, crying out his name as she felt him erupt inside her at the same moment.

"I love you, Cat." She heard his gentle whisper as sleep began to overtake her.

"I love you, Luc. Forever..."

Also by Lora Leigh

❧

About the Author

෨

Lora Leigh is a wife and mother living in Kentucky. She dreams in bright, vivid images of the characters intent on taking over her writing life, and fights a constant battle to put them on the hard drive of her computer before they can disappear as fast as they appeared.

Lora's family, and her writing life co-exist, if not in harmony, in relative peace with each other. An understanding husband is the key to late nights with difficult scenes and stubborn characters. His insights into human nature and the workings of the male psyche provide her hours of laughter, and innumerable romantic ideas that she works tirelessly to put into effect.

Lora welcomes comments from readers. You can find her website and email address on her author bio page at www.ellorascave.com

Enjoy this excerpt from
Coming in Last

Copyright © Shiloh Walker 2004

∽

"So what's eating you?"

Sliding Mick a glance, Jamie lifted his shoulders in a disinterested shrug and said, "Not much." Flipping through the file on his desk, he skimmed the account information they had received, and cursed mildly the sense of family obligation that had him agreeing to drive two hours south and stay there, for heaven only knows how long.

Of course, it wasn't like he had anything more interesting to do at the time.

"You know, you've had that same damn look on your face for about the past six months, like nothing on this earth can hold your attention for longer than five minutes."

Flashing Mick a grin, Jamie said, "Well, anything having to do with your ugly mug is gonna bore me senseless in five seconds. What's your point?"

"Just wondering when you're gonna snap out of this, that's all." Mick shrugged, lifting his shoulders as he sipped from his coffee before flipping a page and studying the next. "You know, this is really a waste of time. Time and money—his money, our time."

"His money. He can afford us. And this was slick, slick and pat. There may well be more missing than what is showing," Jamie mused, eyeing the accounts.

"There is that," Mick said with a nod. "So when are you gonna snap out of it?"

"Snap out of what?"

"This funk."

Jamie sighed. "Mick, I'm bored. Okay? Just bored." He laughed, recalling the scene with Erin from the previous weekend. "I can think about business while I'm getting a blowjob, and a damn good one. Tell me what in the hell the problem is here?"

"You need to let me have the woman while you get your head examined?" Mick offered blandly.

Jamie rose, the tailored suit falling into place over his gun as he strode over to the window and stood staring out into the clear summer day. "Something is just…missing, Mick. I'm bored with all of this. Everything. All of it. Not the business, but my life. Erin was just the exact same as every other woman I'd gone out with before her. And the next one will be just like her."

* * * * *

There was something about a woman surrounded by kids, Jamie mused. Some guys tended to be put off by the sight, but Jamie loved it — loved watching women as they held and rocked, soothed and played with children.

Her laugh floated above the higher-pitched laughter of the kids as she unlocked the pudgy little arms from her leg and lifted the baby. Settling him on her hip, she answered one question after another as she wove her way through the maze of toys and games already spilled out on the floor.

The high-pitched peals of laughter and the squeak of excited voices had his head pounding again. Wincing, Jamie pressed his hand gingerly to his throbbing temple, wishing for a bit of peace and quiet. Hell, he had planned on coming down here with a feigned injury, not a real one.

Right before he could open his mouth, she stopped mid-stride and turned her head, meeting his eyes across the room. Light reflected off her glasses, keeping him from seeing her eyes. She turned her head and the chunky teenager took the baby from her.

"Hello."

Squinting against the bright light, cursing the throbbing in his head, he managed to growl out, "Hi."

"Looks like you bumped your head," she said. Without asking, she laid one hand on his arm and guided him around the perimeter of the room, sidestepping toys and toddlers with ease. "The clinic is right over here."

Moments later, laying flat on his back, eyes closed against the harsh glare of light, Jamie mumbled around the thermometer, "Is all this really necessary?"

"Company policy," she replied as she wrapped a blood pressure cuff around his arm. Competent, quick hands checked his vitals while Jamie lay there waiting for the Motrin he'd taken to kick in. Strong, cool, slender fingers wrapped around his wrist. It was just the pain that caused his pulse to race, Jamie told himself.

A subtle scent wafted over to taunt him. God, she smelled good.

Through the fringe of his lashes, he watched as she rose from kneeling on the floor and smoothed down the plain, simple white utilitarian scrubs she wore. As she turned away, his eyes locked on the long red braid that hung between her shoulder blades. Her hips swayed as she moved around the small office, gathering up paperwork, asking questions that he replied to as quickly and tersely as possible.

A soft wail rose from the other room and he waited for her to respond. When the wail continued for more than ten seconds, he asked, "Aren't you going to check on whoever that is crying?"

"It's Amy, our newborn. And she's hungry. Abby's got to get her bottle ready." She glanced at the simple band of braided leather on her wrist.

"Quite a lot of A's."

With a grin, she said, "This is the A-team. We have Andi, which is me, Abby, Alex, Amy, Aaron, Aspen, and Arnie, the pet hamster." Another glance at her watch, and a few seconds later, the tiny cry was silent as laughter and excited voices filled the air.

Her skin was smooth and pale, not a single freckle marring her milky complexion. And up this close, he doubted that shade of red came out of a bottle. Her eyebrows were the same shade and so was the super fine hair he could see scattered across her arms. Her eyelashes looked to be darker, but behind the glasses, he really couldn't tell.

"Hectic job," he said.

With a roll of her eyes, she said, "Any job that involves anybody under the age of thirteen is hectic."

"What happens after thirteen? Does it become less hectic?"

"No. After thirteen, it just becomes more traumatic. Ever had to deal with a thirteen-year-old girl who was convinced the world was going to stop turning on its axis because the boy from math didn't call the way he said he would?"

"Actually, yes. I have two sisters."

"Then you should already know what happens after thirteen."

Lowering herself to the rolling stool, she asked, "Dizzy?"

Some twenty minutes later, he was ushered out into the relative quiet of the hall, and he had to admit, he agreed with Johnson.

She didn't fit the image of a corporate thief at all.

And she smelled better than he ever would have imagined.

Her mouth, hmm, well, her mouth was probably going to be giving him some sweaty dreams for a night or two. Those naked, pouty lips put only one thing in a man's mind. And the thought had his cock stiffening up like a pike. Just the thought of her putting that mouth on him—

"Enough, McAdams," he muttered, stalking down the hall, absently rubbing his temple. "The girl is a damned embezzler."

Why an electronic book?

We live in the Information Age—an exciting time in the history of human civilization in which technology rules supreme and continues to progress in leaps and bounds every minute of every hour of every day. For a multitude of reasons, more and more avid literary fans are opting to purchase e-books instead of paperbacks. The question to those not yet initiated to the world of electronic reading is simply: *why?*

1. *Price.* An electronic title at Ellora's Cave Publishing and Cerridwen Press runs anywhere from 40-75% less than the cover price of the <u>exact same title</u> in paperback format. Why? Cold mathematics. It is less expensive to publish an e-book than it is to publish a paperback, so the savings are passed along to the consumer.

2. *Space.* Running out of room to house your paperback books? That is one worry you will never have with electronic novels. For a low one-time cost, you can purchase a handheld computer designed specifically for e-reading purposes. Many e-readers are larger than the average handheld, giving you plenty of screen room. Better yet, hundreds of titles can be stored within your new library—a single microchip. (Please note that Ellora's Cave and Cerridwen Press does not endorse any specific brands. You can check our website at www.ellorascave.com or

www.cerridwenpress.com for customer recommendations we make available to new consumers.)

3. *Mobility*. Because your new library now consists of only a microchip, your entire cache of books can be taken with you wherever you go.

4. *Personal preferences are accounted for*. Are the words you are currently reading too small? Too large? Too...**ANNOYING**? Paperback books cannot be modified according to personal preferences, but e-books can.

5. *Instant gratification* Is it the middle of the night and all the bookstores are closed? Are you tired of waiting days—sometimes weeks—for online and offline bookstores to ship the novels you bought? Ellora's Cave Publishing sells instantaneous downloads 24 hours a day, 7 days a week, 365 days a year. Our e-book delivery system is 100% automated, meaning your order is filled as soon as you pay for it.

Those are a few of the top reasons why electronic novels are displacing paperbacks for many an avid reader. As always, Ellora's Cave and Cerridwen Press welcomes your questions and comments. We invite you to email us at service@ellorascave.com, service@cerridwenpress.com or write to us directly at: 1056 Home Ave. Akron OH 44310-3502.

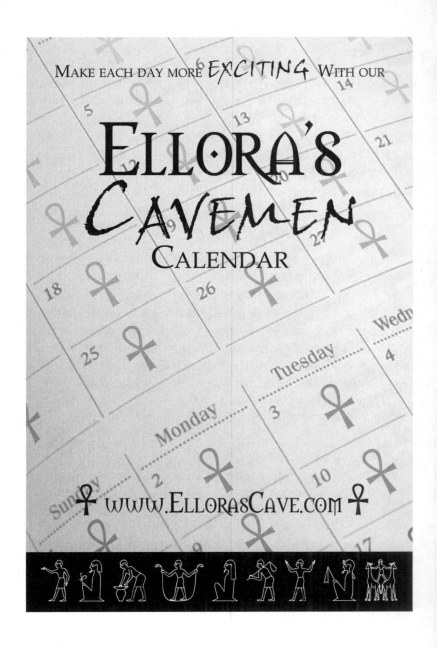

THE
☥ ELLORA'S CAVE ☥
LIBRARY

Stay up to date with Ellora's Cave Titles in
Print with our Quarterly Catalog.

TO RECIEVE A CATALOG,
SEND AN EMAIL WITH YOUR NAME
AND MAILING ADDRESS TO:

CATALOG@ELLORASCAVE.COM
OR SEND A LETTER OR POSTCARD
WITH YOUR MAILING ADDRESS TO:

CATALOG REQUEST
c/o ELLORA'S CAVE PUBLISHING, INC.
1056 HOME AVENUE
AKRON, OHIO 44310-3502